She's an empath who's alv  *e a*
supernatural storm o
Fᴀᴛ

Toni Dusi grew up knowing everyone's business and everyone knowing hers because in Moonstone Cove, you can't pass a restaurant, farm, or winery that doesn't have at least one Dusi involved. Despite her family, Toni has managed to carve out a private niche for herself. She has a car shop she loves, a country cottage all to herself, and has carefully avoided any long-term romantic commitments.

Then fate handed Toni a shot of supernatural empathy that threw all that out the window of her prized vintage Mustang.

Now she's feeling the mood swings of everyone from her parts guy to her reluctant crush to her second cousin going through a messy divorce. She's losing her temper, she's crying a river, and she's definitely giving in to temptation.

But when the body of a longtime family rival turns up at her cousin's winery, Toni realizes her inconvenient feelings-magic has turned her into one heck of a lie detector. She and her new friends, Katherine and Megan, might be the only ones who can clear her cousin's name.

When fate throws a final curveball in Toni's direction, will she drop everything with disastrous consequences? Or can a forty-one-year-old empath learn enough new tricks to keep the life she's built without sacrificing new happiness?

Fate Actually is a paranormal women's fiction novel and the second book in the Moonstone Cove series by *USA Today* best-selling author Elizabeth Hunter.

For my very own crazy clan
Related by blood, marriage, or choice
I love you all.

FATE ACTUALLY

MOONSTONE COVE BOOK TWO

ELIZABETH HUNTER

Fate Actually
Copyright © 2020
Elizabeth Hunter
ISBN: 978-1-941674-61-1

Cover: Damonza
Content Editor: Amy Cissell, Cissell Ink
Line Editor: Anne Victory
Proofreader: Linda, Victory Editing

Recurve Press LLC
PO Box 4034
Visalia, California 93278
USA

CHAPTER 1

*A*ntonia Dusi slicked a clay face mask over her olive-toned skin and set the timer for five minutes.

Five minutes.

She leaned on the edge of the counter and glanced to her right, drumming her fingers on the edge.

Four minutes, fifty seconds.

What was she supposed to do with four minutes and fifty seconds? Toni hated sitting still. She hated wasting time. She had too much going on in her life to waste time. It was Wednesday morning, she had a dozen things to do at her garage that day, and her dad was supposed to be coming in; she wanted to get her butt going out the door.

Four minutes, thirty seconds.

Drip.

Drip.

Drip.

The rhythmic drip of water at the bottom of her sink snagged her attention. She cocked her head and put her

1

finger to the faucet. It was one of those little jobs she hadn't quite gotten around to doing since she bought the old cottage at the bottom of the hill.

It was probably just a washer. She could fix that in five minutes.

She glanced at the counter and the numbers ticking by. Okay, four minutes, fifteen seconds.

Toni opened the bathroom door and walked through her bedroom and toward the kitchen where she kept her toolbox under the sink. Eventually she'd move her tools to the laundry room, but right now the laundry room was torn up while she refinished the cabinets in there.

Just as she grabbed her tools, she felt her phone buzzing in her pocket.

She slid it to answer. "Morning, Dad."

"Toni, you're not at the garage."

He was early. Of all the days.

"I'm just running a little late. I'll be there soon."

"There's like three guys just sitting around in the bay."

She looked at the clock on her phone. "It's five till eight. They're not on until eight."

Bobby Dusi huffed and muttered something about "his day."

She walked the toolbox back to the bathroom. "Dad, I'm sure Glenn has them all scheduled. It's a busy day and he knows what's going on."

"Is this Glenn's garage or yours?"

It's mine, you old coot! "Dad, do I go to the club and tell you how to play bocce ball?"

"You act like I didn't run this place for forty years."

"You act like I haven't run it for the past fifteen." She could feel her temper start to rise. So much for that careful meditation she'd been practicing every morning since she'd been struck with unexpected psychic powers earlier in the year.

The traumatic near-shooting that had triggered her empathy was a fading memory, but the unexpected wash of emotional energy still took her by surprise most days.

If she was happy, she could make other people ecstatic. If she was pissed, she could start a fight. Not to mention the emotional sponge she'd become. Most days she hardly knew whose feelings were swimming through her body.

Her two new friends, Katherine Bassi and Megan Carpenter, were dealing with changes too. Katherine was still having flash visions she couldn't control, and Megan had become telekinetic. Megan seemed to be most devoted to understanding their new situation, and she'd been the one to suggest meditation for Toni.

Meditation worked. Until your seventy-five-year-old dad went and blew your Zen to hell.

"Dad, I don't have time for this." Shut it down. Shut it down. "Listen, I'm not sleeping in. I have a leak in the bathroom I'm fixing."

"A leak?" Her father calmed down. "Ah, I know how that is. Take care of it, and I'll see you here. It's a good old house, but we all know how old houses can be."

"I know."

"I helped build that house, so I know how solid it is. But everything needs maintenance."

"I know, Dad."

"You need any help?"

"I got it." She reached under the sink to turn off the water lines. "If you can help Glenn out this morning, I can take care of this. But really, don't worry about it, because Glenn's got everyone scheduled for the day." Her foreman had been working with her for ten years. Glenn could likely run the entire garage on his own, but then what would she do for fun?

"Okay, honey. I love you. Mom made us lunch today."

Her stomach rumbled, then gurgled, despite the tea she'd sipped that morning. "That sounds great. I'll see you later."

She hung up the phone and glanced at the counter. Two minutes.

Okay, so she'd fill a couple more minutes than five. She'd just gotten her pliers around the faucet when her phone rang again.

"Seriously?" She hit the button and put it on speaker. "What now?"

"Toni?" It was Glenn. "Did you know your old man is here?"

"Yes, I'm sorry. I didn't know he'd be in so early. There's a leak in the bathroom I have to fix. I'll only be a few minutes late." She heard the timer go off and quickly hit the button before she continued. "Just uh..." She glanced down and blinked. "Just keep my dad occupied for a while until I get there, okay?"

"All right." Glenn cleared his throat. "I might have him help the new kid at the parts counter. I really don't want him trying to change tires again."

"I know, I know." She swept everything on the counter to the side so she had room for the faucet parts. "Bobby tends to forget he's not thirty-five." Her dad might have retired, but he wasn't very good at taking it easy.

"I'll take care of things here."

"Sounds good." She stared at the glossy edge of water forming at the lip of the faucet.

Drip.

"Okay, I'll see you when you get in."

"Thanks, Glenn. You're the best."

Drip.

Toni blinked and grabbed a red rag before she started taking the faucet apart.

Drop.

She had the faucet head in her hand when her phone rang again.

"Seriously?" she grumbled. She glanced at the screen.

Henry.

Nope. Not today, Satan's better-looking brother.

No, that wasn't fair. Henry wasn't Satan or even in Satan's extended family. He was good, so ridiculously good that she didn't know how to handle him that morning.

"Go to voice mail," she muttered. "Take a hint."

She pried the old washer out of the faucet and set the cracked rubber on the counter. "Out with the old, in with the new."

It was kind of her motto for everything these days. When she bought the house, she knew it needed work. That's why she got it for such a low price. The old stone cottage was at the base of the hill that marked the boundary of her cousin Nico's winery and his nearest neighbor, Fairfield Wines. She was ten minutes from Moonstone Cove, fifteen minutes from the beach, and smack in the heart of Central California wine country in a seventy-year-old cottage surrounded by a stand of oaks.

It was heaven, leaky faucets and all.

She was putting the new washer in when her mother's name flashed on her phone's screen.

Toni groaned. "How? How do you all know the exact worst time to call?"

No matter. She hit the green button because if she didn't, she'd regret it later. "Hey, Ma."

"Toni, your dad says a pipe burst in the bathroom. Did you call Nathan?"

Oh, for Pete's sake... "It's a leaky faucet, Ma. I don't need to call Nathan."

"He's your cousin; he wouldn't charge you for going out there."

"I'm good. I've already got it fixed." She tossed the red rag on the counter and reached under the sink to turn on the water.

"I knew that house was just going to be a money pit, Antonia. A *money* pit."

The house had been the old foreman's place on the Dusi family winery, but no one had lived in it for nearly twenty years. It was taken over by spiders and mice, had a family of rabbits living in the back bedroom, and generations of cats ran wild in the old red barn. But the house was solid.

"My house is not a money pit." In fact, she'd insisted on a very thorough inspection by someone she was *not* related to before she agreed on the price. "It's just maintenance stuff. Already done." She tossed the washer in the trash and glanced at the clock on the counter. Ten minutes. Not bad at all. "I better say goodbye. I gotta feed Shelby and head in to work."

Other than her overfed grey shorthair, Toni lived alone and she liked it that way. The cottage was her haven. She'd scooted the bunnies out the door, called the Humane Society for most of the cats, and adopted one gnarly-looking tomcat to keep the barn free of mice and gophers.

She'd had the old man neutered, and he still hadn't forgiven her. Enzo ran from her every time she got close. He was the fastest cat she'd ever seen, hence the name.

Her own house cat, Shelby, had barely left her sunny perch in the living room window since she'd moved in the year before. She watched the birds flitting outside but knew that Toni would never let her out.

Enzo might have evolved to evade coyotes, but Shelby would be lunch.

"I made you and your dad lunch," Rose Dusi said quickly. "And we're having Sunday dinner at our place, and Luna and the kids are coming down too."

"Sounds good. I'll be there." She ran some hot water and wiped the cracked clay mask off her skin, which looked fresh and glowing. "Have a good day, Ma."

"You too, baby. I'll see you later—be nice to your dad."

"When am I not nice to Dad?" Leave it to her mom to throw that in at the end.

"Oh, you know what I mean. Love you." Her mother blew kisses and hung up the phone.

"No." Toni spoke into the empty bathroom. "I have no idea what you mean."

She'd fixed the sink, but in the back of her mind, she could still hear it dripping.

Toni was getting in her car when her phone rang again. "Why do I know so many people?" she yelled into the barn. "Hello?"

"Oh. Bad time?" It was her friend Katherine. "I was just calling to remind you about Wine Wednesday. It's tonight."

"Thank God," she breathed out. "I'll be there."

"Bad day? It's not even nine o'clock."

"Isn't it?" Everything that morning had moved fast. The ocean fog had even burned off for the day, leaving the grass-covered hills glowing gold in the sunlight. "I think everyone and their uncle decided to call me this morning specifically, just to fuck with me."

"Well, just make it through the day and tell us all about it tonight. Have you been meditating?"

"Yes?"

"That sounded like a question."

"That's because I am, but I'm not sure it's helping. That is, it would help if I could magically make my entire family disappear and not talk to me ever, but I don't think that's really an option."

"Seeing as you're related to half the town, making your family disappear seems like it could lead to disaster and a fairly significant economic downturn."

"Thanks, Professor."

"You're welcome. Come at six. We have wine and food."

In the six months since they'd met, Katherine and Megan had become the closest Toni had ever had to "girlfriends." She'd always been the girl who played with the boys. As an adult, she was close to her mother, her sister, and her myriad female cousins. But girlfriends? Not much. She hadn't had time to cultivate friendships until fate had basically forced her into it. Now? She couldn't imagine life without Wine Wednesday, Katherine's adorable husband, and snarking at Megan, who gave as good as she got.

Toni's life was full.

So very full.

Too full?

Her phone rang again and she nearly cried. She looked at the screen and only picked up because it was her cousin Nico, who hardly ever called even though he was her closest neighbor.

"Yo." She started her vintage Mustang and backed out of the barn.

"Toni, please tell me you're not under a car right now."

"No. In fact, I haven't even left for town. What's up?"

"Thank God." He let out a breath. "Can you come up to the house? We're supposed to start picking the pinot today, the harvest crew is all here, and the tractor won't start. I'm panicking."

"I'm not a diesel mechanic, Nico."

"I know I know I know, but I need to know if it's a quick fix or if I need to call a neighbor to try to wrangle a favor."

"I'll come." She pulled out of her driveway and turned left, taking the gravel road up to Nico's house at the top of the hill. "You owe me two bottles of wine."

"If you get it started, you can have a case."

"Seriously?" She smiled for the first time that morning. "Awesome."

People always thought she could grab as much wine as she wanted since her cousin owned the farm, the winery, and the whole operation. Unfortunately, she was one of dozens of cousins. If everyone got free wine, Dusi Heritage Winery would go out of business. She had to pay just like everyone else.

When she pulled behind the barn, she could see dozens of workers hanging out along the edge of the field. Though all the wine grapes were cut by hand, the tractor pulled the bins through the rows. No tractor meant way more walking, a much slower harvest, and very pissed-off employees.

"What's up?"

Nico was standing next to the small tractor with a grimace on his face, looking completely stressed out. "I have no idea. Henry and Danny are in Paso Robles to pick up some valves and they're on the way back now, but everyone is waiting. I don't have time for this. It was working fine yesterday."

Oh good. Henry was gone.

Nico gestured to the trailer stacked with empty crates. "And we've got to get the rest of the pinot today or I'm fucked. The temperatures are going to spike tomorrow."

"Hey." She tried to use her superpowers for good by putting her hand on Nico's forearm and giving it a little squeeze. "Relax. I'm sure it's fixable."

Nico immediately chilled out. Toni could feel his stress leave him and soak into her. It didn't do much for the queasy stomach she'd been battling all morning, but there was considerably less tension floating around her.

"Thank you for coming up," he said. "You know I wouldn't call if it wasn't an emergency."

"Okay, keys out?" She walked over and stepped up on the

running board. As soon as she flipped up the seat, she spotted the problem.

"Okay, well, if you knew a fraction as much about engines as you do about grapevines, you'd be able to figure it out. Someone cut the line on your primary safety switch."

"The what? Someone messed with a switch?" Nico craned his head. "How do you know?"

She pointed to the cut wires. "I mean, it's pretty obvious. They put that in there so if the driver falls off, the tractor shuts off. Without a working safety switch there, the engine could be perfect and the tractor still won't start. I don't know of any way to bypass it."

Nico's face turned red. "Could it be an accident?"

"I mean..." She shrugged. "It looks cut to me. The wires are pretty clean. You're gonna need to get someone out here to rewire it if Danny can't do it." Henry was the winemaker, but Danny Barba was his foreman on the farm and kept all the equipment working. "I'm gonna say at least a couple of hours."

"Shit!" Nico slammed his hand on the top of the tractor, and Toni heard something fall from the tractor with a thunk.

She hopped down and stared at what had fallen in the dirt. "Oh my God."

She covered her mouth with the back of her hand. The queasy stomach she'd been battling all morning roared up with a vengeance. Toni ran for the edge of the field and puked into the grass.

"Toni?" Nico ran to her, but she shook her head and waved him back. "What the hell?"

"Finger." She cleared her throat and tried not to retch again. "Nico, look."

"What are you...? Oh *fuck*."

That was two fucks in one day. Yep, her Aunt Marta was going to be hearing about that one.

But then again, what else were you supposed to say when a bloody human finger fell out of your broken tractor?

CHAPTER 2

*D*etective Drew Bisset stood over the lone finger
sitting in the dirt, watching with a frown while
one of his officers documented the scene with a camera. He
was a handsome man with dark brown skin, dark hair and
beard, and a medium build, who carried himself with confident ease.

Drew was the head detective at the Moonstone Cove
Police Department. He'd moved to town around five years
ago, so people still considered him a newcomer, but he was
well liked. Toni had met him the year before when her cousin
Max had joined the police department, and she had a lot of
respect for the man's straightforward personality.

Toni had gotten to know Drew better when she, Katherine, and Megan were trying to figure out what had caused the
near-shooting that triggered their powers. A mystery that
involved one student had grown to be a conspiracy that
involved students at the university, a hijacked psychological
study, a shady professor, and a grad student with secret
empathic abilities like Toni's.

Not that Drew knew about that last part.

He was frowning at the finger. "And you said it fell out of the tractor?"

Toni nodded and avoided looking at the bloody digit. "According to Nico, the tractor was working fine yesterday, no weird sounds or anything, so I flipped up the seat to see if there was something interfering with the safety switch."

"And the wires were cut?" He scribbled something in a small notebook.

"Yeah. I flipped up the seat and saw the wires there. They didn't look worn down or anything, like they were rubbing up on anything—nothing like that—the ends were cut clean."

Drew looked up at the tractor, then back to the finger. "Could someone have been trying to mess with the tractor and gotten their finger cut off? Lost it in the engine or something?"

Toni shook her head. "I guess anything is possible, but you'd have to be pretty inept to lose a finger cutting a couple of wires. They're not exactly hard to find."

Drew crouched down. "The edges of this are pretty rough. It doesn't look like a clean cut. Almost like it was torn off. And it looks like it's been exposed for a while."

Toni shuddered. Accidents on the farm or at the garage were not unheard of, and they were one of the reasons she didn't wear jewelry, not even tiny earrings. Still, she had no idea how a finger could be torn off while cutting two exposed wires.

"If I'd been checking a belt or something, I could kind of see it but..." She shrugged and tried to calm her stomach, but she wanted to puke again. "Honestly, I have no idea. You're gonna have to examine the engine, I think. See if there're any traces of blood in it. Maybe the safety switch isn't the only thing that was tampered with."

Nico let out a low groan, and Drew looked up.

Toni tried to send out good vibes, but it was a lot harder to change the temperature of someone's emotions when she wasn't in direct contact.

Drew said, "Sorry, Mr. Dusi, but there's no way that this tractor is going to work today."

Nico ran a frustrated hand through his hair. "Can I at least get my crew going?"

Drew frowned. "Is there a reason you need to rush them out of here?"

"The pinot grapes," Nico said. "We have to get them today. I'm gonna make some calls about a tractor." He stalked off toward the barn.

"Pinot grapes?" Drew looked at Toni. "These grapes gonna go bad in a day?"

"It's the sugar," Toni said. "The daytime temperatures are supposed to head way up tomorrow, and he's afraid the sugar levels will spike with the heat, which would throw off the fermentation and change the character of the wine." Toni glanced at Nico, who was on the near side of the barn, looking like he was about to deck Henry. Or Danny. Or both.

How about that? Henry was here.

Focus on the bloody finger, Toni.

Toni looked away. "That's his winemaker, Henry Durand, and his foreman, Danny Barba. Henry's the one who kind of determines what the sugar levels should be.

Then Nic's gotta get the grapes in so they can start the crush."

Drew pursed his lips, glanced at the men, and nodded. "Okay, I'll make sure the officer gets all the employees' names and numbers and we can follow up later. Go tell your cousin he can get his guys working."

"Thanks." She glanced at Drew, then back at the finger. Then at Drew again. "One thing."

"Yeah?" Drew pulled out his phone.

"Can I take off too?" She was dying to get out of there. Not only was the temperature starting to climb, she could see Henry walking toward the workers.

Nope. Nope, nope, nope. Of all the days, not this one.

"Yeah." Drew waved at her. "Take off. I got your number."

"Okay." She hightailed it toward her car but wasn't fast enough.

"Toni!"

She turned just as she reached her car. Knowing Henry, if she tried to take off, he'd just sit on her hood or something.

Toni looked up. "Hey."

Henry Durand was the size of a smallish tree. He had narrow hips and a lean torso. He'd told her once he used to mountain climb, and she could see it in the lanky lines of his body. He was about as opposite from her short curvy frame as was physically possible.

And he was cute. So damn cute she had to steel herself every time they interacted.

"Hey, Henry." She wiped her expression clean. "What's up?"

"You didn't answer my call this morning."

"Nope. I was busy."

He bit his lower lip. "Everything okay?"

That is such a loaded question I don't even have an idea of how to answer it. "Fine. Just have a lot going on. And I need to get back to the garage, so—"

"Do you need any more help with the cabinets in the laundry room?" He shoved his hands in his pockets. "I've been meaning to ask."

"No." She swallowed the maniacal laugh that threatened to erupt. "I've got it."

The first time she'd met Henry, she'd felt the sparks between them, but Henry was an "aw, shucks" clean-cut farm boy from Washington State, and he was about ten years younger than Toni.

Or so she thought. She honestly had no idea, and she was too afraid to ask.

"Just..." His cheeks turned a little red. "If you need any help, I'm happy to lend a hand."

Oh, he'd lent her a hand all right. The first time she'd accepted his help, they'd gotten the entire fireplace surround cleaned and the woodwork sanded down before they'd ended up naked on a drop cloth in the freshly painted bedroom.

Toni had been scrubbing drops of Coastal Plain green off her backside for an hour the next morning.

The second time, he'd helped lay tile in the new shower.

The third time it had been refinishing the floors.

Every time Henry lent a hand with the house, he lent something else as well. Which was a lot of fun and a complete disaster waiting to happen, but she couldn't seem to help herself.

Worse, ever since the incident at the gym, she could *feel*

Henry's emotions. The man had none of the mental shields she'd learned to distinguish on people. Nearly everyone she'd met, from her mother to Detective Drew Bisset, had some kind of shield. Her mother's was whisper-thin, but it was there. Drew's were thick as stone walls, and she was pretty sure she'd never be able to influence him.

Henry? He had none. None! The man wore his heart on his sleeve, and she could feel his affection bouncing around her as enthusiastically as the floppy-eared rescue dog he'd adopted.

Toni quickly slid on her sunglasses. "I'm good, Henry, but thanks. Appreciate the offer." She opened her car door and got inside. "I need to get to work."

"Have a great day." He patted the side of her car. "Be safe, Toni."

You darling, innocent man. "Thanks. Hope all the grapes get in."

His smile was a little crooked. "If I have to harvest all night, we will get those pinot grapes in the barn."

Henry was an incredibly hard worker, and Nico—the cousin with three sisters—treated the younger man like a long-lost brother. The winemaker had grown up at a vineyard in Washington, but as one of six kids, he'd taken off to make his own fortune in the world.

He'd actually said that. "Make his own fortune in the world." Who said things like that?

Henry, of course. And Regency romance heroes maybe? Missionaries? Earnest Canadian Mounties?

As her grandma would say, "*Six of one, half dozen of the other, Antonia.*"

Toni carefully backed out of the parking spot by the barn

before she pulled forward and headed down the paved driveway that led to the highway. She didn't look back. She couldn't afford any more distractions.

But all the way back to town, Henry kept circling her thoughts.

Drip.

Drip.

Drop.

KATHERINE BASSI SET an open bottle of red wine on the table along with three glasses. Toni looked away from the crashing waves of Moonstone Cove and stared at the wineglasses.

Shit.

She stood and walked toward the house. "I think I need some water actually. I was so busy today. If I have wine, it'll go straight to my head."

Megan lifted an eyebrow. "Your dad at the garage today? You look stressed."

If anyone knew stress, it was Megan Carpenter. The woman had uprooted her life, left her event-planning business in Atlanta, and moved with her husband and three children to the Central Coast, only to find out that her husband had started fooling around with a woman half his age behind her back. She'd kicked him to the curb and was in the process of a messy divorce, all while trying to start a new business and deal with three kids.

Toni couldn't even imagine that kind of stress.

Just her and the cat. Cats. Not that Enzo was high-maintenance.

"You know, it was a lot of little things." Toni opened the door. "But let me get some water first."

She walked into Katherine's house to see Baxter, husband extraordinaire and math professor, making a cheese-and-fruit plate to take out to them.

"Thank you," Toni said. "Can I get that?"

Baxter lifted the tray and held it close. "Did you think I was sharing?"

Toni grinned. "My mistake."

"You know how I love pears." Baxter smiled and handed her the tray. "If you can get this, I'll slice the baguette from the market."

"I know I'm probably too old to be adopted, but I would pick you for a big brother over my own any day." Toni reached for a tall glass and filled it with water from the fridge.

"Family friction?" Baxter asked. He had a charming accent that was half Hong Kong and half London. "I'll let my brother know that we have an honorary sister. He'll be thrilled; we always wanted one."

Toni snagged a pear and bit into it. "I just think I have too much family, you know? It would be one thing if they'd spread out a bit, but they all stayed here."

Baxter motioned to the large windows looking over the ocean. "Can you blame them?"

"Not really." Moonstone Cove was nestled in a curve of the Central California coast, smack between the coastal range and the Pacific Ocean. The weather was mild, the breeze was cool, and there were far more sunny days than overcast.

Baxter and Katherine taught at the local state university that specialized in marine biology and had a thriving agricultural and viticultural school. Nearly all of Toni's family—brothers, sisters, and cousins—worked locally, and many hadn't even left town for college.

"There's just so many of them," Toni said. "And they all have opinions. About everything."

"I heard a writer once compare family to an octopus," Baxter mused.

"That's not... inaccurate," Toni said. "Some days it's a thin line between hugging and strangulation."

"Indeed." He finished cutting the baguette into thin slices. "Let's see if food makes a difference, shall we?" He patted her shoulder and motioned her out the doors. "Or do you want to stay in here and hide from the perceptive ones?"

"Tempting, but they'd find me." Toni popped a slice of pear in her mouth and grabbed her tall glass of water. "I better face the music."

Baxter ushered her out to the back deck and set down the basket of bread while Toni scooted the wine bottle out of the way and set down the tray of snacks. Baxter gave Katherine a kiss on the cheek and then promptly decamped to the study to leave the women to their own devices.

"Here." Megan held out a glass of red wine to Toni. "For when you're done hydrating."

Toni hesitated a moment before she took the wine and sat next to Megan. "Thanks."

Katherine leaned her elbows on the table. "Out with it. I'm not an empath, but the worry is rolling off you like waves. Even I can feel it."

"Cheers." Megan clinked her glass with Katherine's.

"Here's to Wine Wednesday and girlfriends. Together we can solve the mysteries of the universe."

Toni nodded and took a long drink of water. "Okay, cool. What do you want to start with? The detached finger I found while trying to fix my cousin's tractor this morning? Or the fact that I'm pretty sure I'm kind of pregnant?"

CHAPTER 3

Katherine promptly spat a mouthful of wine across the table. Megan, with her lightning-fast reflexes, diverted the wine with a swipe of her telekinesis before it could hit the cheese. It splashed next to Katherine's chair as she sat coughing into a napkin.

"Well, at least I saved the cheese." Megan gave her a sideways glare. "You have fun giving us a heart attack like that?"

"What was it? The severed finger or the pregnancy?"

"The pregnancy of course." Megan rolled her eyes. "Who hasn't seen a severed finger or two? You getting knocked up, on the other hand—"

"Please don't say knocked up," Toni said. "I'm not a teenager."

"Could have fooled me, Miss I Don't Know What Condoms Are." Megan shook her head. "Are you sure?"

"Well, you're the one with three kids. How positive is a week of bathroom pee tests that all say 'pregnant'?"

"Yeah, you're knocked up."

"Will you not?" Toni reached for another slice of pear.

23

Her stomach was in full revolt. She hadn't eaten anything since lunch, and she was getting more nauseated as the day went by, not less. "I thought it was called morning sickness, not evening sickness."

"Have some bread." Megan handed her the basket. "It doesn't follow the clock a lot of the time." She sighed a little. "What were you thinking, Toni?"

"I was thinking I haven't had sex in like... five years and hot man and ooooh, orgasms! I wasn't thinking about birth control anymore." She bit into a slice of bread. "I'm not twenty-five."

"Did you think your uterus just stopped working?" Megan snatched the glass of red wine from Toni's hand. "Did you come equipped with an ovary gauge that I don't have? Women can get *more* fertile in their forties, Toni. It's like a going-out-of-business sale down there."

Toni closed her eyes. "I wasn't thinking *clearly*. Obviously."

Katherine was staring at Toni and not saying a word.

Megan took a long drink of wine. "I think you broke Katherine."

"I didn't mean to."

"You know, I have these discussions with my teenagers," Megan quipped. "I didn't think I needed to have them with my girlfriends too. Are you keeping it?"

"I..." It hadn't even occurred to her *not* to keep it. She'd been too absorbed with how she was going to manage her mother finding out. "I guess I am. I mean, I'm financially independent. I own my home. I have a big support system. I'm perfectly capable of raising a child."

"But do you *want* kids?" Megan asked. "It's not for everyone."

"I don't *not* want kids," Toni said. "I always imagined having them, it just didn't happen the way I thought it would. Men weren't exactly beating down the door to marry Bobby Dusi's daughter, who could beat them up and fix a car better than they could, you know? So I didn't get married. So I didn't have kids. It wasn't a deliberate choice. Life just happened."

"Well, life definitely just happened here. Speaking of men beating down your door, who's the daddy?"

Katherine finally spoke. "Henry?"

Toni nodded.

"Who's Henry?" Megan's eyes went wide. "Why haven't I heard about this man? Who is he? How long have you been in a relationship? Do you have pictures?"

"No, we're not in a relationship. Exactly. And it's not—"

"You have a picture," Katherine said. "I saw it pop up on your phone once when he called."

Toni pointed at her. "You are not to be trusted."

"Oh bullshit." Megan held her hand out. "We are going to support you whatever happens, and you know we've got your back walking through literal gunfire, Antonia Dusi, but we're gonna give you shit about this first. Show me the man."

Toni took a deep breath, opened her contacts, and tapped the picture next to Henry Durand's name before she handed her phone to Megan.

She grabbed the phone, pulled it close, then held it at a distance and squinted before she gasped. "He is so cute! He looks like that..." She snapped her fingers. "Who's the actor I'm thinking about?"

Katherine said, "I'm a seer, not a telepath."

"You know, the young one who was in all those Disney musical shows." Megan's eyes went wide and her head whipped around to Toni. "He's young! How young is he?"

"Thirtysomething," Toni muttered. "I don't know exactly. And he doesn't look like Disney Musical Guy."

"He kind of does though, you cougar."

"See? This is why I was dreading telling you guys about him. I'm forty-one; I'm not a cougar."

Katherine took the phone from Megan, looked at the picture, and smiled. "He's not *that* much younger than you. I think he just has a young face. Have you told him?"

"No." She couldn't even imagine it. "He'll probably want to marry me."

"And you don't want to get married?" Katherine asked.

"Do you know how many of my cousins got married because they got pregnant? Only one of them is still happy. I don't object to marriage completely, but I don't want to do it just because I got pregnant."

"Agreed." Megan handed her the phone back. "It's not 1950. You're an independent woman with a good support system. Have the baby. Work out the coparenting. Let the relationship be a separate thing."

"Thank you."

"Are you sure he'd want to get married?" Megan asked. "A lot of men don't."

"Henry is very..." She sighed. How could she explain? "He's very *good.*"

Megan snorted. "Tell us more."

"Not like... Okay, he's good at that too, but I'm talking about his character. He's traditional, but not in like the narrow-minded way, just like in the... *good* way." She wasn't doing this well. "He grew up on a winery; went to college in Washington State for viticulture. My cousin hired him about a year ago to be his winemaker. He's incredibly gifted, and I know he's traveled a lot for his education, but he still seems kind of... sheltered. Added to that, he doesn't smoke, doesn't drink except for work, and he volunteers at the homeless shelter. He... picks up trash on the side of the road. He already adopted a rescue dog, for heaven's sake."

As if on cue, Katherine and Baxter's adorable goldendoodle scratched at the door. Katherine rose to let him out. The sun was setting over the ocean as Archie came over and promptly laid his head in Toni's lap.

"Look at you." She rubbed his head. "How do you know?"

"He's very empathetic," Katherine said. "You probably have a lot in common. Henry sounds like a wonderful person who would make an excellent father. What's the problem?"

"He's *too* good." Megan narrowed her eyes. "Right?"

Toni nodded. "I hate to be cynical, but I just feel like... no one can be that decent, right? What am I not seeing?"

Katherine smiled. "I think you're overthinking this. At the end of the day, it doesn't matter. Like you said, it's not like you have boyfriends coming out your ears. He works with your cousin and knows your family. You're not going to be able to hide the pregnancy forever, and they're gonna know who the daddy is."

"I know. But just... for a while, can we pretend it's not real? I'm trying not to get too attached to the idea anyway. The chances of miscarriage when you're older are a lot higher." The mention of losing the ephemeral baby already felt like a splinter in her heart.

Megan nudged her arm. "You want this."

Toni took a deep breath. "It's not what I imagined. At all. But I think it's fate, you know? This is probably it. This is probably my last chance to be a mom. And I always imagined I'd be a mom. I think... I'd be a fool not to take it."

Katherine's smile was wide and glowing. "You're going to make a wonderful mother."

Toni blinked back the tears that threatened her eyes. "I don't know how to do much domestic stuff, you know? And this is like... *super* domestic stuff."

"You've got us," Megan said. "We got your back; you can ask me anything. And I have three kids who will make awesome babysitters."

"And I am a very enthusiastic aunt," Katherine said. "I'm also excellent at helping with homework."

Toni held up a hand. "Okay, can't go there quite yet. Can we talk about the severed finger for a while? That's a lot less scary than thinking about babies."

AFTER KATHERINE GOT a ginger ale for her, Toni sketched out her morning, starting with the call from Nico at the farm.

"So someone was messing with his tractor and lost a finger?" Katherine winced. "Painful. But why wouldn't they have taken their finger and gone to the hospital? In all but the worst cases, they can usually reattach them."

Megan made a face. "Really though? They don't turn black and fall off?"

"That does happen, but the success rate is quite high. Around seventy percent or so. Vascular surgeons can do amazing work. They might have sent him up to San Francisco..." She turned to Toni. "I'm assuming, but I shouldn't. Was it a male finger?"

"It looked pretty big to me. I'd say probably male."

"Could you tell which one?"

She shrugged. "Not a thumb. That's about it." She closed her eyes. "No."

"No what?"

"No, there's something else about it that seemed different." She kept her eyes closed. "What was it?"

"Not a thumb," Megan said. "Was it a clean cut?"

"No. Ragged, like it had been torn off. Or... bitten?" That. That was what she'd noticed. "The nail was really neat. Like, *really* neat."

Katherine frowned. "So probably not someone who works with his hands."

"But someone who was trying to tamper with a tractor?" Megan shook her head. "I'd expect anyone who knows how to disable a tractor to have workingman's hands."

"Neat. Clean." Toni could see it in her mind now. "I'm pretty sure he'd had a manicure. His cuticles were all neat like mine are when I get my nails done."

"You get your nails done?" Megan asked.

"Every time a Dusi or Lanza woman gets married, I do." She reached for another piece of bread. "He had a manicure, neat fingernails, and clean hands. No grime on the finger other than a little grease from the engine and dirt."

"Who would want to mess with your cousin? Didn't you say this would mess up his pinot noir harvest?"

"I texted him before I came over," Toni said. "He'll be okay since his neighbor loaned him his old rig. They're going to have to work late and finish up first thing in the morning, but they did get most of the fruit today. And tomorrow morning shouldn't be too cold."

"Is Henry out there with them?" Megan asked.

"Don't know why that would be important." Toni nabbed a piece of cheese. "Drew Bisset was at the scene."

"Isn't he the one who predicted the Cove was gonna go back to 'normal'?" Megan used air quotes around normal. "Oops."

"I mean, people do lose fingers," Toni said. "It's probably one of the more common agricultural accidents."

"But this guy was messing with someone else's tractor, got his finger torn off, and left his finger in the tractor!" Megan said. "Who does that?"

"Makes you wonder," Katherine said.

"Makes you wonder what?"

"Why?" Katherine lifted her shoulders. "If someone came into the emergency room with a detached finger, they'd ask him how he detached it, but I doubt they'd ask that many questions. He could just say he was fixing a tractor. They'd never know he was doing anything criminal."

"So you're wondering why he didn't seek medical care?"

"And wondering why he left his finger behind."

Toni said, "Maybe it fell in the engine and he couldn't get it out because he was bleeding everywhere."

"Was there a lot of blood at the scene?"

Toni thought about it. "No."

"Hmm." Katherine looked troubled.

"Maybe it got cut off and someone took it," Megan said. "Or the finger got lost on the way to the hospital."

"You think someone accidentally misplaced a finger?" Toni asked. "Maybe left it on the roof of the car and drove off like it was a cup of coffee?"

"Did any of the local clinics report someone coming in with a missing finger?" Katherine asked. "If they didn't, that leads us to a whole other set of questions."

"Like what?" Toni asked.

"Well..." Katherine's eyebrows went up. "The most obvious one would be: Was the person alive when the finger was detached?"

Aaaaaand there went Toni's stomach again. "I'm gonna say that's something Drew can figure out without us."

CHAPTER 4

Toni woke up on Saturday morning and stretched with languor in the sunbeam that crossed her bed. Her foot hit something, and Shelby gave her an annoyed yowl when she fell off the end of the bed.

"Oops." She glanced over at the cat. "Sorry."

Shelby jumped back on the end of the bed and promptly attacked Toni's foot.

"Ow!" She pulled her legs up. "Jeez, cat."

The grey shorthair glared at her and let out another loud meow.

"Let me guess, a tiny portion of the bottom of your food bowl is showing."

Shelby turned her back and showed Toni her tail, which whipped back and forth before she jumped to the windowsill.

Toni swung her legs over the bed and let her feet touch the newly refinished floorboards. The wood was cool to the touch, so she toed on her slippers and grabbed a thin cotton robe before she wandered out to the kitchen.

It was only when she got to the kitchen that she heard the distant sound of a gardening pick.

Toni closed her eyes and sighed. "Henry."

She quickly checked Shelby's food bowl, picked it up, and shook the kibble to the bottom of the bowl to cover the bare patch. Then she set it down and Shelby promptly began eating.

"Weirdo," Toni muttered. She walked to the door and wrapped her robe tight before she stepped out onto the wide porch built onto the front of the house.

Her home was a Spanish-style bungalow; an ancient grapevine covered the open wooden porch, creating a thick green shade across the front of the house during the warm summer months. Now that it was fall, fat purple grapes hung over her head, and she could see the edges of the lush green leaves curling up as they started to get dry.

Across the front yard, between the stand of oaks and her peeling red barn, she saw Henry with his pick and a wheelbarrow.

She slid into her garden boots and walked across to the barn.

"Henry," she said. "I told you I was going to do that."

He looked up and wiped a thin sheen of sweat off his forehead. The smile he shot her was brilliant. "Hey."

"I told you I could clear that out," she repeated.

He leaned his pickax on the ground. "It's not a problem. I told you and Nico I'd help."

She squinted into the rising sun. "You don't have enough to do at the farm?"

"Danny and the other guys already started processing. And if I want to clean up these old vines and get some cuttings to propagate them before next year, I need to get some healthy shoots going before it gets too cold."

Along the east side of the barn, there were eight rows of ancient grapevines pruned in a goblet style. Nico guessed they were nearly one hundred years old. They'd gone completely wild in the past twenty years, but they'd survived rain and fog, so Toni knew they had to be hardy.

The small vineyard was in a part of the garden that was completely overgrown, and it wasn't until she'd cut the long grass back that she even realized they were there. She called Nico to take a look to see if they were worth salvaging, and Nico had sent Henry, who'd become obsessed.

"You know these could be some of the original vines planted on the property," he said, swinging the pick over his shoulder to dislodge a large chunk of concrete that had been tossed between the rows. "If I can get decent cuttings off them—and if the grapes are any good—we could propagate or clone the original varieties that were grown on this land." He turned to her with a wide grin. "Don't you think that's exciting?"

She couldn't help smiling a little at his schoolboy enthusiasm. "Hey, if you're going to clean up my yard, I'm not going to argue."

His eyes were dancing in the sunshine, and his smile was dazzling. His dark hair fell over his forehead, and she could see a little stubble on his jawline. His shirt was long-sleeved, but he'd opened it at the neck and the cords of muscle on his neck nearly had her drooling.

Oh God, he does look like a Disney prince.

"Uh..." She blinked and turned to look at the house.

Must. Escape. Dazzle. "I was gonna make some coffee. Do you want some?"

Wait. Shit. Was she allowed to have coffee? Was that bad for the baby?

Don't think about the baby.

"I'd love some coffee." Henry put his fingers to his mouth and let out an ear-piercing whistle. "I should call Earl. He's been gone a while."

"You don't worry about him getting lost?"

Henry looked at her like her head was damaged. "No."

Earl was the dog of mysterious origins that Henry had adopted. Within seconds of the whistle, she heard him crashing through the brush as he raced across the oak grove that led down to the dry creek bed.

Toni braced herself.

If there was anyone more enthusiastic about life than Henry, it was Earl. He was the size of a small horse, with a ruddy tan coat and floppy ears. He looked a little like what Toni imagined would happen if a yellow lab and a quarter horse had a baby.

"Hey Earl!" Toni put her hands out. "Sit. Sit!"

Earl, who was mostly legs and panting tongue, managed to stop just before he ran into Toni's legs and knocked her over like a bowling pin.

"Hey, buddy!" Henry grinned and spread his hands in a helpless gesture. "Sorry. He loves you."

The waves of happiness were impossible to resist. It was early in the day, and Toni's emotional receptors were wide and clear. Joy and affection rippled off Henry, then bounced off Earl and onto her. It was nearly enough to make Toni light-headed. Earl stuck his head under her outstretched hand and woofed. It was impossible not to be charmed.

"Hey, buddy." She picked a foxtail off his ear. "You need to be careful with him."

"I check him every night." Henry propped his pick against an old vine and walked over to pull another foxtail off Earl's shoulder. "I don't suppose I could ask you for a bowl of water. He's still afraid of Enzo and won't go in the barn."

At the sound of the Enzo's name, Earl whined.

"It's okay." Toni rubbed his ears. "I know you were only trying to be friendly. He's a cranky old man."

"Don't let him in the house," Henry said. "I'm fairly sure he rolled in something."

"Okay." Toni patted her leg, and Earl followed her while she walked back to the house. "You're going to have to pine from a distance then."

Earl trotted ahead of her and promptly sprawled in front of Shelby's favorite window.

As if she'd been waiting for her cue, the grey cat jumped into the window and paced back and forth with her tail held high as Earl let out excited yips.

"Chill." Toni opened the door and yelled at the cat. "Stop teasing him, you hussy."

Shelby and Earl adored each other in a way only possible between divergent species. Shelby bestowed her presence upon Earl, and Earl whined helplessly and cast her longing stares from outside the house.

Toni got a large bowl of water and took it out to Earl before she went back in the house and put on the electric kettle for coffee. She could make a couple of pour overs. That way she could give Henry caffeine and she could drink the decaf she got for her mom until she found out what was and wasn't on the "bad food" list.

No alcohol. No coffee. No sushi? Was that still a thing? It had been a few years since either of her sisters had been pregnant.

So far, pregnancy sucked hard.

Her nausea actually seemed to calm down when she opened the coffee, as if the scent alone was enough to calm her quickly escalating anxiety.

You're pregnant, Toni Dusi, and the father of the baby is cleaning up your garden and has no idea.

"I can do this." She repeated her mantra from the day before. "Katherine says I'll be a great mom, and she's like the smartest person I know." She got two filters from the cupboard and filled the first with decaf and the second with regular. Then she poured the piping-hot water over the ground coffee and let it sit.

She went to her bathroom, washed her face, and put on a pair of work pants and a long-sleeved shirt. She wasn't going to let Henry do all the gardening alone, and she'd already been planning on digging out some of the weeds on the far side of the house.

The little stone house had a decent-sized porch and a wide, stone-covered patio under the oaks on the north side. When the weeds were cleared out and the grass grew back between the stones, it would be a shady spot perfect for a dining table and chairs. Maybe she could even host Wine Wednesday at her house someday.

You're going to have to unless you find a babysitter.

Toni sat on the edge of the bed and stared at the cracked plaster wall. The enormity of changes threatened to pull her under a rising wave of panic.

"Toni?"

She blinked hard, pressed the heels of her hands to her eyes, and took a deep breath. "Yeah?"

"There's an old rose in the middle of one of the rows. It's pretty beat up, but I can transplant it if you have a spot."

She took two deep breaths. "Yeah. Sure. That sounds good. I was going to turn the bed in front of the porch into a rose garden." Actually that had been her mother's idea, but it was a good one. Toni wasn't a fan of cut roses, but she liked the ones on bushes. They were pretty and they were hard to kill.

"Okay great. I'll move it over there. It's thorny, but it's a really beautiful red."

"Great." She stood and slapped her cheeks, pulled on some socks, and walked down the hall, only to see Henry standing in front of the mantel, staring at the fireplace.

"It turned out great."

"Yep." She refused to think about that day. Things were too complicated. Toni turned to the kitchen, and Henry reached for her wrist.

"Just tell me why," he said quietly. "Is there someone else?"

"*No.* That's not it." Toni shook his hand off and continued to the kitchen to finish making the coffee.

"Then why?" He walked over to the kitchen, bracing his arms in the doorway. "Because I work for Nico?"

"I mean..." That was part of it. Toni pushed the filters down and let the dark brewed coffee drain into the mugs. She had a feeling Nico wouldn't be too thrilled that she and Henry—

"He knows, if that's what you're worried about."

Toni spun around. "Nico knows *what?*"

Henry held up his hands. "Just... that I'm into you. That's all. I asked him if you had a boyfriend and he asked me if I was thinking of asking you out and I told him yes. So like... he knows that I'm into you. That's all. Not that we... you know."

She could tell from his expression he was telling the truth. Who was she kidding? Henry always told the truth. She was the one lying. "What did Nico say when you told him you wanted to ask me out?" She was surprised her older brat of a cousin hadn't said anything.

"He just laughed." Henry frowned. "I don't know why."

"Probably because he thought you were joking."

"Why would I be joking?"

Because big handsome hunks don't generally ask out older women who routinely make grown men cry. "I just... don't date a lot."

"I know you're busy. I just think—"

"Yes." She went with that. "I am busy. So... *damn* busy right now. You know the car show is coming up and we have, like, four different clients we've been juggling."

"Right." He knew she was lying. "It's fine. I can be patient."

"Good. I mean" —she cleared her throat— "patience is a virtue and all that."

What was she going to do with him?

Kiss him. Tackle him to the floor, tear off his shirt, and—

"Coffee's done." She handed Henry his mug and reached for the milk in the fridge. She dosed her coffee and opened the jar of biscotti on the counter.

"Are you done with the...?"

"Yeah." She handed him the milk. "Do you want the...?"

"Yeah." They moved around the kitchen in a dance that was a little too familiar for Toni's taste. Henry was too accustomed to her home; he fit into her routine a little too easily.

Is that a bad thing?

Yes?

"So does Nico know who messed with the tractor yet?" She took a bite of the homemade biscotti. It was her grandmother's recipe and the one thing she could bake and not ruin.

"The police haven't said anything, but you know Nico. He always blames Fairfield." Henry reached for the jar of biscotti. "It's not just the tractor either."

"What do you mean?" She grabbed her coffee and walked to the door.

Henry followed her and waited for Toni to slide on her garden boots before he shut the door behind them. They sat on the two creaking chairs that faced the barn.

"There've been a lot of little things lately," he said. "Uh... the tractor. A fermentation tank that was tampered with. A call to the labor contractor that changed the day we were supposed to start the pinot harvest. That was the one right before the tractor."

"Seriously?" Toni frowned. "So someone is definitely trying to mess with him."

"The pinot we bottled last year is looking good, and the conditions this year look even better. The other varietals are our bread and butter, but the pinot is the one that's going to start winning consistent awards for us, I'm dead sure of it." He finished his biscotti in two bites. "That's why Nico was kind of pushy the other day."

Toni kicked her feet up on the low railing around the porch and let her senses settle. Dog flopped on the porch and cat sunning in the window. Tall drink of man lounging next to her. Morning birdsong, the wind through the trees, and silence.

Forget Megan's meditation. This was all she needed.

"Did you end up getting all the grapes in the other day?"

Henry nodded. "The pinot, yeah. Some of the last boxes might be a little high on the Brix, but I can work with it. I have some ideas."

"And Nico blames Fairfield, huh?"

Whit Fairfield had been the bane of Nico's existence for nearly five years. He'd originally come down to Moonstone Cove as a Silicon Valley millionaire looking to pour money into a winery as an investment. He quickly realized that there was still land available in the hills of the small but growing wine appellation that he could obtain at a bargain if he offered cash. He had pressured landowners to sell and amassed a commanding amount of acreage before he poured a bunch of money into a high-end tasting room and a Napa Valley marketing team.

Fairfield Family Wines bought black-and-white pictures to hang on the tasting room walls and presented themselves as a Moonstone Cove institution. Tourists ate it up, and local vintners rolled their eyes.

"Is Fairfield still pressuring him to sell that acreage along Ferraro Creek?"

Henry nodded. "Yeah. I don't think Nico's tempted even with what Fairfield is offering, because the cabernet vines that grow along there have been amazing the past few years and they're the backbone of our estate red blend. Danny told me Fairfield doesn't even want to plant it. But it's right across the creek from his tasting room, and he wants to expand his event space."

"Are you serious?" Toni rolled her eyes. "What an asshole."

"Yeah." Henry glanced at Toni. He looked nervous. "Someone told me they saw Marissa and Fairfield having drinks in town. Have you heard about that? Do you think Nico has?"

Toni's eyes went wide. "Are you kidding me?"

"Nope."

"You think it's just gossip?"

Henry shrugged. "No idea. The two of them deserve each other, if you ask me."

The only harsh word Toni had ever heard from Henry was about Marissa, Nico's ex-wife. Or... almost ex-wife. He'd been trying to get her to sign the papers for six months. She'd up and left him and their two kids a couple of years ago, but Marissa was still hoping to wrangle some of the winery from the Dusi clan.

"I used to think it was kind of shitty that Grandpa Dusi never signed that land over to Nico outright since he was the one who loved it the most and was obviously the one who would take over eventually, but now I am so glad he didn't."

"I think Nico's happy about that too." Henry finished his coffee. "But I still hate the idea of Fairfield fooling around with Marissa and messing with Nico that way."

"I don't think he'll care," she said. "It'll bug the kids though." She narrowed her eyes. "If it really is Fairfield messing with Nico, I hope that finger we found is his."

Henry chuckled. "So vengeful."

"You should know this about me." She looked over at him. "I have a mean streak."

"I know. I think it's cute." He stood and handed her his mug. "I better get back to cleaning up those vines before it gets too hot. Really appreciate the coffee, Toni."

"Sure." *And thanks for knocking me up with your thirty-year-old super-sperm and upending my entire life. Really appreciate that, Henry.*

Toni took both mugs back in the house and shot Shelby a dirty look as she rolled around in the window, baring her belly to a retreating Earl. "Have some dignity, woman." She shook her head. "You know, *this* is what happens when you let a man in your life."

CHAPTER 5

*S*unday dinners with the Dusi clan were a rotating affair. They were mainly held at Bobby and Rose Dusi's house where they'd retired, but now that her parents were a little older, her brother Frank sometimes hosted them at his ranch house out in the country, or Nico hosted them at the giant Mediterranean house at the winery.

Toni's house, thankfully, would never be big enough for Sunday dinner.

Regular attendance from her and her brother was expected. Her older sister Luna and her family lived in Monterey and could skip out on most of them. Nico and his two kids were usually in attendance, especially in the years since Marissa had left.

And mixing into that core group were various aunts, uncles, grown cousins, and myriad third-generation Dusis, Lanzas, Herreras, and Mendoncas. In all, Sunday dinner was usually between thirty to fifty people, all eating copious amounts of tri-tip barbecue and homemade pasta in the garden behind her parents' house.

Sunday dinners were some of Toni's favorite times with her family, but they'd become a minefield since her empathy had developed. She had to be cautious, or she'd quickly become overwhelmed.

She grabbed a plate of food and settled in her favorite spot at the picnic table in the back corner. That concentrated family drama on two sides instead of four. Within minutes, her sister Luna joined her.

"Where's your wine?" Luna didn't sit down. "Did you forget it? I'll get you some."

"No." She motioned for her sister to sit. "Not drinking anything today."

Luna was instantly concerned. "Nico brings brand-new bottles and you're passing? What's wrong?"

Not wanting to be hit with another coffee-type situation, Toni had come prepared with a cover story. It wasn't that her family were alcoholics—none of them had a drinking problem that she knew of—but in a family of farmers and winemakers, not drinking the new wine was noticeable.

"Okay, it's kind of weird and it may be an overreaction—"

"Oh my God, what's going on?" Luna's emotional temperature spiked.

"My blood pressure is a little high. Chill." Toni held up a hand. "My doctor told me it might just be stress but to cut back on caffeine and alcohol and stuff for a while until we can follow up."

Luna's eyes were wide. "Blood pressure? Did she put you on any meds?" Luna was a marine biologist, but the operating word there was *biologist*. She was keenly interested in anything medical if it had to do with her family. "Did you tell her about Dad?"

"I told her about Dad."

"And Auntie Gina? Did you tell her about Gina?"

"I told her about Gina too. Like I said, she's being cautious and wants to just see what happens if I cut out the wine and coffee and try to get more sleep."

Luna pursed her lips. "What did I say, Toni?"

"Yes, I know. Welcome to my forties."

The satisfied smirk was infuriating. "And you were soooo sure—"

"Can we not?"

"I'm just saying."

"I know you are." Toni adored her big sister. Luna drove her crazy sometimes, but Toni adored her.

A few minutes later, they were joined by their sister-in-law, Jackie. Jackie's family were vegetable growers, and Frank and Jackie had been high school sweethearts. Toni hardly remembered when her sister-in-law hadn't been part of the family.

Jackie sat down and let out a long sigh. She motioned for Luna and Toni to scoot together. "If you guys just scoot a little closer together, I don't think the kids will be able to see me."

With Jackie's presence, the emotional energy in Toni's small bubble turned up to eleven—that was just how her sister-in-law rolled—but Toni didn't mind. Jackie was a lot, but she always cracked Toni up.

"Where's Rani?" Jackie asked. "I didn't see him around."

Luna waved a hand. "He was scheduled to go out on the boat with a group of doctoral students from Central Coast State this weekend. He couldn't change it."

"Gotcha."

Luna's husband, Ranil Abaya, was a marine climatologist who'd come to Monterey via the Philippines and South Africa before he'd gotten a job in California. He and Luna had been working together for barely a year before they'd announced they were getting married. Having a Filipino son-in-law might have been a surprise for their parents, but since Rani was Catholic, they had no issue with it.

And as Toni learned at Luna and Rani's wedding, large Filipino families were as fun, crazy, and nosy as large Italian families, so really Luna and Rani were made for each other. Their two kids were twelve and thirteen and currently shouting across the basketball court with their Dusi cousins.

"Is Rani getting an electric car?" Toni tried to change the subject and not be jealous of Luna's wine. "He texted me about it two weeks ago and I never heard another word."

"He's a climate scientist. He kind of feels like he has to even though in his heart he wants a muscle car."

Toni took a bite of steak. "We'll get there. You know, there are shops that will take old cars and put electric engines in them now."

"Are you thinking about doing anything like that?"

"I'm considering it." Toni shrugged. "Gotta plan for the future, right? It's going to be a growing wing of custom work."

"Yep."

Jackie took a sip of wine. "Give me any car I can fit four children into and not spend a fortune on gas. That's all I want." She glanced at Toni. "You're not drinking? You okay?"

Luna said, "She's got a blood pressure thing her doctor said."

"It's minor," Toni said. "She's just being careful."

"Did you tell her about Dad and Gina?"

"She told her," Luna said. "Relax."

"I'm just saying she's young to have a blood pressure thing."

"Hey." Toni leaned closer to her sisters and tried to change the subject. "Have you guys heard anything about Marissa dating that Whit Fairfield guy?"

"Seriously?" Jackie kept her voice low. "Are they a thing now? What a pair. They deserve each other, I guess, but that's so trashy. He was her neighbor."

Luna shook her head. "Nico's poor kids."

Nico's kids were about the same age as Jackie's. The oldest was just about to graduate from high school, and the youngest was just going in. Since Frank and Nico were as close as brothers, Jackie had spent more time with Marissa than either Toni or Luna.

"That woman," Jackie said, "is the most selfish person I think I've ever met. Ever. After the way she treated Nico, I hope she gets a UTI every time she has sex."

Luna almost snorted wine out her nose.

"Harsh." Toni bit back a smile. "But probably deserved."

"I know Nico's kids are teenagers, but they're still kids," Luna said. "They're gonna care about their mom dating someone who's been so horrible to their father. If nothing else because it'll make people in the Cove talk."

"Please," Jackie said. "I'm pretty sure I saw Beth text Rosie a meme about one of the real housewives of something or other with her mother's face pasted over the picture."

Toni winced. "Ouch."

"Supposedly Marissa has been trying to get something out of Nico. Some piece of the winery that she wants for herself or she's never going to sign the papers and never give him a divorce and contest everything." Jackie shook her head. "What a mess."

"That sucks. Did... uh?" Toni cleared her throat. "Speaking of the winery, did you two hear about what I found at Nico's last week?"

"Oh holy shit, are you talking about that finger?" Jackie's eyes were the size of saucers. "Frank and Nico were talking yesterday. What is that? Who loses a finger and just leaves it in someone's tractor? Did Nico flip his shit?"

"What?" Luna's eyes went wide. "Someone lost a finger?"

"But no one knows who!" Jackie said. "Nico says it's not any of his guys. Danny says none of the harvesting crew got hurt. But some asshole's been messing with Nico's crews and stuff, so Frank thinks maybe whoever is messing with Nico is the one who lost a finger."

"What happened?" Luna said. "It got cut off?"

"Honestly, it looked more... ripped off." Toni shuddered. "It was really gross."

"Are the police doing anything about it?" Luna asked.

Jackie shrugged. "What are they gonna do? They asked at the hospitals, according to Max, and no one came in with a missing finger."

"You ask Leah?"

"I asked Leah too. None of the nurses have seen anything like that."

"What about Aunt Gloria?"

"She's a large animal vet," Toni said. "Do you really think someone's going to go to a vet if they lost a finger?"

"Maybe." Luna narrowed her eyes. "Was there a lot of blood?"

Toni shook her head. "Hardly any. On the finger or the tractor where we found it."

"Huh."

Her older sister was a scientist like Katherine. Toni wondered if her mind was going to the same place. "You're wondering if there's a whole body out there."

Luna shrugged. "I mean, it would make sense. Nico's place is pretty remote."

"I know. That's why I like living out there."

"Luna's right," Jackie said. "If there was a body out in those hills, it could turn into a mummy before someone found it. There's no cell reception or anything. If you got lost..."

"Who's lost though?" Toni asked. "If it was someone from Moonstone Cove, someone would have reported them missing by now. Don't you think?"

"Maybe a weekender?" Luna asked. "There're a lot of people from LA and the Bay Area with vacation homes around here now."

"True." Jackie shrugged. "Well, if no one finds it, eventually the coyotes will."

Toni finished her dinner and wandered out to the side yard where a bunch of the guys were playing horseshoes. Or rather a convoluted Dusi-rules version of the game with way more than four players and a lot more wine. It was a gathering of grown men who immediately reverted to teenage antics as soon as they were around their cousins.

Toni adored all of them.

"Hey, boys." She leaned her elbow on an old wine barrel they were using as a table.

"Toni, get out of here!" her brother Frank shouted. "Nico, you better not—"

"Antonia!" Nico spread his arms with a grin that said he was on his third glass of wine, minimum. "A case of wine if you're on my team."

"You dickhead," Frank hissed. "She's my sister."

"She's my neighbor." Nico held out a horseshoe. "Take the horseshoe. Turn to the dark side."

She squinted at Frank, then at Nico. "Don't you already owe me a case of wine for fixing your tractor?"

"Technically you didn't fix it, but all that will be forgotten if you join my team." Nico stepped between her and Frank. "Forget him. Remember when he cut your hair?"

"I was seven!" Frank said. "And I did a good job."

"If you'd been blind, you did a good job." Nico blocked Frank. "Just come on my team, Toni. We're already six up."

"Sorry." Toni shot Frank a dismayed grin. "He's right. About the haircut and the neighbor thing."

"Oh man!" Frank stalked back to his side of the horseshoe pits, ignoring the betrayed faces of his team members.

It was well known among the Dusis that Toni was preternaturally gifted at horseshoes. She readily admitted it was her only athletic skill. As she lined up behind her cousin Ray, she elbowed Nico.

"What's up?" Nico threw a careless arm around her.

"Any news from Max or Drew on that finger?"

"Nothing." He shook his head. "And no one is talking around the ranch either. I thought for sure someone was going to cop to messing with the tractor when the police started questioning them, but not a word. I told Max they needed to go out to Fairfield's place."

Max was their younger cousin who was on the police force. He was working his way up to detective and idolized Drew Bisset.

"They haven't gone out there yet?"

"Max said— Hold on." Nico stepped forward, set down his wineglass on a large barrel, then tossed the horseshoe. It hooked once around the center stake before it jumped off and fell in the sand.

Nico cursed under his breath as Frank jeered him from across the lawn. "Serves you right, you rat!"

Nico flipped him off and walked back to the barrel to grab his wineglass. "Max said they called out to Fairfield's office, but the secretary said he was in the city. Didn't know when he'd be back."

There were two more throws before hers, so Toni hung back and spoke in a low voice by Nico's shoulder. "Did someone tell you about him and Marissa?"

He gave her a dark look. "I heard. Not from her, of course. She can't be bothered to spare me or the kids any bit of embarrassment. They had to hear it from some shitty little gossip at school."

"You know I think she's an idiot, but there is an upside to all this."

"Oh?"

It was Toni's turn. She stepped forward and, ignoring the whistles and shouts from across the lawn trying to distract her —an accepted and expected part of Dusi-rules horseshoes— landed a perfect ringer around the center stake.

The cousins across the lawn booed and her own team cheered.

"Nine up!" Nico shouted. "Suck it, Frank!"

"Nico!"

Everyone fell silent when Toni's mom called from inside the house.

"Yeah, Auntie Rose?"

"Watch your language, young man."

Toni put a hand over her mouth to keep from laughing.

"I will."

"Serves you right," Frank yelled.

"Frankie!" Toni's mom called again. "Come inside and talk to your father."

The "oohs" and laughter rose from the lawn as Frank Dusi grabbed his beer and walked inside without a word.

"You know he probably wants to talk about the farm," Nico said. "Your dad doesn't care that Frank called me a dickhead."

"Probably because you kind of are."

"Harsh." Nico elbowed her. "See if I send Henry over to help with your vines again next weekend."

Don't be suspicious. Don't be suspicious. "Please, you know he's obsessed with my vines. You can't keep him away." Shit, was that suspicious?

Nico cast her a glance. "He's obsessed with something, all right."

She kept her voice low. "If you say anything about that man to my sisters—"

"Relax, I don't want to torment the poor guy. I'm sure you do that enough, extinguishing all hope in his little crush."

Little crush? Oh, that was great. "So as I was saying about Marissa and your nemesis—"

"Oh yes, can we get back to literally my least favorite subject in the world?" Nico grumbled. "Please, can we?"

"I'm just saying that if they have something going on, maybe she'll finally sign the divorce papers. It's not necessarily a bad thing."

"From your lips to God's ears," he said. "But I'm not holding out much hope. He's probably just messing with her to needle me."

"You think he hates you that much?"

"I think he hates that people see me as a real winemaker and him as an out-of-town wannabe." Nico threw his head back and finished his glass. "Trust me, if Whit Fairfield could get rid of me by snapping his fingers, he'd do it in a heartbeat, and it wouldn't be because of my ex-wife."

CHAPTER 6

"So what do you know about Whit Fairfield?" Drew Bisset didn't wait for her to close the door to her office before he began questioning her.

Toni blinked and kicked the door shut. "You came to my place of business to ask about Whit Fairfield?"

"Did you think I just wanted to hang out?"

"I thought we bonded last spring, Drew."

Drew let out a clipped laugh. "Sure we did."

"Why are you asking me?"

He'd interrupted Toni when she was working on a new project, which was kind of annoying, but it also gave her an excuse to retreat into her office and recharge because she was feeling the urge to crawl under her desk and sleep as soon as the clock hit two o'clock these days.

Because you're pregnant, dumbass.

She ignored her own mental chiding because she was also firmly in denial.

Drew sat in the chair on the far side of Toni's desk and slouched down. "I'm asking you because you know nearly everyone in town in a way that I don't, you're incredibly perceptive, and you and your friends tracked down a serial offender last spring."

Toni spoke carefully. "Those are all sort-of-true things."

"And I trust your read on people."

Silently, Toni said, *Since I can tell when anyone is lying and can usually tell what their motivation is, that's a smart move, Detective.*

Out loud she said, "I mean... I know what I know. Don't you have a read on people too?"

He frowned and folded his hands, resting his chin on his fingers. "I got a read on your cousin. I got a read on this Fairfield guy. The problem is, there's a whole other layer I know I'm not seeing." He pointed at Toni. "And I think you might be able to shed some light on it for me."

"You know there are rumors that Fairfield's seeing Nico's ex, right?"

He waved a careless hand. "I heard, but from what I can tell, that's good riddance on your cousin's part, right?"

"Yeah. Marissa's the one who filed for divorce, but now she won't sign. Nico pretty much hates her guts, but he'd be thrilled if she got a serious boyfriend because she might actually sign the divorce papers then."

"Sad." He shook his head. "That's a sad situation for both of them."

"Yeah, it is." Toni sighed. She could feel that the sentiment from Detective Bisset was sincere. "No one in our family celebrated when she left him even though most of us don't like Marissa much."

"So the read I get from over at the Fairfield place is that the employees like their boss, he pays them well, and that Fairfield isn't all that bad, he just comes across as kind of an asshole at first. Also, they all think your cousin is arrogant, stubborn, and old-fashioned. And that Nico likes to make things difficult for Fairfield and his whole crew just because your cousin doesn't like the guy."

"You got that from his employees?"

Drew nodded.

"So... you got the 'he's not that bad' bit from the people that Whit Fairfield *pays*?"

Drew shrugged. "Fair point. But they seemed pretty sincere."

"And what did you get from Nico's people?"

"That Nico's a hard boss, but everyone respects him. He minds his own business and the only thing he's really obsessed with is winning awards for his wine while Whit Fairfield is the devil incarnate who wants to raze the Dusi winery, burn the oak trees, and turn all of Moonstone Cove into a wine theme park."

Toni pursed her lips. "I mean... that may be slightly exaggerated, but the wine theme park idea has merit."

Drew cracked a smile. "So I'm pretty clear what your cousin and his employees think about Whit Fairfield. What do you think about him?"

"Me?" Her eyes went wide. "What does it matter what I think?"

"For all the reasons I said when I came in. You're a good judge of people and you know everyone."

Toni glanced at the 1968 Chevy Corvette she'd much rather be working on in the garage.

Or a nap. A nap would be good.

"Am I getting paid a consultant's fee or something for this?"

"My wife makes excellent brownies."

Toni considered the offer. Her sweet tooth was already acting up. "Deal." She cleared her throat and leaned back in her chair. "So what do I think about Whit Fairfield?"

"Yep."

She reached into the small fridge sitting on her desk and pulled out a ginger ale. Maybe the sugar would wake her up. "You want one?"

Drew narrowed his eyes. "I'm good."

She cracked it open and took a drink. "I know it's not just my cousin. No one in town really likes Fairfield. Lots of people put up with him because he has so much money. He's an arrogant SOB who thinks he knows more about making wine because he hired a fancy guy from Napa Valley to come down here and show everyone up. He may have thought he was hiring an expert, but this isn't Napa, and people didn't take it that way. People think that Fairfield thinks he's better than people from the Cove."

Drew glanced down at her desk calendar, then met her eyes. "And people from the Cove think he's less because he's not local."

"Speaking from experience?"

"This town can be brutal to new people."

"I know." She thought about how much Megan used to hate Moonstone Cove. "It takes a while for people to break out of their shell around here. But once we do, we're loyal. And people in the wine business around here? They're suspicious of fancy packaging."

"Whit Fairfield is fancy packaging?"

"Oh yeah. Personally, I think his wine is... fine. Nothing special. But he's cozied up to enough wine reviewers who buy into his plans for the town that they tend to cut him slack. He set the bar low for himself, so he leaps over it every time."

"Slack they don't cut your cousin?"

She took a deep breath and tasted the temperature of the air. Drew was searching for something, but he seemed genuinely curious. She didn't pick up any negative vibes when the man mentioned Nico, nor did he seem antagonistic toward Fairfield.

Toni leaned forward. "Okay, real talk? The winery was never a big deal in the family until Nico decided to change that. My grandpa liked to diversify, if you know what I mean, but the vegetable farm was the moneymaker. Still is, to be honest. So Grandpa grew some grapes, raised some cattle, helped my dad and my uncle start this place, helped my Aunt Gina start her restaurant. All that stuff was good. And the vineyards always made money."

Drew nodded. "Okay. I'm getting the picture."

"But we never really made Dusi wine—like an upscale label—until Nico went to my grandpa and asked for the reins to do something bigger than just grow the grapes. And making really good wine is way different than growing grapes. So for him, making a name for himself and Dusi wine really is an obsession. He's worked his ass off to start to get critical respect for a winery that a lot of people around here considered kind of on the level with stuff you buy in jugs, you know?"

"Okay. And he resents Fairfield because...?"

"The guy bought his way in. He didn't work at it. He just

threw money at the idea, and because he was a new name with fancy credentials, critics and restaurant people around here ate it all up and thought Fairfield walked on water when a lot of them would barely answer Nico's calls."

Drew nodded. "Interesting."

"Yeah. So I get that some of Fairfield's employees are annoyed that people don't like their boss, but to be fair, he's made a lot of enemies with his attitude. And he's not above playing dirty tricks. He used shell companies to buy all his property. No one knew he was accumulating that much acreage. And the people who didn't want to sell? A lot of them got harassed big-time."

"Harassed how?"

"Oh..." She spread her hands. "Broken equipment. Busted wells. A barn fire once. Hiring extra harvesting crews just to keep them from picking for someone else."

"I've never heard anything about any of this stuff," Drew said. "Are you sure it's not just rumors?"

"People aren't going to report shit like that. It's not the way things work around here. Did my cousin call the police when his tractor up and quit? No. He called me. Plus no one ever linked anything back to Fairfield. The guy's not dumb. But you tell me it was a coincidence that every single person who resisted selling to him ended up doing it in the long run."

"And you think Nico's next on the list?"

"I think Nico has land Fairfield wants. And if playing dirty worked in the past, why not keep doing it?"

Drew rubbed his chin. "I'm gonna have to think on all this." He sat up straight. "But thanks, Toni. I really appreciate the time. You've given me a much better picture of the situation."

"So are you going to question Fairfield about Nico's tractor? And that finger? Because honestly, what the hell? Who just leaves a finger lying around?"

Drew walked to the door and opened it. "I definitely want to ask him some questions. When I can find him."

Alarm bells started going off all over Toni's brain. "What do you mean?"

"I mean when I got the message from his secretary here that he was in the city, I called up to the Fairfield Enterprise offices in San Jose. And they told me that he was down 'at the ranch' for a while."

Toni blinked. "So his office up there thinks he's down here?"

Drew nodded. "And his office down here thinks he's up there."

"So what you're saying is... he's missing."

"Except no one has reported him missing."

"Oh." Her stomach sank. "Shit."

"Yeah." Drew grimaced. "Shit."

MEGAN HELD a few carved stones in a small leather pouch, moving them from hand to hand with her eyes closed.

"Is Whit Fairfield somewhere in Moonstone Cove?" Megan opened her eyes and cast the stones into the middle of a circle outlined with a long leather strip. The collection of crystals and polished stones bounced onto the wooden table.

Toni tried to keep her face straight. She glanced at Katherine, who was watching the stone casting intently.

"The Mars stone and the Saturn stone are in a cluster

here with the place stone I got from around your house," Megan said. "So... that's interesting."

Toni wasn't going to ask, but Katherine would. Katherine would always ask.

"Why is that interesting?"

"I've met Whit Fairfield more than once," Megan said. "My ex was desperate to get that man's account, so he completely sucked up to him. Whit was very aggressive. Very dominant. Very arrogant."

"Traits associated with Mars," Toni muttered.

"Exactly." Megan examined the circle of stones that she'd divided into four quadrants with two more leather strips. "And Saturn is in the same cluster. That is associated with really negative energy. Misfortune. Pessimism."

"And the place stone?" Katherine asked.

"Well, I'd think that would indicate he's around here." She pointed to a bright green stone on the opposite side of the circle. "And his luck stone is all the way over here. He's in the opposite place of lucky right now."

Don't roll your eyes. Don't roll your eyes. Don't roll your eyes.

Katherine leaned her elbows on the table and examined the circle of stones carefully. "Megan?"

"Yes?"

"You're a confirmed telekinetic."

Megan nodded. "Yes. But I've been reading a lot. And psychic energy can be channeled in ways that aren't always obvious. A lot of it is just practice."

"Noted." Katherine frowned a little. "But my question is, since you can move objects..."

"Yes?"

"And the rocks are objects..."

Megan pursed her lips. "Uh-huh."

"Is it possible that you're subconsciously moving the stones into a pattern that answers questions the way you want them answered?" Katherine leaned her chin on her palm. "In theory."

Toni bit her lip to remain silent.

Megan looked thoughtful. "I mean..."

Katherine looked at her with wide eyes. "After all, the stones did tell you that we should order from Rio Rancho Cantina last week, but I had a feeling that was just because you really like their enchiladas."

Megan started gathering up her stones. "You know what? Forget it."

Toni laughed a little. "Oh, come on. She has a point, Atlanta."

"Just because I'm trying to stretch my psychic abilities and you two are trying to forget you have them," Megan said, "doesn't mean that you get to tease me. Some of us prefer not to live in active denial." She sent a loaded look toward Toni.

"What's that for?" she asked. "Don't give me that."

"Have you told Henry you're pregnant?"

"It's only been eight weeks."

"Have you made a doctor's appointment?"

"No," she muttered. "But I bought vitamins that are the size of horse pills and I'm taking them every day, okay?"

Katherine asked, "And the extra folic acid? Your pregnancy is considered geriatric."

Toni felt like punching both of them even though she knew they were being responsible friends.

"Toni, I can feel your aggression from across the table, but you know we're right. This isn't just about this pregnancy—this is going to be hard on your health even though you're in fantastic shape. You need to see an OB."

"Fine!" She huffed out a breath. "I'll call this week."

"No more living in denial," Megan said. "It's not healthy."

"I'm not living in denial," Katherine said. "Or at least I'm not trying to forget I have visions. That would be irresponsible. If I hadn't had my first vision, Justin McCabe might have murdered all of us. I am feeling a little blocked right now." Katherine twitched her nose. "I'm starting to wonder if ragweed allergies can cause psychic blockage."

Megan handed her the stones. "Okay then, maybe you need to study these instead of me."

Katherine looked at the stones in the leather pouch. "Is there some kind of... textbook I can study?"

"Yep. I'll drop it off tomorrow."

That seemed to cheer Katherine up. If there was a textbook involved, Professor Bassi was always up for the challenge.

"So getting back to Drew's question," Toni said. "Megan's magic stones are telling us he's around here, but he's having bad luck? That seems too vague to take to the police."

"Agreed," Megan said. "What about sniffer dogs? They always bring those out in Georgia when kids go missing."

"There doesn't seem to be any true indication that he is, in fact, missing," Katherine added. "After all, he's a grown man with varied business interests. Who's to say that he didn't simply meet up with someone or leave on a trip without telling anyone?"

"According to Drew, his secretaries in both offices

confirmed that in the years they've worked for Fairfield, he's never taken off without leaving directions on how to reach him. Even when his father passed away."

"Interesting." Katherine tapped her chin with one finger. "Well, if I can provoke a vision, I will. Do either of you have a picture of the man? That might help."

"I don't," Toni said. "I could tell you what he looks like but—"

"Oh!" Megan pulled out her phone. "I think I actually do. Give me a minute. It was from a Christmas party last year."

"Speaking of Christmas, is your mom coming back out?"

Megan rolled her eyes. "Of course she is. And bringing my daddy too. They're distraught about the kids."

"The kids who haven't even spoken to their father in months?"

Megan's children were not being understanding about their father cheating on their mom. Her son, in particular, was furious with his dad.

"Here it is." Megan held up her phone. "There he is on the end, horning in on Jodi Vanderwall. He was being kind of creepy with her, and her husband was piiiiiiissed. That's him in the green shirt."

Katherine narrowed her eyes, then reached for her glasses on the table. She put them on and immediately stopped squinting. Her eyes went wide as saucers.

"This woman's husband is in green? Or the Fairfield man?"

"Whit Fairfield," Megan said. "He's the one in green."

"What is it?" Toni reached for one of the saltines that Katherine had set on the table. Her stomach had started to churn again. *This fucking morning sickness that only comes at night...*

The professor's face was pale. "If that's the case, I don't think I need to have a vision about Whit Fairfield."

"Why not?"

Katherine set the small bag of stones on the table. "I'm relatively sure I already had one. And I'm relatively sure that Whit Fairfield is dead."

CHAPTER 7

*T*he next free afternoon they all shared was on Friday. Toni had finished tuning a particularly touchy Jaguar that afternoon, so she was feeling accomplished as she led the way up the slightly overgrown trail between her house and Nico's winery. "Okay, I'm not saying this is definitely where your vision was, but it's a possibility."

"The creek sounds right." Katherine spoke from behind her. "Toni, you have a growing *Centaurea solstitialis* problem on your property."

"What?" Toni turned her head to see Katherine pointing at the yellow thistles in the brush. "Oh yeah. Nico's got people burning them all over the place. They're impossible to get rid of."

"Yellow star thistle is very invasive and resistant to burning," Katherine said. "Tell him to hire goats."

"Goats?"

Katherine nodded cheerfully. "Goats are extremely effective in keeping thistle infestations down. I can give him a few numbers if you'd like."

"Sure."

Megan was panting behind Katherine. "How long is this trail?"

"About half a mile. We're almost up to the winery." She glanced at Katherine. "You still haven't seen the oak tree?"

"Not yet. But I think I'll recognize it."

Katherine's vision had seemed innocuous at first, which was why she hadn't been alerted to any violence. She'd seen a man who looked like Whit Fairfield with heavy bruising on his face, sleeping under an oak tree near a stream. The vision had been in the middle of the night more than a week ago, days before the morning that Toni had been interrupted by a million calls, a broken tractor, and a severed finger.

In retrospect, a vision about Fairfield "sleeping" was far more ominous than originally perceived.

Toni had immediately suspected the old walking trail that led from the Dusi winery to the highway. It followed Ferraro Creek down to Toni's house, and past that, the highway. If you wanted to sneak into the winery without leaving your car in a noticeable place, that would be the way to go, and the creek was lined by hundreds of oak trees.

"Anything yet?"

"Not yet."

They were nearly to the top of the hill when Katherine stopped and looked around. "There's something we missed."

Toni was flushed and tired from walking, but she didn't want to complain. "What's up?"

Katherine turned to look down the trail. "Perspective. Trees look different from different directions."

"So you're saying we might have already passed it?"

"I can't hear the creek anymore," Katherine said. "Can you?"

"Not really," Megan said. "Just barely because I know it's there."

"But I definitely heard it in the vision. We need to go back." Katherine started walking back the way they'd come. "We may have passed it."

Toni sighed. "Maybe we're just in the wrong place." If they kept going up the hill, there was a bathroom at Nico's house. She really needed a bathroom.

Really, *really* needed a bathroom.

"Katherine—"

"She's already walking back," Megan said. "You doing okay?"

"Yeah." Toni started down the trail. "It's not really that far back to my house—I just have to pee."

Megan motioned to the deserted trail. "You have a Kleenex? Pee. There's nothing around here but trees and bushes. And thistles. Don't squat in those."

"That's a good idea." She patted her pockets. "I don't have anything."

Megan reached into the small backpack she'd slung over her shoulders before they started walking. "Here you go." She handed her a small pack of Kleenex. "And don't forget this." She gave her a small bottle of antibacterial gel. "Do you want wet wipes too?"

Toni blinked. "Do you just carry that stuff around all the time?"

"I got a whole range of snacks too. It's called being responsible for growing humans." Megan patted her shoulder. "You'll get the hang of it. They start out pretty simple. Diapers. Wet wipes. Boobs. That's pretty much all they need at first."

Toni was frozen in her tracks. Tissue in one hand, hand sanitizer in the other, and existential dread a tightly curled ball in her chest. "Megan, I don't think I can do this."

"Pee outside? Just find a tree, honey. No one's around but us."

"No. I don't think I can be a mom."

"Oh." Megan's face went soft. "Yeah, you can." She drew Toni into a firm hug. "I promise you can. You're going to be a wonderful mom."

Toni felt stiff in Megan's embrace. "I've only ever taken care of myself."

"Are you kidding?" Megan pulled away. "You've got a huge family. You're telling me you never babysat? Never watched your sister's or brother's kids? Never held a cousin's hand when they needed it or cleaned up someone else's mess? Not to mention all your employees. You take care of everyone, Toni. Don't minimize those skills just because they're not what commercials make mothering look like. You're gonna do great."

"I'm not like you though." She took deep breaths and tried not to leak her rioting emotions all over Megan just because she was in emotional striking distance. "I don't have the planner and the superclean house. I don't decorate for holidays. I don't... bake."

"You don't have to mom like me!" Megan laughed. "There's a million ways to be a mom. You're gonna find your own way of doing things that works for you. Remember, it's your own little family. You get to set the rules."

Toni nodded and blinked back tears. "Okay."

"Okay?"

"Okay."

"Good. Go pee before you explode. I remember those first few months." Megan patted her shoulder and sent her off into the bushes. "I can't lie. If I'm being honest, I'm a little jealous."

Toni walked behind a bush and squatted. "Why?"

Ahhhhhhh, relief. Like, relief so profound she nearly cried from it.

You nearly cry from everything these days.

"Those early years are work," Megan said, "but they're a lot of fun too. And little kids are hilarious. Teenagers..." She sighed. "It's a whole other level of drama."

"But they can feed themselves."

"I can't lie, that's a bonus."

She cleaned up, used the hand sanitizer, and walked back to the trail. "Okay, I'm thinking more clearly now."

"Good. Let's go find Katherine before she gets lost."

"The trail is pretty clearly marked."

"This is Katherine we're talking about. She could end up seeing an interesting bug or bird and if it flew off, we'll never see her again."

"Good point."

THE SHARP, antiseptic smell of Megan's hand sanitizer was Toni's only saving grace when they found what was left of Whit Fairfield along the edge of Ferraro Creek.

Megan and Toni stood at a distance while Katherine got far too close to the body for either of their comfort.

"Yes," Katherine said. "Definitely scavengers. Coyotes probably. Feral cats too. Maybe some buzzards."

Oh Enzo, what have you done?

"Katherine, we need to get back to the house and call the police." Megan waved at her to come back. "Step back, honey. You know what they show on TV. They're not going to want anyone contaminating the crime scene."

"I'm fairly sure he was shot." Katherine held a handkerchief over her face and leaned over the body. "There's a lot of blood."

Okay, that was it. Toni walked back to the trail, across a small clearing, and puked her guts out under a tree. She stood up straight after losing her lunch and took several deep breaths.

"Toni?"

"Here." She spit and reached for her water bottle to wash out her mouth. "I'm okay."

Megan waved from the trail. "We're here." She had Katherine in tow. "Let's head back to your house and call Drew."

They were deep in the hills above Moonstone Cove, in the folds of the coast range mountains, and mobile phone service was a joke. They'd be in range once they got back to her place. "Should we mark where we went off trail?"

"I already did," Megan said. "Tied a handkerchief on a branch right on the trail."

"Okay." Toni walked back toward them.

Katherine rubbed her back. "Feeling better?"

"How on earth can you just look at... that and not be affected?" Toni asked.

Katherine shrugged. "I guess because it's interesting. I never studied gross human anatomy, but the human body is fascinating to me even in stages of decomposition."

"Well, I am grateful we have scientists like you who can examine things like that," Megan said. "Because I'm with Toni on this one. I nearly lost my lunch at the smell. The scavenger thing certainly explains the finger, doesn't it?"

Whit Fairfield had been killed about halfway between Toni's house and Nico's. A coyote or a cat must have taken the finger from the body and dropped it at the ranch. According to Katherine, there was more than one finger missing.

"Drew will likely have problems finding all the pieces of Mr. Fairfield," Katherine said. "Ecologically, of course, it's for the best. Human preservation practices for the dead are very unnatural." She smiled. "Baxter and I have already arranged to be cremated and planted in a memorial forest in Big Sur. With the proper soil amendments, of course. Human ashes are harmful to plants on their own."

"I did not know that," Megan said. "I will keep that in mind."

Toni felt her nausea coming back. "Can we change the subject please?"

"Sure." Megan held out a tube of saltines. "Here."

"Thanks, mom."

"Do you have any trail mix?" Katherine asked.

"Of course."

Toni's stomach was feeling more settled by the time they

reached her house. That was until she saw Henry's truck sitting in her driveway.

She spotted the beat-up blue vehicle and turned. "You know what? Maybe I'll go wait by the body. That's a good idea. Someone should stay with poor Mr. Fairfield."

"Who is that?" Megan's eyes lit up. "Could it be...?"

"Oh look." Katherine waved at the tall man walking around the house. "Henry is here."

Kill me now.

"Hey!" His face lit up when he saw Toni and the girls. "I was wondering if you'd gone for a hike. I was just about to go looking—"

"Whit Fairfield was murdered." Toni decided to cut off any pleasantries at the gate. "We just found his body on our walk."

Henry's eyes went wide. "Oh my God, Toni, are you okay?"

"Girl, he is so sweet," Megan murmured. "She might need some help." Megan waved him over. "She threw up a couple of times from the smell."

"I hate you so much," Toni hissed. "I'm fine!" she said louder. "We'd better call the police."

Katherine pulled out her phone. "I'll call Drew right now." She held out her hand. "Hello, you must be Henry. I'm Katherine Bassi, Toni's friend."

He shook Katherine's hand, but he didn't take his eyes off Toni. "Okay, let's get you inside. You look pale."

"I'm Megan Carpenter, and it is so nice to meet you." Megan introduced herself and somehow passed Toni off to Henry in one fell swoop. "Toni's told us so much about you."

Toni was walking under Henry's arm and halfway to the house before she understood what was going on. "Henry—"

"I'm going to make some tea," he said. "I know you like coffee better, but you still look a little sick. I can't blame you; that had to be upsetting."

Toni studiously ignored how nice it was to tuck herself under Henry's tall frame. It was one of her favorite things about him. When they were together, she felt surrounded and safe. It was annoyingly comforting. "Tea sounds good."

"Was it bad?"

I'm actually puking because I am pregnant with your love child, but sure, let's go ahead with the dead-body explanation. "It was pretty shocking. He's been out there for a while."

Henry curled his lip. "Coyotes?"

"Yeah. Probably some cats too."

He glanced at the barn. "Do you think Enzo—?"

"I'm going to allow my brain the fiction that Enzo wouldn't have gone near a dead human body, okay? I keep him well fed."

"Right." He helped her up the steps and followed. "So you and your friends were just out for a walk?"

"Katherine and Megan both had a free afternoon and they love Nico's wine, so I told them about the trail between our houses. I thought we could hike up and say hi."

"Shoes off." They went in the house. "That's a pretty walk, especially in the spring."

"Usually it is. We smelled something about halfway up the trail and Katherine went to look—she's a biophysicist and she's curious about everything. She's the one who spotted him."

"That's awful." Henry deposited Toni on her couch and went to the kitchen. "Do you have chamomile tea?"

She heard him filling the electric kettle. "I think so."

"Is your stomach bothering you? Mint might be better."

She couldn't stop the smile. "Look at you. You like to fuss, don't you?"

He leaned against the doorway to the kitchen and hooked his thumb in his pocket. "Keep teasing me. I'll tell you to put on a hat."

"You really are an old Italian nonna, aren't you?"

Henry walked over, looking very *not* grandmotherly. His jeans were worn in all the right places, and his work shirt was open at the collar. He knelt down on the floor in front of her, bringing his face to the same level as hers. He nudged her knees apart and braced his large hands on either side of her hips before he leaned in, inches from her face.

"You think I'm grandmotherly?" he said, his voice low.

"Teasing you." She swallowed. "Obviously."

"You must be feeling better if you're teasing me like that." His breath was close enough to her lips that she felt its warmth. "Your stomach settled down?"

"Uh-huh." She couldn't look away. His eyes were hypnotic and he smelled amazing. Like sunshine, sawdust, and a little red wine.

Damn you, hormones!

He leaned closer. His left hand started squeezing her hip. "You smell good."

"I smell like motor oil."

Henry smiled. "You smell like lemons." He nipped the edge of her jaw. "You taste like salt."

"Sweaty from... walking." She swallowed hard. "Henry—"

"Don't care." Henry captured her mouth and swiftly parted her lips in one movement. His hand moved from kneading her hip to cradling her neck while his thumb ran along her jaw.

Toni's head swam from the intoxicating taste of red wine and Henry. She gripped the front of his shirt with her fist and spread her knees so he could lean in closer.

Her head fell back against the back of the couch and Henry groaned into her mouth.

The door opened.

"Sorry!" Megan squeaked.

The door slammed, and Toni blinked back to awareness as Henry ended the kiss.

He was pressed against her, practically humping her on the couch while one of her hands was fisted in his shirt and the other was tangled in his hair.

"Right," she panted. "People."

"Tell them you need to rest." He ran his lips along her neck.

"Uh..." Why was that a bad idea again? "Police, Henry. Dead body. Murdered... person."

He pulled away, and she saw his lips form the word *fuck* even though he didn't say it.

The fact that he only cursed silently and usually only when they were intimate made him even sexier. He had a vocabulary with manners and a mind with none.

Hormones. They would be the death of her.

She released his shirt, and he sat back on his knees. "Okay. Um... tea?"

He glanced down, back to her, then stood, adjusting himself quickly before he walked away. "What kind of tea do you want?"

Whichever one tastes like you.

"Uh... mint." She rubbed her flushed cheeks. "Let's go with mint."

CHAPTER 8

*D*rew sat on the edge of the recliner, facing the couch where Toni, Katherine, and Megan all sat. Henry was sitting next to Toni, a dining room chair flipped around so he could straddle it.

Focus on the stern police detective, Toni. Not Henry's thighs.

"Why'd you decide to take that trail today?"

Toni could sense Drew was suspicious. He didn't want to be, but he was.

Toni shrugged. "I hike that path a few times a month. It goes right behind my house and leads all the way up the hill to the winery. I've been bringing Nico's wine over to Katherine's for months now and—"

"We just wanted to see the winery," Megan said. "Thought it would make a fun Friday afternoon."

"A fun Friday afternoon for the county forensics team," Drew said. "I don't know that we'll be able to find every part of that body before next week."

"You're welcome to park here as long as you need," Toni said. "It's probably the closest access to the trail."

"Yeah, I noticed that."

Henry piped up. "I already called Nico. If you need to widen that trail at all, we can bring a little Bobcat tractor down from the barn. We have one narrow enough to get down that trail and clear it out a bit."

"Thanks," Drew said. "I'll let you know. For right now, we're still trying to pick up evidence."

"How long?" Katherine asked. "Was it about a week and a half? I was looking at the insect life on the cadaver and—"

"I can't tell you that, Katherine. You know that." Drew cleared his throat. "Can you tell me why you ladies keep showing up any time there's a violent event in Moonstone Cove?"

Megan's eyes were wide and innocent. "What do you mean?"

"Near shootings. Car crashes. Ambulance accidents." He slid his eyes toward Katherine. "Don't think I've forgotten about that one, Professor Bassi."

"The important thing is, we found out who the finger belonged to," Toni said. "That was really bugging me."

"Was it?" Drew's voice dripped with sarcasm. "So glad we could clear that up for you."

Toni shrugged. "What? I'm not saying I'm glad he's dead or anything. Just that the mystery was annoying me."

Drew rubbed a hand along his beard. "Okay, so if Katherine is right and he was killed about a week and a half ago, that would have been..." He thought quickly. "Saturday or Sunday weekend before last." He looked at Toni. "You're the closest house to the crime scene. Did you hear or see anything suspicious?"

She shook her head. "I was home, but I didn't see anything weird. Sometimes during the spring, tourists will walk along the creek, but I didn't see any hikers that weekend that I can remember."

"Did you hear anything? He was shot. Did you hear gunfire? Anything that you thought was a car backfiring maybe? Anything like that?"

"Not that I can remember. If it was the middle of the night, I'm a pretty sound sleeper."

Henry opened his mouth but closed it quickly when she shot him a look.

"Also, you'd be amazed," Toni added. "The way the hills are around here, sometimes they just swallow sound. The creek runs right behind my house, but unless it's really high in the winter, I hardly even hear it."

"So you didn't see or hear anything strange when Whit Fairfield died," Drew said. "And it looks like your footprints are the only ones we found on the trail so far."

"I mean, it's rained since then, so even if there were prints, they'd probably be gone."

Megan asked, "Did you find any bullets? Casings?"

"Better than that, we found the gun." Drew crossed his ankle over his knee and his arms over his chest.

"You did?" Megan said. "That's great news!"

"It was in the creek," Drew said. "Covered in mud. We'll see what we can get off it, but I'm not very optimistic."

"Oh." Megan deflated. "That's not good."

"The main problem I've got is that I have a murder victim, and it seems like half the town didn't like him much."

Henry snorted. "At least."

"Exactly." Drew nodded at Henry. "Whit Fairfield pressured people to sell their land, had numerous affairs with married women, and lied... a *lot*. But specifically..." Drew frowned. "He was actively pressuring your cousin to sell his land and appeared to be tampering with his business."

"Hey." Toni sat up straight. "Nico didn't have anything to do with this. He's not a hateful person, and he'd never get involved with anything violent."

"Fairfield was messing with him, pressuring him to sell his land, and flaunting an affair with his estranged wife."

"Ex-wife except on paper. Nico doesn't care about that shit. He *wants* her to sign the papers and move on. Ask anyone. He's not jealous about Marissa. And the tampering with the tractor happened after Fairfield was already dead! So that must have been a coincidence."

Drew shifted in his seat. "His body was found on your cousin's land, Toni."

"It was found on a trail! Lots of people know it's there. It's marked in hiking guides. There's a sign on the highway for it. Ferraro Creek Trail. Look it up. It's not exactly a secret." Toni felt her anger rising. "Whoever killed Fairfield probably killed him there to make it look like Nico was guilty. Have you thought that someone may be trying to frame him?"

"It's possible, but I can't ignore all the other coincidences," Drew said. "I have to look at your cousin."

Toni felt like Drew had punched her in the chest. "You told me you trust my judgment. I'm telling you, Nico would never do anything like this."

"I have to look."

Henry put a hand on Toni's shoulder. "You can look at

Nico for this," he said, "but you're not going to find anything. You're barking up the wrong tree, Detective Bisset. I promise."

"Trust me, I'm not stopping with your cousin," Drew said. "We don't have a lack of suspects—we have too many." He looked at them meaningfully. "So really, *anything* you can give me to narrow it down a little would be very appreciated."

Toni exchanged a look with Megan and Katherine, but both of them looked as clueless as she was. She had no idea who might have killed Whit Fairfield.

"Not Nico. That's all I can say right now," Toni said. "My cousin had nothing to do with this."

"Do you think he knows?" Megan stood at the sink, staring out the kitchen window as the sun started to set over the hills. The last of the police cars were pulling away.

"Who?" Toni was drained. Henry had left a few minutes after Drew, telling her he was going up to the winery to let Nico know what was going on. She wanted to crawl in bed and fall asleep, but she knew she needed to eat something, and Megan had offered to cook.

"Knows what?" Katherine added. She was staring at Toni's bookshelves, which were mostly filled with classic-car manuals and gardening and home-repair guides. "You have very little fiction here."

"I keep the steamy romance novels in my room."

"Oh."

Katherine might think she was joking, but she wasn't. Toni loved romance novels. She always knew how they were going to end, and with all the stress in her life, she liked knowing that things in a book would always end well.

She'd read a book with an intriguing cover that her mom had raved about and read in her book club. At the end, everyone died except for like two people, and the romance she'd thought was developing had been part of the main character's delusions.

Worst. Book. Ever.

"I mean, do you think Drew knows about *us*?" Megan walked back to the living room. "About our abilities. Did you notice he brought up the ambulance thing with Katherine? How we're always in the middle of violent stuff in town?"

"Maybe he thinks we're secretly serial killers or something," Toni said.

Megan rolled her eyes. "And then he said if we could give him 'anything to narrow it down' that would be really helpful. I mean, why would he think we would know anything unless we... knew things."

Katherine turned. "But we don't know anything. I didn't see Mr. Fairfield get killed. I just saw him dead. Rather, I thought he was sleeping, but obviously he was dead."

Toni frowned. "You didn't think it was weird that you saw a guy sleeping on the side of a creek?"

Katherine raised her eyebrows. "I see a lot of things far stranger than that. Psychic power has opened my eyes to the peculiarities of human behavior, that's for sure."

"So who had a motive to kill Whit Fairfield?" Megan asked. "It can't be that many people."

Toni raised an eyebrow. "You said you met him."

Megan grimaced. "Okay, there were probably quite a few."

Katherine frowned. "Was he really that unpleasant?"

"He struck me as completely self-centered," Megan said. "A narcissist, probably. Very focused on money and making himself look good. Very dismissive of anyone who wasn't useful to him in some way or another."

"We should stay out of it," Toni said. "I don't want anything I do to make it look like I'm covering up for Nico or anything. The last thing he needs is me accidentally pointing fingers at him. Or making it look like I'm trying to cover something up on his behalf. Plus I have work! I can't keep asking Glenn to pick up the slack for me at the garage while I'm off solving mysteries."

"Has he complained?" Megan asked. "Are things falling behind?"

"No." Of course Glenn hadn't complained. The garage could probably run without her, but that wasn't the point. "I just need to work." *To maintain the last shreds of my sanity.*

Katherine was staring into the distance with pursed lips, clearly not listening to anything Megan and Toni were talking about. "If Megan is correct about Mr. Fairfield, we do have a lead. And a possible suspect other than your cousin."

"Who?" Megan asked.

"Nico's former wife," Katherine said. "If he was a narcissist, then any relationship he initiated would be transactional in nature. He'd only spend time with someone who could give him something. What did this woman have that could interest him? Was she wealthy?"

"Marissa?" Toni asked. "No. She sells real estate and she's pretty good at it, but she's not rolling in money. Nico has to give her some spousal support, but she doesn't own any part of the winery. The house and the land all belong to the family trust set up after Grandpa Dusi died. Nico gets a salary like the rest of the staff."

"So Fairfield wouldn't want her money. Would she burnish his reputation in some way? Were her social connections good? Is she notably beautiful?"

"She's beautiful, but is she more beautiful than half a dozen other women in her social circle?" Toni sighed. "I don't know. I'm not the right person to judge that stuff."

"Well, I only skirted the edge of that crowd for a little while with Rodney, but Marissa Dusi wasn't considered a social queen bee or anything close to that," Megan said. "I moved here around the time she and your cousin were breaking up. I never met Nico, but most of what I heard about Marissa was other women saying she was a fool for leaving him." Megan cleared her throat and smiled a little. "There might have been a few comments about Nico being back on the market too."

"Weird." Toni shook her head. "I guess he's good-looking enough, but he's like my brother, so he'll always be a gross teenager to me."

"So we have one mystery we can try to solve," Katherine said. "And one that wouldn't be likely to point fingers at Nico. We can find out why Whit Fairfield was dating Marissa. There has to be a reason."

Megan nodded. "Agreed. He wouldn't date someone unless he was getting something in return. Something more than sex, because Fairfield was good-looking enough to get sex if he wanted it. I can see him as being one of those guys who'd just pay for sex if that was all he was after. So Marissa must have something he needed."

Toni shook her head. "I don't know about this. I still think we should keep out of it. Just clear out completely and let Drew do his thing."

"Listen, we can find out things that Drew can't," Megan said. "This case has to be solved for your cousin's sake and your whole family."

"Why? No one is crying about Whit Fairfield being dead, Megan. He wasn't a good person. I'm not saying I'm glad he was murdered or anything, but I'm not broken up about it either."

"It has to be solved because I know how people are," Megan said. "And you do too. If the police can't prove who killed Whit Fairfield, then everyone will just assume the most obvious suspect did it and the police couldn't find enough evidence to arrest him."

Katherine said, "And right now..."

"Right now Nico is the most obvious suspect." Toni groaned. "Okay, you're right. Count me in."

Glenn was going to kill her.

CHAPTER 9

On Sunday afternoon Toni put on her only dress, fixed her short hair in loose curls with a tailored headband, and added a dab of makeup before she drove her vintage Mustang out of the vineyard and up the hill to Moonstone Cove Country Club.

It was hard not to tug at her dress. She hadn't worn one since the last Lanza cousin wedding, which had been in Santa Maria, and it felt more like a costume than an actual item of clothing.

In a way, it was a costume. They were going into the foreign environment of "ladies who lunch" on Megan's invite in order to see if they could gather more info on Marissa Dusi and why Whit Fairfield had hooked up with her. Since the country club had a dress code for Sunday brunch, Toni had donned her costume.

They also wanted to gather more gossip about Fairfield's murder, and there was no better place to overhear gossip than the country club.

The winding driveway leading to the country club was

lined by olive trees and the rolling lawns of the golf course. The main building sat on a hill overlooking the ocean, and Toni had to admit the view was stunning.

She pulled into the lot and found a spot under a cedar to park her car. The club's parking lot was filled with a wide variety of luxury cars that screamed "conspicuous consumption" and very little taste. She recognized more than one customer by their license plate.

Megan was waiting near the front of the building, looking at her phone.

"Hey."

The blond woman looked up and blinked. "You're wearing a dress."

"I am. Isn't that the dress code?"

"Dress, skirt, or dress slacks. Collars for the men. I usually wear a dress. It's the easiest."

"Since I don't own slacks and leather pants probably aren't considered dressy enough, I figured the outfit I wore to my cousin Marie's wedding would have to do."

"You look nice!" Megan cocked her head. "Weird, but nice."

"I think that's what Marie said too." She leaned against the railing and stared at the view. "I didn't know you were a member here."

"It's become a point of contention in the divorce." Megan smirked. "As of right now, we're both still on the member roll. I don't particularly want the membership, but I also know Rodney does because all this" —she waved a hand in a general circle— "is his thing."

"So it's leverage."

"Absofuckinglutely." The corner of her perfectly painted

red lip turned up. "I gave up a thriving business to support that man on our move out here. He's going to work for every penny he gets out of our marriage."

Toni watched Megan from behind her sunglasses. The devastated woman who'd walked in on her husband cheating was long gone. All Toni saw in Megan anymore—at least relative to her ex-husband—was a ruthless businesswoman.

"I genuinely feel sorry for any man who has to negotiate with you."

Megan glanced around. "When we're not here, I'll let you in on the latest, but the last thing I want is anyone around here getting the slightest clue about my personal business." She waved at a carefully coiffed older woman walking into the club. "Mrs. Sharp, how are you? Your hair is stunning. Did you just have it done?"

"I certainly did."

"It's just darling. And I heard about your granddaughter getting engaged. How sweet is that? Are y'all excited? You must be."

"We are—he's a lovely young man..."

As they waited for Katherine and the brunch crowd began to roll into the country club, Toni watched Megan playing her part of the rich, well-connected divorcée. She could tell that the older women especially were charmed by Megan's Southern accent and manners. The younger women resented her ease and charm.

Megan's cutting sense of humor was so lightly applied that Toni knew most of the women didn't even realize they were the butt of a joke. More than one walked away from Megan, smiling but with an edge of uncertainty.

Toni could sense their confusion from six feet away.

During one lull in the traffic, Toni shook her head and said quietly, "This place is exhausting."

"You're telling me."

"No, I mean empathically, it's exhausting. Nothing about the outside of these people matches the inside. I have never been more grateful for my oversharing family."

"Ha! I want to meet your family sometime. They sound like a hoot." Megan smiled and waved at someone walking in with a group of men in business suits. "I should talk to her before I leave."

"Who's that?"

"Pamela Martin. She strikes me as a good egg. Events director of the club. She's all business. If I'm going to have any kind of event-planning business, I need to get on her list."

"How's all that going?"

"It's going okay, but what I'm discovering is that a lot of the event planning in this area is driven by location. Most venues have their own planners, and people don't always think about hiring an independent coordinator of their own even though it would probably save them money."

"Oh, I see what you mean. So if someone wanted to have a wedding here at the club, they'd call that Pamela lady—"

"Exactly. And she'd coordinate the food and flowers and all that. Most of the wineries are the same way. But when you do that, you're kind of stuck with whoever the club or the winery likes for services."

"Interesting." Toni wasn't too interested in fancy events, but she did enjoy talking about business. "I don't think Nico has an event planner."

"Does he have a good venue?"

"Oh yeah. There're two houses on the winery, and

they're both Mediterranean. Nico and the kids live in the larger one, and they rent out the smaller one for events. But there's a big formal Italian garden that my grandmother planned from the ground up. It's gorgeous. They've hosted parties and stuff, but it's like you were talking about—planners just hire the location. The winery doesn't really do anything except provide the wine."

"Interesting." Megan seemed to be mulling something over. "I wonder—"

"Katherine's here. Thank God." Toni flexed her ankles. "These shoes are killing me."

Megan looked down. "You're wearing kitten heels."

"I know." Compared to the work boots she normally wore, they were excruciating. "This place better have a decent spread. I am starving."

KATHERINE WAS LOOKING around the formal dining room of the country club with wide eyes. "This is fascinating."

Megan smiled. "This is why I got us a table in the corner. I knew she was going to enjoy the people watching."

Toni was unimpressed. "Looks like a whole bunch of fancy jerks to me, sprinkled with a few genuinely nice old people."

"The relationships and power dynamics though..." Katherine pointed to a table full of women in the center of the room. "I've been counting the number of people who approach that table and noting how long they stay in relation to other tables in the room, and I can say that the women there definitely display the most overtly powerful social influence."

"Queen bees," Megan whispered. "You're exactly right."

"And who is the woman we're investigating?"

"Marissa," Toni said. "She's about two tables to the right of the queen bees. Dark hair and a plum-colored dress." She craned her neck and caught Marissa's eye. Toni gave her a fake smile and lifted a hand. Marissa gave her an equally fake smile and waved politely.

"Interesting." Katherine narrowed her eyes. "That's very interesting."

"Why?"

"I noticed her earlier. She's watching the room the same way we are." Katherine shrugged. "Well, she's probably not as acutely aware of the social dynamics from an outside perspective, but she's definitely observing." Katherine's eyes went momentarily distant and she froze.

Toni looked at Megan. "Is she having a vision right now?"

"I think so," Megan murmured, sipping the mimosa that came with the brunch buffet. "Just leave her."

Katherine's eyes fell closed, and Toni could see her eyes darting back and forth as if she was in a dream. A few seconds later, her eyes opened and she reached for Toni's hand. "There's going to be a scene. In a few minutes, you should go to the ladies' restroom. Marissa is going to run in there, and she'll be upset."

Seconds later, Toni saw Poppy Carmichael, one of the queen bees that Megan had identified at the center table, stand up and walk over to Marissa's table. She pulled up an empty chair and spoke quietly to Marissa.

"What do you think she's saying?" Katherine said. "Do you think she's asking about Mr. Fairfield?"

"From what I heard at the buffet, that's the hot topic today. Everyone is speculating about what happened."

Toni asked, "Do they knew any details?"

"Not many." Megan dabbed her mouth and kept her voice low. "A few people said he was murdered. Bunch of other people seemed to think he probably died from natural causes."

Was it wrong of Toni to feel superior for knowing the facts of the case? "Did anyone mention us?"

"No. That doesn't seem to have slipped out, but everyone *is* talking about how he was found on your cousin's land."

"Great." Toni watched Marissa. She could see the tension around her mouth as she struggled to control her expression.

"Almost," Katherine murmured.

Poppy took Marissa's hand and put an arm around the other woman's shoulders. If you didn't see the undercurrents involved, it would have looked comforting.

It wasn't comfort.

Poppy finally leaned back and Marissa stood rapidly, her lips pursed as she looked at the diners around her. Poppy sat back, her eyes wide and seemingly concerned.

"Thank you." Marissa's voice was audible across the room as the club fell silent. "For your concern, Poppy. You're so... considerate."

"Go now." Katherine nudged Toni.

She stood and walked to the women's bathroom that they'd passed on the way in.

Marissa's voice rang clear in the dining room. "It's just

so... thoughtful how concerned you all are about Whit's passing."

Oh, she was pissed. So very pissed. Toni nearly laughed out loud.

She ducked into the bathroom and looked under the stall doors. No one. She waited in the plush outer lounge where there were couches and mirrors along with a counter to fix makeup and freshen up with mints, mouthwash, and tiny toiletry items.

Toni took the opportunity to grab a few for her purse.

Handy.

Seconds after she'd nabbed a bunch of the breath mints and extra toothbrushes, Marissa walked in. Her eyes went wide when she saw Toni.

"You."

Toni swiftly walked over to the door and locked the dead bolt. "Hey, coz."

"What are you doing?" Marissa walked to the door and reached for it, only to have Toni block her.

"I wouldn't do that if I were you." She gestured toward a chaise. "How is that going to look? Where else are you going to go?"

"What do you want, Toni?" Marissa stepped back, but she didn't sit down.

"I want to have a quick conversation about Whit."

Marissa snorted, which Toni appreciated. The gloves and the masks were off. "You and everyone else. I'm not exactly broken up about it, okay?"

"You're upset though." She stared at Marissa's face and tried to sort through the emotions rolling off her.

Anger was obvious.

But under that was irritation. Confusion. Worry. Fear?

"You know he was murdered," Toni said. "Don't you?"

"That detective already called me. I also know he was found on our land."

"It's family land, Marissa. When you left the family, you left any claim to it. Don't even try it with me."

Marissa sneered. "Whatever, Toni. At least I'm not one of the Dusi puppies, forty-six and still sucking at the family teat. Nico's probably the one who killed Whit. He was always jealous."

"Did you tell Drew that Nico killed Whit?"

"Maybe." She shrugged. "If he didn't do it, he has nothing to worry about."

"Wow." Toni blinked. "You are an ignorant bitch. How were you married to Nico for nearly twenty years?"

"Good question." She narrowed her eyes and smirked. "It did have a few perks. Nico's fantastic in bed."

"You're so trashy." Toni tried not to gag. "And yet you left him and ran off with Whit Fairfield of all people. Hard to imagine he was very attentive to anyone but himself."

Marissa's cheeks went red. "Whit was a great boyfriend."

"Was he?" She smiled. "Was he really your *boyfriend*, Marissa? Or were you a convenient place to put it? I mean, no judgment, whatever works for you. But it's not like he was taking you home to meet the family, was he?"

Marissa's chin went up. "Whit knew exactly how valuable I was. Unlike Nico."

"Okay. Sure." Toni shrugged. "Too bad Whit's *dead*."

"Fuck you, Toni."

Marissa blinked hard, but Toni wasn't feeling any real grief from her.

Toni curled her lip. "You're not even sad about him. You feel sorry for *yourself*."

Marissa narrowed her eyes, and Toni knew if they were anywhere but the country club, she'd be going for Toni's eyes with those manicured fingernails. "At least I'm not the sad little spinster aunt with grease under my nails. Nico always wondered: Why hasn't Toni ever gotten married? Why can't guys see how great she is?"

It was a common poor-Toni tactic, even in her own family, unfortunately. Toni rolled her eyes. "Maybe I'm not married because I didn't want to get married. Is that too hard for your little brain to understand, Marissa? Some of us don't need a man to make us feel complete in life, okay? You'd probably be better off if you understood that."

"And you'd be better off if you understood that men don't like women who make them feel emasculated." Marissa's face was all pity. "Putting on a dress doesn't change who you are."

Had this conversation outlived its usefulness? Probably. "Okay. Whatever, Marissa. Why was Whit Fairfield dating you? Or sleeping with you anyway. Was it just convenient, free sex?"

Marissa's mouth curled up in the corner. "Like I said, unlike Nico, Whit understood exactly how valuable I am." She turned and walked to the counter, opening her purse and taking out a tube of lipstick. "By the way, how's Henry?"

"Henry?" Toni schooled her features carefully. "Nico's winemaker?"

"You know exactly who I'm talking about." Marissa laughed a little.

"He's fine. Why do you care?"

Fuck, fuck, fuck. Why was she asking about Henry? What did that mean?

"No reason." Her voice was breathy. "Such a promising young man. We all know he's the only reason Nico's wine is starting to win awards. I'm surprised he's still working for him. Henry's so... talented." Her lips curved into a mauve-slicked smile.

Toni wanted to slap Marissa, yank her hair, and smash her fist in her smug mouth for letting Henry's name cross her lips. "Sure, Marissa. Whatever."

"Nice to see you, Toni. You should go now. We both know you're not even close to being a member here."

"That's a feature, not a bug." She unlocked the door and looked over her shoulder. "So what was that with Poppy earlier?"

Marissa's eyes went cold.

"Let me guess." Toni flipped through what she knew about the ladies who lunched and what Megan had told her on Friday. "Poppy was warning you—now that you foolishly kicked Nico to the curb and your new sugar daddy is gone—not to go looking for any new hookups at the club, right? No one trusts you around their husband. Did I guess that right?"

The red spots on Marissa's cheeks told Toni she'd nailed it in one.

Toni pretended to wince. "Harsh. But kind of smart. After all, we all know you don't have any money of your own, Marissa. Without Whit Fairfield, whatever will you do?"

And with that last bomb thrown, Toni walked out of the bathroom and back to the hornets' nest of the Moonstone Cove Country Club. She sat back at the table with Katherine and Megan, who were both staring with curious expressions.

Toni sighed. "You know what?"

"What?"

"Not being able to drink free champagne sucks." She glanced down at her still-flat stomach. "This better be worth it."

CHAPTER 10

"So Marissa thinks she was valuable to Fairfield in some way." Megan sat on Katherine's back porch, sipping wine and staring at the ocean. "How? Does her family have money?"

"No. Her mom and dad are normal middle-class folks. Dad was a farmer and Mom was a teacher. I have no idea where she got the idea that her shit doesn't stink."

Katherine asked, "Does her family have land Fairfield might want? Does she have any kind of inheritance?"

"I don't think so. Pretty sure her brother is still running their farm and it's all vegetables. Not the right area for wine at all."

"Hmm." Megan tapped her finger against her cheek. "Oh, by the way Toni, your read on what got Marissa all riled up was dead-on. I heard a bunch of Poppy's friends talking about how Marissa wasn't even going to let Whit get cold before she hooked up with someone new, and it sure as hell wasn't going to be their husband. That kind of thing."

"Did they know he's already been dead for about a week and a half?" Katherine said. "He's far past cold."

"Pretty sure it was a figure of speech."

Katherine nodded. "Right."

Baxter came out, carrying a tray of enchiladas and a salad. "Dinner is served."

"Oh, thank God." Toni was starving. She'd barely picked at her lunch that afternoon because she'd been focused on getting information from Marissa and surfing the emotional waves at the country club.

"Toni!" Baxter smiled. "You look lovely. I don't think I've seen you wear a dress before."

"Thanks, Baxter." Toni would accept a compliment if Baxter Pang was the one offering. But maybe just him. "I got the dress for my cousin's wedding."

"It suits you," he said. "But not as well as your blue jeans, I think." He winked at her and sat at the table that Katherine had set. "Dig in, everyone."

Archie the goldendoodle sat next to Baxter's chair and sighed deeply.

"Don't feed him," Katherine said. "You heard what the vet said."

"Just a little bit of chicken," Baxter said quietly. "It's rather rude not to, don't you think? He helped me cook."

"He waited by your feet and grabbed any scrap that fell on the floor, Baxter."

"Exactly. And now we have a clean kitchen floor." Baxter kept his eyes on Katherine as he broke off a bit of chicken and let it fall to the deck. "I have to pay my sous chef, darling."

"You guys are completely adorable." Toni served herself a hearty helping of chicken enchiladas. "Marissa tried to needle me this afternoon about why I never got married, and it's because of people like you." She pointed at them. "Especially now. It's Baxter-and-Katherine levels of happy or nothing for me."

Katherine's cheeks turned a little red. "Oh, I don't know that we're all that unusual. Lots of people have happy marriages."

Baxter said, "Statistically, in fact, the majority of married couples classify themselves as happy. The numbers are quite consistent."

"Don't buy it," Megan said. "I would have called my marriage happy two years ago too. And he ended up cheating on me."

"That was definitely his loss," Baxter said. "But Toni, what about the young man that you're involved with? Do you have plans to continue the relationship?"

Megan snorted. "Sure looked that way on Friday."

Toni threw her napkin at Megan. "I'm not *opposed* to marriage," she said. "But it's more complicated now with a potential baby."

"Did you go to the doctor?" Megan asked.

"I have an appointment on Tuesday, okay? Calm down, mom."

"Good." Megan took a bite of enchilada. "I need this recipe. My kids would love this. Trina's been cooking more lately, and she'd want to try making this."

"I'll write it down for you," Baxter said. "So what did you learn about the victim's girlfriend today?"

"I think Katherine is right," Toni said. "They had a reciprocal relationship of some kind. I'm just not sure what Marissa was bringing to the table. Fairfield was obvious. He was decent-looking and had money and status, all things Marissa wanted."

"One thing I don't understand," Megan said. "The women at the club have talked enough that I'm pretty convinced they find your cousin Nico a catch. Why would Marissa leave him if she was just after money and status?"

"Nico does okay, but he's not independently wealthy. Just like the family owns part of my garage, they own part of Nico's winery too. Marissa didn't buy into that side of the family business. She wanted everything to belong to her and Nico."

"And the status thing?"

"Nico..." She shrugged. "He doesn't really care. I don't think he actively dislikes the people over in that social set like I do, but he's not going to voluntarily hang out with them, you know? He can do the salesman thing when he needs to, but I'd call him a little rougher around the edges. He didn't play the game. Didn't feel like he needed to if he wanted to sell wine. My brother Frank is more in that group than Nico is."

"Okay." Megan nodded. "I get that. So Marissa got a taste of the fancy life and she decided that's what she wanted, but Nico didn't care that much. So she hooks up with Whit Fairfield, and she must think he's her ticket in."

Katherine said, "But Fairfield—from what we know about him—is probably a narcissist or had those tendencies. He wouldn't have a real relationship with her unless he was getting something. And Marissa herself said she was valuable to him. How?"

"I don't think we can answer that," Toni said. "I think we need to talk to someone who worked with Fairfield."

"Would Nico know anyone?" Megan asked. "I mean,

they both worked in the wine business. They had to know a few of the same people. Is there anyone over there you think we could trust?"

"I don't know," Toni said. "But Nico would."

———

TONI WAS at her garage on Monday morning when Drew Bisset dropped by again. She was leaning over the engine of the Corvette, and she shook her head as he approached.

"Nope," she said.

Drew spread his hands. "I didn't say anything."

"The last time you came here, you asked me for my read on a guy that ended up being a murder victim, and now you're trying to pin his death on my cousin."

"Please." Drew straightened the front of his button-down shirt. "I'm not trying to 'pin it' on anyone." He rolled up his sleeves and leaned on the car. "So what are you doing here?"

"After I replaced the alternator, I discovered the ignition system needed some cleaning up, so I did that last week and now I'm tuning it." She glanced at him. "You know cars?"

"Absolutely not." He looked intently at the engine. "But I feel like I should."

"You know how to change a tire?"

He nodded. "I do know that."

"You know how to change your oil?"

"I do, though I will admit that I take it to the drive-through fifteen-minute place over on State Street instead of doing it myself."

"If you know how to change oil and a tire, you know more about cars than about ninety percent of the population." She stood up straight and placed her torque wrench on her work cart with a small sigh of regret. *Goodbye, beautiful, distracting engine.* "Let's go in my office. I don't need you putting Everett on edge."

Everett, her German car mechanic, had known a few too many cops in his past life to ever be comfortable around them. He was a magician with classic German engines and a nervous wreck around cops.

Toni led Drew into her office and reached into her mini fridge for a ginger ale. "Drink?"

"Any kind of cola you have."

Toni tossed him a Pepsi and sat down. "So what's up?"

"The coroner narrowed down the time of death based on decomposition and evidence at the scene."

"And?"

Drew frowned. "Nico doesn't have an alibi. Said he was sleeping at home, alone in his room. Which has a door that leads outside, so he could have snuck out without the kids even hearing him."

Toni groaned. "Or he's just a normal father of two who was home exactly where he said he was on the night Fairfield bit it."

Drew raised his hands. "I agree. It's far more likely that's the case. Unfortunately, I can't eliminate him. I was hoping he'd have an alibi once we had a time of death."

Toni took a long drink of her soda to settle her stomach. She was going on nine weeks pregnant and so far, the morning sickness had been more of a problem at night. She was hoping it stayed that way. She knew she wouldn't be able to hide the pregnancy from her guys forever, but she didn't want to deal with their questions quite this early.

"So why are you here?" she asked. "You want me to help you get more insight into the guy who made Nico miserable? How's that going to help my cousin?"

"I'm more curious why you were questioning Marissa Dusi yesterday at the country club. She mentioned it when I talked to her today."

Toni crossed her arms over her chest. "Did she?"

"She said you were, and I quote, 'intimidating her.'"

She snorted. "Marissa would find a stiff breeze intimidating. I was giving her shit about her dead boyfriend because she annoys me and I'm a horrible person. It was nothing."

Drew wasn't buying it. She could feel the doubt rolling off him in waves.

"What exactly did she say I did? I'm surprised that the Moonstone Cove Police Department is that interested in country-club gossip."

"When that gossip involves the woman a murder victim was known to be sleeping with, we get interested."

Toni cocked her head. "The woman he was *sleeping* with? Not his girlfriend?"

"According to friends in San Jose and his secretary there, Whit Fairfield is engaged to a woman named Angela Calvo. In fact, they're considered a 'power couple.' She works in finance, is the daughter of a city council member, and has a business degree from Wharton."

"Huh." So Whit Fairfield had a country girlfriend to keep him busy when he was slumming it in Moonstone Cove. Toni wasn't surprised. Did Marissa know? Did she have delusions that she was going to get Whit to leave his fancy, well-connected girlfriend in the Bay Area and make things with her permanent?

"So Marissa wasn't nearly as important to him as she thinks she was," Toni said. "I'm petty enough to be happy about that, but what does it mean for the investigation?"

"It's possible that this all stemmed from old-fashioned 'other woman' problems and had nothing to do with wine." Drew crossed his arms over his waist and knit his finger together. "If you knew anything that would support that... I would be happy to listen."

"I wish I did, but I don't. I will say that Whit Fairfield doesn't strike me as the kind of guy who'd waste his time on any kind of relationship—even a casual one—unless he was getting something out of it."

Drew nodded. "You are not the first person to mention that."

"Oh yeah? Who else is talking about Fairfield that way?"

"Your... friend," Drew stood and opened the messenger bag he'd brought with him. "Henry Durand."

Henry again.

What the hell was going on?

"Well, Henry's a smart guy."

"He thinks very highly of you. And your cousin."

"Right." Toni nodded. "That's nice. I better get back to work."

"Better not forget the real reason I came."

"Oh yeah?" She stood and waited while Drew pushed papers around in his bag before he took a blue plastic container from the bottom. "What's that?"

"Brownies." He set them on her desk and tapped the top of the Tupperware. "They are as good as I told you. Don't wait too long to eat them."

"That won't be a problem." Toni couldn't stop her smile.

"Thanks, Drew. And... I know you're not trying to pin anything on Nico. If I hear anything else that might be helpful, I'll let you know."

"You or your friends," he said. "For you three, I'm all ears."

CHAPTER 11

"*I* think Drew knows we're psychic." She mumbled into her phone. She'd only been able to get Megan's voice mail for the past two days, and she was starting to get annoyed. "And I'm at the doctor *alone*. Call me."

She was walking into her usual gynecological office after a somewhat embarrassing conversation with Dr. Patel, the grandfatherly doctor she'd been seeing since she was sixteen. He'd known her for over half her life, and she could tell he was shocked to hear she was pregnant.

Kind and professional? Always. But shocked.

It's only the beginning...

Her mind drifted to every shocked reaction she'd have to deal with. Her parents? Brutal. Her sister? Fine. Her brother? Preachy.

Her employees? Awkward.

And maybe the most complicated of all? Henry.

She sat in the waiting room and opened one of those mindless games on her phone. She'd spent the past nine weeks pretending none of this was really happening, and now she was going to have to face the music.

A ball of panic started to spin wildly in her chest.

"Hey!" Megan's voice snapped her out of her panic spiral. "Sorry. It is not easy to find a parking spot around here."

Toni stared at her. "You came to my doctor's appointment?"

"Katherine was going to come, but she has class today and she couldn't miss it for some reason, so she called me because I'm closer." Megan shrugged. "We couldn't let you go alone, could we?"

Toni blinked back tears that Megan very carefully ignored. "Thanks."

"No problem." She sat next to Toni and took out her own phone. "But the next one should be Henry with you. Unless he's an asshole about it, in which case he will be banished and burned in effigy."

Toni sniffed and sank into her chair. "He won't be an asshole about it."

"I kind of get that feeling too." Megan glanced at her. "He's in love with you. You know that, right?"

"He likes me. It's not—"

"That man is in love with you." Megan kept her voice low. "You are a freaking empath, Toni. If you were honest with yourself, you'd know I'm telling the truth. Added to that, he's sweet and takes care of you with Baxter-level consideration. If you don't love him, that's one thing. But I think you better stop dismissing his feelings for you because he's younger."

"It's not because he's younger."

"Yes, it is."

"No, it's not."

"Okay, what is it then?"

"I don't know." *It's because he's younger.*

Shut up, inner voice of honesty!

"Antonia Dusi?"

"Yep." She stood and Megan followed her. They walked back to the nurses' station, and Kerry, Dr. Patel's regular nurse, took her vitals and weight. Then she and Megan were ushered into a back office to wait.

Toni took a deep breath and blew it out slowly.

"That's good," Megan said. "You're practicing your breathing already."

"Oh, will you shut up."

"Nope." Megan picked up a magazine. "Katherine and I are walking a very fine line in all this with you. We want to be supportive, but do you know how many lectures I've listened to in the past couple of weeks about the abysmal maternal mortality rate in the United States as compared to other developed countries? She is extremely worried, and you cannot just ignore this and pretend like nothing in your life is going to change. Beyond the baby, you have to take care of your health."

"I'm processing, all right? Remember how long it took me to accept that I was a supernatural fucking feelings wizard?"

Megan narrowed her eyes. "I did not put any language on your official wizard mug. You take that back."

"Fine." Toni leaned her head against the wall. "I don't want to get rid of this baby, Megan. I just don't know how any of this is going to end well. Everything about my life is going to turn upside down. And I liked my life."

Megan put down the happy mommy magazine she'd been perusing. "Before you got pregnant, what did you envision your life was going to look like... a year from now?"

Toni shrugged. "I don't know. I don't plan ahead like that."

"Well, maybe that's the problem."

"Okay, enough. I know I should have been practicing safe sex; I already got the lecture about—"

"Not *that*." Megan smiled. "Maybe it's not so much that this baby is going to change the life you liked, it's that you're going to have to start planning ahead. You're going to have to start thinking about the future instead of just letting life happen."

Toni sighed. "Is it worth it?"

Megan's whole face transformed. "Oh yeah. Yeah, it is." Her eyes shone. "Being a mom is... It's gonna sound cheesy, but it's the greatest joy of my life. And it made me a better person. I was so shallow and judgmental and selfish when I was younger." She smiled. "And kids are hilarious. You are going to laugh so much, you have no idea."

Toni stared at the chubby-cheeked baby on the poster on the opposite wall. "Keep talking."

"I hesitate to say that you're going to experience love like you've never understood before because I think that's dismissive of other kinds of love in your life, but it's *different*. It's unique. And if you're the right kind of mom—which I know you're going to be—then you're going to understand empathy in a very new and real way. It'll be one of the most challenging things ever. But one of the most rewarding too."

Toni nodded. "Okay."

"Just let your heart open up to it, and it'll change your life in ways you never expected." Megan reached over and squeezed her hand. "I promise."

An hour later, Toni was holding a small black-and-white photograph of something that looked like a lima bean after what could only be described as the worst ultrasound ever. She felt as if she'd been sucked into an alien ship and probed internally. Nothing magical about that motherhood moment, that was for sure. Megan told her she'd only have to do that kind once though, and she'd be holding her to that.

She'd seen the heartbeat. She'd heard it even.

Wild. Weird. Kinda cool.

She wanted to tell Henry. She wanted to share this with him, but she didn't know how. They'd never talked about the future and definitely hadn't talked about kids. What if he didn't want kids?

Are you kidding? That man has peewee soccer dad written all over him.

Toni tucked the small black-and-white pictures in her backpack and started the car. Megan had taken off shortly after Toni's appointment was over, but Toni was eternally grateful that she'd been there. Megan knew what questions to ask, having done this three times herself, but she never made Toni feel stupid for not knowing about baby stuff.

Baby stuff.

She started imagining what her house would look like. Would her cat like the baby? She'd need a crib and a bunch of stuff. Did she have enough closet space in her house? Maybe she'd need to do an addition at some point.

She was an active enough aunt that she knew babies came with a lot of extra baggage.

Good thing the garage is doing well.

Oh God, she was going to have to tell her dad. Her dad was probably still deluding himself that she was a virgin since she'd never been married and never brought a serious boyfriend home.

"Don't think about that, Toni," she muttered to herself as she pulled into lunchtime traffic in downtown Moonstone Cove. "Think about something more pleasant. Something less complicated. Like murder."

Seriously, why had Marissa and Whit Fairfield been together? Toni was hoping her next appointment might give her some insight.

She pulled into the Depot restaurant a little after two o'clock. Nico had set up this meeting, but she knew who she'd be talking to.

Ruben Montenegro was one of Nico's peers, a skilled farmer and vineyard manager from an old Portuguese farming family who'd graduated from the same viticulture program Nico had at Central Coast State. They'd gone to high school together, and Nico had a lot of respect for Ruben even though the man had taken a job managing Fairfield vineyards two years before.

Toni spotted Ruben on the far side of the back patio at the Depot. He stood and waved her over.

"Toni!" He smiled and held out a hand. "You look great. It's been a long time."

"You too."

He did look great. His dark brown hair was salt and pepper at the temples, but it looked good on him. He was clean-shaven and handsome. His collared shirt was open at the neck, and his sleeves were rolled up, showing off muscled forearms.

Toni sat across from him. "I don't think I've seen you since your mom brought her Cadillac in."

He smiled. "God, she loves that car, and it's so old."

"You tell her to hold on to that old girl. It's a classic again. People are starting to look for them." Ruben's mom had acquired a 1977 Cadillac El Dorado with ridiculously low mileage and brought it to Toni to get it checked out. "It's worth its weight just for the chrome and leather."

Ruben laughed. "I ordered a couple of glasses of the Fairfield claret. You know I gotta show off a little."

"I can have a sip, but I'm on a medication right now, so that's all." She waved her hand. "It's no biggie, but I don't want my mom to give me crap, you know?"

"I know how that goes." Ruben reached for the two glasses as the waitress returned and ordered a cheese plate for them to share. He waited for the server to retreat before he asked, "So Nico said you had some questions about Fairfield? What's up? You become a detective in your spare time or something?"

"I mean... kind of?" Toni shrugged. "It's more personal. I'm just feeling some way about it because he was murdered right behind my house I guess. I don't know."

Ruben raised his eyebrows. "I mean... the police aren't seriously looking at Nico, are they?"

"Oh yeah. They're serious. Everyone knows they didn't like each other, and Fairfield land borders Dusi land."

Ruben waved a hand. "It was all stupid shit."

"Tell the police that," Toni said. "I think he's their main

suspect at this point. All the people who hated Fairfield, and it seems like they're only looking at Nico."

"Well..." Ruben shrugged. "Can you blame them? You know I respect Nico a lot, but the guy can go off half-cocked."

"When someone is harassing him? Of course he can."

"Nico blamed Whit for *everything* though. It was kind of overboard, Toni."

"Was it though? I'm not asking you to talk shit about your ex-boss—"

"I mean, Fairfield's *still* my boss. Or his estate is." Ruben shrugged. "As far as I've been told by the lawyers, nothing has really changed. Whoever owns his estate owns the winery too."

"So business as usual for you guys?"

Ruben smiled. "I mean, Whit won't be butting in, which isn't all bad, but other than that, all the same."

"Oh." Toni tried to get a read on Ruben, but his walls were pretty dense. There was something though... "So was he pretty intrusive?"

"Oh, not that bad. I mean, he was okay, but he really didn't know much about wine."

Ruben was holding back on something. There was a lot more going on between him and Fairfield than he was letting on. The tension emanating from him had gone way, way up. It was enough to make Toni's skin itch.

"But you're still in charge over there, right?"

Maybe Ruben had reason to get rid of his boss too. Even though they had a seemingly amicable relationship.

"Oh yeah. If anything, I'm probably busier now, but I'm sure they'll eventually hire some kind of business manager and I'll have to give my reports to them or something. Long term, I imagine whoever controls everything—"

"Any idea who that is?"

"None." Ruben shook his head. "We weren't buddies. He was a decent boss. Paid well. He could be a pain in the ass about the vineyard, but if I put my foot down, he listened."

Toni didn't sense anything untrue about that. "Huh. Good to know."

"But we didn't talk about personal stuff. I don't think he had any kids, so it's not like there are heirs. He came from money, so maybe his parents? A sibling? Like I was saying, I imagine that long term, we might be sold to another company, but I'm hoping that the value the winery adds to the estate will be enough to keep things going the way they have been."

And keep you in a job.

Toni propped her elbows on the table. "But can we be honest? You know your boss was giving my cousin shit, right? No bullshit, Ruben. We both know he was a dirty player."

Ruben took a deep breath and sat back in his chair. "Do I know that Whit pulled some stunts to make Nico's life a little more difficult? Yeah. He wanted that land along the creek and had plans for it."

"Nico's not going to give up that land, Ruben. It's not even his to sell; it's family land. And why would the family sell any of their land, especially to someone who was so obnoxious as Fairfield?"

"Come on, you guys haven't even owned it that long. Maybe... twenty years or so? It belonged to that weird old guy from Hungary before, didn't it?"

"I've got no idea. Nico knows all that stuff. I just don't

understand why you're covering for Fairfield when he's dead."

"Hey." Ruben raised his hands with a smile. "I'm not covering for anyone. I don't deny that Fairfield was a jerk to your cousin. But I don't think he was involved in anything illegal. He knew I wouldn't back him up on anything like that."

"Tampering with Nico's tractor? Tampering with his tanks? Stealing his crews?"

"You can't steal a harvest crew, Toni. They're independent contractors. If you give them more money than what your cousin's offering—"

"To sit around and *not* harvest his grapes?"

"To do whatever," Ruben said. "I'm not saying I agreed with him, but it's not illegal."

"Tampering with equipment is," Toni said. "Sabotaging a tank is."

"Can you prove any of that was Whit and not teenagers? Or a disgruntled employee?"

"Okay, even if you're right, can we talk about Fairfield literally dating Nico's ex-wife and flaunting it?"

Ruben's cheeks turned a little red. "I don't know anything about that."

"Oh, come on, Ruben. Why on earth would Fairfield be seeing Marissa of all people unless it was to piss off Nico?"

"All I can say is the few times I overheard Marissa and Fairfield talking, it wasn't Nico's name that came up."

"No?"

"No." Ruben looked at her dead in the eye. "It was his winemaker. Henry Durand."

CHAPTER 12

*T*oni waited in her Mustang, debating whether to go in or not. She wished she had Katherine's gift of foresight, because she knew she needed to talk to Henry, and she had no idea what she was going to say.

But no. Instead of foresight or telekinesis, she had the "gift" of empathy. She knew when people were lying to her. She'd always had a fairly good bullshit detector before the incident at the gym. Now? It was foolproof, and Toni wished it wasn't.

Most people had no idea how many tiny deceptions people told throughout the day, many of them for innocent reasons. To spare someone's feelings. To ease through an uncomfortable conversation. To gloss over an inconvenience.

Toni felt them all. It was one of the reasons she really appreciated spending time with cars more than people.

Now she was sitting in the driveway of Henry's small apartment on the outskirts of Moonstone Cove and wishing she could turn all her psychic power off. In the silence of the early evening, she could admit that.

If everything between them had been a lie, she didn't want to know.

Someone tapped at her window and she started.

"Hey." It was Henry carrying a bag of groceries. His smile lit up the evening gloom. "This is a nice surprise."

She opened her door and looked at his blue truck. "Can I help you carry anything in?"

"Nope." He lifted the paper bag. "It's just this. What's up?"

"Do you mind if we...?" She motioned toward the stairs that led to his second-floor apartment.

"No." He was concerned. "Everything all right?"

"Yeah. I mean... I'm sure it is." There had to be a good explanation. A logical one. There had to be.

This was Henry. And Henry was good.

"Okay." He looked confused but still happy. "Come on up."

She walked up the stairs and squeezed into a corner of the landing while he opened the door. He hadn't even locked it.

Typical, trusting Henry.

"Woof!" Earl's deep-throated bark greeted them as the door opened.

Okay, maybe not all trust. Any burglar who ventured into Henry's house would be greeted with a hundred pounds of awkward canine. Toni knew Earl was harmless, but most criminals probably wouldn't.

"Hey, Earl." She bent over to rub the dog's floppy ears while Henry put the groceries away. "How you doing?"

He sniffed her legs thoroughly, whining a little.

"Sorry, buddy. Shelby's at my house."

Earl sighed and lay down at her feet.

Henry came up behind her, put both his big hands on her hips, and squeezed. "Back off, Earl. She didn't come to see you."

She leaned back into his chest, closed her eyes, and let the warm wave of desire wash over her. It wasn't only desire. There was affection. Surprise. Delight.

And maybe, worst of all, hope.

"Henry, I didn't come over here for that." She turned and his hands slid around her hips. "I wish it was just that, but I need to ask you a question."

He frowned. "What is it?" Worry. Pure worry. "Is everything all right?"

"I've kind of been looking into what happened with Whit Fairfield."

The flavor of Henry's worry turned sour. "Okay."

"And... I've been trying to figure out one main thing. Him and Marissa. Why would he be with her? What did he get out of it?"

Henry let go of her and stepped back. For the first time ever, Toni felt a solid wall rise between them. His face shut down. His emotions shut down.

"I mean, probably just to irritate Nico, right? What does it matter?" Henry asked. "Do you think Marissa's a suspect?"

Toni felt an ache knotting her stomach. "I don't think so. But according to Drew, Fairfield had a fiancée in San Francisco, which meant that whatever he had with Marissa here was just... a fling. Maybe less."

"And?" He cleared his throat. "I mean, it's shitty, but men like Fairfield cheat on their girlfriends pretty frequently."

"But Whit Fairfield was so calculating. So... careful. Why

risk pissing off your fiancée to fool around with Marissa of all people? It's hard to imagine that it was just to piss off Nico."

"Why not? I mean, he's an asshole. *Was* an asshole." Henry crossed his arms over his chest. "It seemed like both of them were pretty horrible people. They deserved each other."

"You said that before," she said. "At my house when you told me someone saw them having drinks."

"Well, it's true." He walked to the kitchen. "You want a beer?"

"No."

"I want a beer."

Her heart was pounding. "Henry, why did Marissa ask about you when I saw her at the country club?"

Henry slammed down the beer bottle he'd just picked up and spun around. "What did she say?" His eyes were wide and angry.

"Nothing much." She swallowed hard. "I, uh, I didn't know what to say when she asked about you. I wasn't expecting that, you know? You always sounded like you hated her."

Henry's eyes were wild. He looked down at the counter. Out the window. Anywhere but directly at Toni. And his emotions were all over the place. Toni felt anger. Embarrassment. Shame.

"I do hate her," Henry said. "She was horrible to Nico and the kids."

"That's not why." She could feel it. There was something he was hiding.

"What are you trying to say?" His jaw clenched tight and he stared at her, his stance alert like an animal ready to flee. "You don't believe me?"

If she put her hands on him, she could make him relax. She could make him tell her whatever she wanted and she would know he wasn't lying.

And she'd never trust him again.

Toni took a deep breath and put her hands on her burning cheeks. She was upset, but she was trying to remain calm. "Henry, I need to you to be honest with me. For... so many reasons. I need to know why Marissa and Whit Fairfield would be talking about you."

"I don't know why that sonofabitch and that woman would be talking about me."

She closed her eyes and tried to stop the tears. "You're lying."

"I'm not..." He gave a sharp, bitter laugh. "It doesn't matter."

"What doesn't matter?"

He abandoned his beer in the kitchen and walked across the room, raking a hand through his hair. "Everything I've done. The months I've spent..." Henry turned, and the look he gave her cracked her heart open wide. "There's no win here. Nothing I did for Nico is going to matter, and worst of all, you're never going to..." He gripped his hair in his hand and clenched hard. "Fuck!"

Toni walked over to him and took him by the shoulders. "Henry, just tell me. Tell me everything. I can't help you if you—"

"There's nothing to help!" His eyes tore her apart. "I had a fraction of a chance with you before tonight, and now I'm going to have nothing. It's not the job. I don't care about the job; I can get another one if Nico fires me, but us..." He shook his head.

"Did you sleep with her?" The thought twisted her guts, but she needed to know.

"No!" He swallowed hard. "She tried. It was right after I moved here and started working at the winery; it was pretty obvious she and Nico were unhappy. I was trying to be nice, and maybe she took it for something else. I don't know. I'd had a little too much to drink after a Friday staff party, and she cornered me in the barrel room." He closed his eyes and stepped back, crossing his arms over his chest again. "She kissed me. I didn't react fast enough—my head was swimming—but I realized what was happening and I pushed her away."

Toni felt the worst of her anxiety release. He was finally telling the truth.

Henry didn't look relieved though. He looked ill. "She *laughed* at me." His cheeks were flaming red. "She laughed and said it could be our little secret. Don't tell Nico, she said. Don't tell anyone. If I did, she'd tell them I came on to her."

It was the truth. She could feel his shame and his anger. "Henry, that wasn't your fault. She was your boss's wife. She had the power in that situation and she abused it."

"I realize that. Now. But I didn't say anything, not even after she left him. I should have told Nico what had happened and been honest. But by the time she'd left, I'd met you." He blinked hard and reached across the space between them.

Henry ran a finger down her cheek, his thumb brushing the edge of her lip. "I'd met you, and I just thought you were so... cool." The corner of his mouth turned up. "You weren't like anyone I'd ever met before. You were so funny and smart. You didn't care what anyone thought about you. You were so bold, and I've never felt that way. I always worry what people think."

"You could have told us. Me or Nico."

He dropped his hand. "You are so damn loyal to your family, Toni, and your family may like me, but I am not one of theirs. If Nico got angry with me, you'd have sided with him. And I was still working up the nerve to make a move with you. I didn't want to mess anything up, so I just…"

"Tried to pretend like nothing happened."

Henry nodded. "Yeah."

It was the truth. He was telling her the truth, but he wasn't telling her everything.

"What happened after?" She held her hand out. "Tell me, Henry."

He let out a long breath and crossed his arms over his chest. "It was about a month after we'd won our first medal at the Central State Fair. It was a really big deal, remember? First gold medal for a Dusi wine, and it was the first pinot noir that Nico and I had worked on together."

"I remember. He called you his lucky charm."

Henry's smile was bitter. "Fairfield approached me— came here, in fact—and at first I was confused. I didn't know much about him, but I knew what Nico said about the guy. I about shut the door in his face, but then he told me he knew about me and Marissa."

Toni's heart fell to her stomach. "She told him."

"She told Fairfield that we'd had an affair. I told him he was full of shit and she was lying, but he said it didn't matter if she was." Henry shrugged. "Fairfield said, 'In a little town like Moonstone Cove, a rumor is all it takes to ruin a life.'" Henry swallowed hard. "I never forgot that. A rumor was all it would take to ruin things. My job. My relationship with my boss. My relationship with you."

"A year ago. So we'd just started..."

Henry nodded. "The mantel."

"That damn fireplace mantel."

Henry hooked a finger through her belt loop and tugged a little. "It's my favorite part of your house. I'll always love that mantel."

"Henry—"

"He threatened to tell Nico that Marissa and I'd had an affair. Said it wouldn't matter if it was true or not; Nico wouldn't trust me again because I hadn't told him in the first place. And if I wanted him to shut up, all I needed to do was give him a little bit of information every now and then."

Her heart sank. "What did you do?"

"I didn't say no." He wouldn't look at her. "And I will always feel guilty about that. I should have gone to Nico that night. I should have told him the truth. I should have told you—"

"You could have trusted me, Henry." That was the part that hurt the most. "I understand when things happened with Marissa. You didn't know us that well. But later? You should have known we would have believed you. Why didn't you think we'd trust you?"

"I was... so afraid. Everything had been going great. Better than I ever could have expected. And then Fairfield made me feel like I was the guilty one, you know? That it was my fault for not telling Nico about Marissa in the first place." He shook his head. "I know I should have known—should have trusted both of you—but it's like that asshole crept into my head and knew everything. He played on every single thing I was most afraid of."

Toni felt like there was lead in her stomach. "What did you tell Fairfield? Were you the one who was sabotaging—?"

"No!" Henry bent down and took her face in his hands. "Not once. Not ever. I swear on my mother, Toni." He closed his eyes and breathed out. "And I don't know who it was. But every time something happened, I felt guiltier. More trapped." When he opened his eyes, they were distant and angry. "I never even told Fairfield anything valuable. I kept stringing him along. Kept trying to figure out how I could get rid of the guy. Get him off my back." Henry's eyes went wide. "I didn't kill him."

Toni blinked. "I didn't think you did." It honestly hadn't even occurred to her. She could tell he was being honest with her. All the walls he'd thrown up were completely down. "But you and I are going to go to Nico's house right now. Tonight. I will go with you. You're going to tell him everything, and he is going to forgive you."

Henry stood straight and his face was a mask of pain. "Toni, he's gonna be furious. You know how he is about people playing straight with him. He's gonna fire me. He's gonna make sure no one around here will ever hire me. I'll have to leave town and—"

"Nope." She took a deep breath. "He's not gonna do any of that shit, Henry. I promise you."

Henry sat down on the couch, and Earl came and sat between his knees. He looked defeated. Resigned. "I know you're one of his favorite cousins, but I don't think you realize how furious he's going to be about this."

"Oh, he might be furious." She sat next to him. "He could

very well have you cleaning out fermentation tanks for a year, but he's going to forgive you."

He reached over and tentatively played with a piece of her hair. "How can you be sure?"

"Because I know my cousin." She took a deep breath. Henry had been completely honest and vulnerable with her. It was time to return the favor. "And because I *am* one of his favorite cousins. And because I'm going to have a baby." She turned to Henry, frozen next to her. "And you're the dad."

CHAPTER 13

"When were you going to tell me?" Henry stared ahead at the twisting road that wound away from the cove and into the hills. "When you started showing?"

"It's only been like nine weeks, okay? I've only been sure of it for a couple, and the chances of miscarriage are still kind of high." She crossed her arms. "I was kind of shocked, okay? At my age, I didn't think that was something I needed to worry about."

"You're not that old!" He shook his head. "And we only slipped like... once. That I can remember."

She shrugged. "There were probably a couple of times when we went back for seconds that we didn't remember to..."

"Okay maybe." He sighed. "Are you okay? Have you been to the doctor? How are you feeling?"

"Mostly fine. A little sick. And yeah." She motioned in the vague area of her abdomen. "I went today actually. It was an experience. Everything looked normal."

"Good. I'm coming with you next time."

"That's not actually up to you."

He jerked the car to the side of the road and stopped. "Listen. I want to be very clear, just in case you're wondering how I am dealing with this because I'm kind of all over the place right now."

She'd never seen him so thrown. "Yeah. I'm getting that."

"I am... *ecstatic* about you having my baby. I am obviously nuts about you, and I didn't think you wanted kids and that would never be a deal breaker for me, but I'm not gonna lie, I fucking love the idea of us having a kid together."

Now he was using his rare curse words to express his excitement about fatherhood.

Damn her ovaries!

He continued, "I also don't know what you want from me, and I'm more than a little worried that you're going to try to cut me out of this entire thing because... that's kind of something you would do, Toni."

She muttered, "It's irritating how well you know me."

"I have spent two years studying you in an 'I'm trying to not be a stalker' sort of way. I'm probably a little ahead of the curve on this."

Why was he so damn attractive? He wasn't just sweet and concerned Henry anymore, he was exhibiting a kind of aggression and protectiveness that she found damn near irresistible.

Ugh! She hated being a stereotype.

Toni turned to him. "I'm not going to cut you out, but *don't* try to dictate my life. I'm not some wilting flower, okay? I may be older, but it's not like I was looking to trap some younger guy into fathering my baby so I could satisfy a biological—"

"How fucking young do you think I am?" He glared at her. "I swear to God, you act like I'm a teenager sometimes."

"I don't know..." Her cheeks burned. "Thi-irty?" Please God, let him be thirty. He had to be at least thirty.

Henry threw his head back and laughed. "I don't know whether to be insulted or flattered."

"What does that mean?"

He leaned across the cab of the pickup truck, hooked his hand around the back of her neck, and pulled her into a mind-melting kiss. Toni completely forgot where she was and where they were going. She nearly threw her leg around him and humped him in the car, she was feeling so horny.

Hormones.

"Thirty." He pulled away and tasted his lips. "You're what? Forty-one?"

"Yes." She glared at him as he put the truck back in gear.

"You're such a cougar." He wiggled his eyebrows. "A sexy cougar luring a younger man into your clutches."

"How old are you, Henry?"

He turned to her with wide eyes. "So young. So innocent. Please don't tell my parents I got you pregnant, Toni. They might ground me."

"As soon as we get finished at Nico's, I'm going to beat you up. I'm going to tell him he has to forgive the father of my future child; then I'm going to hurt you."

He reached over and rubbed her thigh. "Just don't strain yourself, okay? At your advanced age— Ow!" He burst out laughing. "Let go of my ear."

"Nope." She twisted his ear in a proven grip she'd used to torment all her boy cousins the moment they got taller than her. "I'm sorry, but you are going to have to die."

"Stop." He batted her hand away, grabbed it, and brought her knuckles to his lips to kiss them. He kept her fingers clutched in his and rested their joined hands on his thigh. "You're so cute when you're mean. Your freckles stand out more, and I want to kiss your nose."

She refused to stop glaring. "How old are you, Henry?"

"I'm thirty-*four*." He glanced at her from the corner of his eye. "Cougar."

"Oh." Toni blinked. "That's only seven years younger than me."

"Uh-huh."

"I guess that's not that much."

"I guess not."

NICO SAT on the couch in his office, looking like he'd just been smacked in the face with a two-by-four. "Okay. Let me get this straight..."

Toni was perched on the corner of Nico's desk, and Henry was sitting in an office chair next to her. "We kind of threw a lot at you," she said. "Take your time."

Nico blinked. "You're pregnant?"

Toni and Henry exchanged a look.

Toni said, "That's the part that's throwing you off?"

Nico spread his hands. "I didn't think you wanted kids."

"I didn't *not* want them, it just didn't happen. I'm not anti-kids. I love kids."

"You love being an aunt. Being an aunt is not being a parent."

"You think I don't know that, dipshit?" Toni rolled her eyes. "Was it a surprise? Yes. Am I happy about it?" She took a deep breath. "I think so? I'm getting used to the idea. I feel better about it now that I know Henry's not freaked out."

"Well that doesn't surprise me," Nico said. "But you..."

"What about me?" Toni narrowed her eyes. "You think Henry will be a better parent than I will, don't you?"

Henry finally spoke up. "Nico, I know I should probably shut up right now, but I would not answer that if I were you."

Nico leaned back and stretched his arms over the back of the couch. He scratched the stubble on his chin. His eyes returned to Henry. "So Marissa sexually harassed you, and you didn't feel comfortable reporting her?"

Henry froze. "I didn't think of it that way."

"Well, you should have. She harassed you and threatened your employment if you told anyone. That's sexual fucking harassment, and you could have sued the winery for it. So... thanks, I guess."

"You're welcome?" Henry looked really confused. "You're not angry?"

"I'm very fucking angry, Henry. I'm *pissed* that you didn't report her at the time, but I'm not going to say I don't get it. You'd just started out, and I always come off as kind of a hard-ass to new employees."

Henry leaned forward in his chair. "Nico, I am so sorry."

"I'm *angry* about Fairfield though. I understand we have a little of the snowball-rolling-down-a-hillside thing going on here—"

"Exactly," Toni said. "Henry didn't want to tell you about

your ex-wife, so then he didn't think he could tell you about Fairfield—"

"—but you should have told me." Nico stared straight at Henry and ignored Toni. "If for no other reason than what he was trying to do was blackmail you. And that's probably illegal, and we could have called the cops on him. Which would have been awesome." Nico shook his head and stared out the window, probably still trying to sort through the deluge of information that Toni had hit him with.

Was it part of a strategy? Yes. She knew her cousin, and she knew he could be kind of a hothead. If she'd hit him with any single piece of Henry's revelations, he might have flipped out. Hitting him with everything—including the pregnancy— had short-circuited the mad.

"So Marissa told Whit Fairfield the two of you had an affair and you'd give him insider info on me to keep it quiet." Nico frowned. "What kind of trade secrets does he think we have around here? It's not like we have a secret fucking ingredient. He would have had better luck messing up the winery if he'd just hired you away from me."

"I would never work for that man."

Nico cut his eyes to Henry. "You swear none of the sabotage was you?"

"I swear it wasn't, Nico. And I don't know who it was either. I would tell you if I did."

"Hmm." Nico was starting to brood. "If Fairfield blackmailed you, he probably has someone else on our crew on his payroll. Or he *did*. Dammit." He huffed a breath. "I hate thinking anyone who works for me is a rat."

"I can ask everyone on the staff if they've taken money from him," Toni said. "I'll know if they're lying."

"Yeah, you were always good at that," Nico muttered. "I don't think it matters now. Maybe a more important question is: Does Henry have an alibi for the night Fairfield was killed? Because you're telling the police all this shit. I don't think we should hide anything at this point. It'll come out eventually—hell, Marissa might have already spilled it—and if you try to cover it up, you'll just look guilty."

Henry frowned. "Okay. Uh... He was killed on Friday or Saturday?"

"Saturday night is the one they keep asking me about. The week *before* the finger thing."

"Oh." He glanced at Toni. "Well, Toni and I were kind of hanging out."

Nico raised a hand. "Never mind. I don't want to know."

"Not that, idiot," Toni said. "I was watching a movie and then Henry called and he turned it on too, and we were kind of watching together. But we hung up around ten or so. We were probably both sleeping when Fairfield was killed."

"Oh, probably." Henry sighed. "Then I don't have an alibi either."

Nico waved a finger between the two of them. "Why were you guys sneaking around in the first place? You're dating, for fuck's sake. You're both adults. Why make it some big secret?"

Toni scoffed. "We aren't dating. Not really."

"Toni, you were watching a movie together over the phone. The man helps you with household projects and yard work. He's your boyfriend."

"I'm here." Henry raised his hand. "Just reminding you."

"Exactly." Toni pointed at Henry. "Who says Henry wants to be a *boyfriend*, Nico? He's a grown man, not a boy."

Henry frowned. "Toni, I've been trying to be your boyfriend for like a year now."

Damn it. She knew she should have brought Katherine and Megan for backup. Toni didn't want a boyfriend. That sounded juvenile. Boyfriends took you to the movies and the high school dance. Boyfriends got caught making out with a cheerleader at the kegger at Sammy Delgado's parents' house when they were on vacation and then you broke up dramatically during lunch break the following Monday.

Not that she was speaking from experience or anything.

Toni was an *adult*. What was the adult word for the man you liked spending time with who helped fix up your house, did your yard work, and got you pregnant?

Toni could practically hear her mother's voice shouting in her ear: *that's called a husband, Antonia!*

Not helpful.

"Can we just table the boyfriend discussion for another time when Nico—and now you—aren't murder suspects?" Toni asked. "It's really not any of Nico's business anyway."

"Have you told your parents yet?" Nico asked.

"Do I look insane?" *Maybe don't answer that.*

Henry frowned. "You told me first, right?"

"I maybe... told Katherine and Megan." She cleared her throat. "For advice."

Nico grinned. "Wait, you told me before you told Luna and Jackie?" He hooted a laugh. "Oh, you are in so much trouble."

"No." She hopped off the table. "No, I'm not, because you're not gonna tell a soul, Niccolo Anthony Dusi. Do you understand me?"

"I'm the first one you told in the family." He couldn't wipe the smile from his face. "I am *so* this kid's godfather." He clapped his hands together. "That's the price. I stay quiet? I'm the godfather."

Toni nearly tore her hair out. "Please, God, shut up, Nico. I swear on Grandma Dusi's lasagna, if you tell anyone about this before we're ready—"

"'I'd love for you to be the godfather of my love child, Nico.' That's all I need you to say, Toni. Say that and my lips are sealed."

Henry was watching all this with obvious confusion. "Wait, is this some kind of competition? I'm confused."

Poor man. You have no idea what you've landed in.

"Everything is a competition with my male cousins," Toni said. "Literally everything. Ask Nico how many godchildren he has."

"Thirteen now!" He crowed. "Lucky thirteen. You're welcome, and I'm officially in the lead."

"You only have that many because everyone wants to have the baptism party here at the winery and you practically make it a condition."

Henry shook his head. "I am so confused right now. Is Nico still mad at me?"

"Fuck no," Nico said. "After all, you didn't tell Fairfield anything important. He's dead anyway. And you're gonna end up marrying my favorite cousin. Of course I'm not mad at you."

"No one said we're getting married!" Toni said. "That hasn't even been part of the conversation, okay? Just everyone slow the hell down."

"Sure." Nico literally walked over and patted her head. "Whatever you say, shorty." He held out his hand to Henry. "Either way, welcome to the family, Henry. Hope you're prepared."

CHAPTER 14

*T*oni stared at the bottle of wine on the center of Katherine's table. "I want a drink so much right now. Or a whole afternoon to myself with a really dirty carburetor that needs rebuilding."

Megan opened her mouth. Closed it.

Katherine said, "I can't help with either of those things. Do you want some chocolate?"

"It has caffeine." Toni closed her eyes and groaned. "Being pregnant is the worst."

"Eat the chocolate," Megan said. "I don't think it's that bad."

"It's milk chocolate," Katherine said. "More sugar than cacao. I have more in the house. My sister-in-law sends it from London. It's much better than American milk chocolate."

"No alcohol. Limited coffee. No sushi. Chocolate may be my last vice," Toni said. "Okay, let's do it."

Katherine left the table and went inside.

Not even a day had passed since her truly insane day of

doctor's appointment, meeting with Ruben Montenegro, confrontation with Henry, baby reveal with Henry, and spilling everything to Nico.

She'd taken the day off. She deserved it and the cars could wait.

"It'll be fine." Megan rubbed her back. "This is your baby. She's gonna be a tough cookie."

"Oh God." She covered her face. "What if it's a boy? I don't think I can handle raising a Dusi male. What if the baby is like my brother and Nico and all my boy cousins?"

"Well..." Megan had no words of comfort for that because of course there were none.

Katherine must have caught the tail end of the conversation when she returned. "Genetically, the baby has a fifty percent chance of taking after Henry," she said. "And Henry is lovely."

Toni reached for the shiny, purple-wrapped chocolate bar Katherine was holding. "I don't know. The obnoxious genes are strong."

"Speaking of Henry," Megan said. "It sounds like he took the news very well."

"He said he's *ecstatic*." Toni bit into the chocolate. Oh, that was good. She felt her erratic emotions start to settle. "He stayed the night at my place last night. No sexy reasons, I was just about to fall over and I didn't want to drive back to his place, get my car, and drive back to my house. I was pretty out of it."

"So he just stayed the night?"

"Yeah." Toni hadn't questioned it. Was it the first time that Henry had stayed all night? Yes. But then again, it was kind of nice having another person hanging around when there was a murderer who'd killed someone within throwing distance of your house.

"And he seems okay about everything?" Katherine said. "I know you said you guys had never even talked about children."

"Honestly, he seems really excited. Definitely surprised, somewhat worried, but he seemed to take it in stride. I mean, it's Henry. He never overreacts to anything."

"Except blackmail threats," Megan said. "But that's understandable."

"God, Whit Fairfield was such an asshole." Toni was nearly finished with the chocolate bar. Why was it so small? "Why are we trying to find his killer again?"

"Because we don't want your cousin or your baby daddy to live with a cloud of suspicion over their heads for the rest of their lives?"

Toni pointed at Megan. "Okay, baby daddy is worse than boyfriend. Don't go there."

"Father of your love child?" Megan asked. "Significant other?"

"Sperm donor?" Katherine added. "Though obviously you went the more traditional donation route."

Toni put her head down on the table and wondered if not leaving the house for the next seven months was an option. Would the guys cover for her at the garage? Maybe she could take extended medical leave? Suddenly the unmarried girls who went off to live with the nuns when they were pregnant made sense. At least with the nuns you only had to deal with Catholic guilt and not social interaction.

"We're not helping," Katherine said. "We should focus on the murder."

"Please." Toni lifted her head. "That's so much easier to deal with than thinking about telling my family."

"So now we know why Whit Fairfield was with Marissa," Megan said. "He thought she had information that would screw with Nico."

"I don't get the obsession though." Toni sat up straight. "Fairfield got better reviews and more traffic at his winery. He has more acreage. Literally the only thing Nico had that Fairfield wanted was that one piece of land by the creek."

"It's possible there's something special about that land, or it could be that he really was extremely petty," Katherine said. "He strikes me as a man who was never told no. Maybe the simple fact that your cousin told him no and wouldn't give in was enough to put a target on Nico's back. The sabotage and blackmail seem like big violations to us, but for Whit Fairfield, they might have seemed quite routine."

"And now," Megan said, "even after he's dead, he's messing with your cousin's life."

"Unfortunately," Katherine said, "Nico and Henry are still the most logical suspects. Even though we know neither of them is guilty."

"I feel stuck," Toni said. "We found out why Marissa was hanging out with Fairfield and why she brought up Henry, but it didn't really tell us anything more about who killed Fairfield."

"No," Katherine said. "But it does tell us something important about Fairfield."

"What's that?"

Megan smiled. "He was a blackmailer." She turned to Katherine. "Right? If he was blackmailing Henry, who knows who else he was blackmailing?"

"Agreed," Katherine said. "I'm not a detective, but I suspect blackmailers rarely have single targets. If that was how he conducted his business, he would have had more than one mark. If we find out who else he was blackmailing, we might find more people with motive."

"How are we supposed to do that?"

Toni stared at the ocean. "I might have an idea."

MARISSA LIVED in a condo not far from the pier in the South Beach neighborhood of Moonstone Cove. It was a fashionable area full of shops, restaurants, salons, and tourist traps of all kinds.

It was about as opposite of North Beach, where Katherine lived, as possible.

Nico's former wife rented the place with a chunk of money she received in spousal support from Nico and her income from real estate.

On Tuesday night following the crazy weekend that had resulted in blackmail revelations, baby revelations, and a frustrating lack of wine, Toni rang the bell with Katherine and Megan behind her.

One of the new guys had dropped a tire jack on her foot that morning. Needless to say, she wasn't in the sunniest mood.

"Are you sure about this?" Megan asked.

"I'm having a 'why the fuck not?' kind of day," Toni said. "So I'm not really thinking about it too closely."

Marissa opened the door, wearing a fashionable set of

rose-colored loungewear that complemented her perfect complexion and dark brown eyes.

"Toni?"

"Hey, Marissa."

The corner of her mouth turned up, and she leaned against the doorjamb. "I don't know what you want, but—"

"That's okay." Toni grabbed her arm, wrapped her fingers around it, and gathered a sense of calm to flood Marissa's senses. "Why don't you just let us in so you can relax?"

Immediately, Marissa's eyes drooped and she blinked slowly. "Um... okay."

"Can we come in?"

"Yeah." She stepped aside. "Come on it. That's fine."

"Holy shit, this is very creepy," Megan muttered behind her as Toni led Marissa into the entryway and past the small front room that looked like a shell shop had tastefully exploded.

She didn't let go of Marissa's arm, not once, as they walked to the living room with a view of bustling South Beach. Broad french doors opened to a balcony that looked over the ocean, and flashing lights from the boardwalk flickered in the distance.

She was pushing calm into Marissa with more force than she'd ever tried before. Her intent was to make Marissa as amenable as possible, but she worried a little bit about making her fall asleep too.

Katherine asked quietly, "Have you ever done this before?"

"Like this? Nope." Toni settled next to Marissa on the overstuffed cream couch and she didn't waste time. "Tell me about you and Whit. Did you approach him? Or did he approach you?"

"He was at the club one weekend. He was so sweet." Her smile fell. "I thought he really liked me, but he just... hated Nico." She slumped against the couch, looking slightly drunk. "I mean... two months after we started fooling around, he tells me he has a fiancée. And she knows about us. They have an..." Marissa attempted to use air quotes and failed miserably. "...open relationship. What the fuck is that?"

Katherine said, "Generally it's an established relationship where both members are allowed to have sexual relationships outside the typical bonds of monogamy, but it's not considered cheating because—"

"Oh my God, I fucking know what an open relationship is." Marissa was starting to sound more than slightly drunk. "I just think they're... bullshit. Like, he's a man, right? He was totally cheating on her. She probably knew and didn't care." The groggy woman waved a hand. "Whatever. All men are trash."

"But you're the one who told him about Henry," Toni said. "Aren't you?"

"Damn." She laughed a little. "Have you seen him? I mean, he's hot. He's built like a tree. I'd climb that twice a day if you let me. But then he's all polite and sweet. He's like a... puppy. Like a cute little... fucking sexy puppy."

Toni didn't even have words.

Megan said, "I wish you could see the face you're making right now. It's truly a thing to behold."

"She's just so gross." Toni tried to relax the expression of disgust, but it was difficult. "And she's talking about my... Henry."

"Watching you dance around your actual feelings for this man is going to be the highlight of my year." Megan had that infuriating smirk again. "For real. It's very amusing."

"Hey, Marissa?" Toni shook her arm. The woman had been dozing off. "Who else was Whit blackmailing?"

"Uh..." She squinted. "More than Henry. He had a safe and... he kept all sorts of stuff in there. Like his accounts." Her voice had taken on a singsong quality. "And some cash. And a couple of guns." She stared at the french doors. "The lights are so twinkly."

"What are you doing to her?" Katherine said.

"I'm pushing all the calm I can into her. Kind of like what I did with Justin when he tried to shoot up the gym, only not as much because I don't want her to fall asleep."

"Twinkle, twinkle..." Marissa blinked. "Little... stars."

Megan kept up the train of questions. "So Whit Fairfield had a book of people he was blackmailing?"

"I think so. I saw him get it when he was going to a meeting with..." Marissa's eyes were half-closed.

"Toni! Too much."

"Oh?" She blinked. "Sorry, I'm getting kind of tired too. That might be rubbing off."

"Marissa?" Katherine snapped her fingers by the woman's ear.

She started. "What? Where am I?"

"At home. You were telling us who Whit was going to meet with his black book."

She giggled. "Oh yeah. The *secret* book. He was going to meet Ruben. He *always* had a meeting with Ruben." She rolled her eyes. "Maybe they had a... an open relationship too." She giggled. "That'd be a good one. Ruben and Whit."

"Why would that be funny?"

Marissa rolled her eyes. "Because Ruben haaated Whit. So much. But he pretended not to. And he wanted me. He told me so. Said if Whit wasn't around, I'd be his." She waved a hand. "Like... whatever, right? He's not my type. I was already married to a farmer once. No, thank you. I don't care about all your plans and... caves and stuff. What is that even?"

"She's starting to ramble," Katherine said. "Ask her about the book again."

"Who else?" Megan asked. "Who else besides Ruben?"

"Not really." Her eyes were drooping and she burped out loud. "S-sorry. I don't feel good."

"Are you making her throw up now?"

Toni felt her nausea rising. "I can't help it. All my morning sickness tends to come at night."

"Do you at least feel it less if you push it into her?"

"Kind of?"

"I do not want this woman throwing up on me," Megan said. "We need to finish up here."

"Who else was he blackmailing?" Katherine asked. "Who else did he have meetings with?"

"Uh... Marla Price at the Ledger. And... Ronnie, his accountant here. He was real mad. Ronnie was always real mad." She blinked long and hard. "Oh, and Pamela at the club. They had a couple of meetings." Marissa's eyes got teary. "I think he was fucking her too."

"Good Lord, this man was vile," Megan said. "Can we wrap this up?"

Marissa was slumped on the side of the couch, holding

her stomach. "I am going to puke. Oh my God, Toni, I'm going to puke."

Toni let her arm go and felt an immediate backwash of nausea. "Okay, we need to get out of here."

"Hey, Toni?" Marissa's voice was plaintive. "Toni, can you tell Nico for me?"

Toni felt a little guilty for prying Marissa's brain open. She sighed. "Sure. What's up?"

"I miss..." She blinked. "I miss..."

"You miss Nico?"

"I miss... *sex* with Nico." Marissa groaned. "He was so much better than Whit. Stronger. More stamina... I mean, he could be bossy, but—"

"Lalalalalala!" Toni stood quickly, covered her ears, and turned to the door. "Okay, it's time to go." She nearly ran for the door. "Brain bleach!"

Megan was cracking up. "You mean you don't want to hear the sexual exploits of your cousin?"

"He's like my brother!" She walked out the door and inhaled deeply as the ocean breeze wafted over her. "Okay, that's better."

Her stomach settled. Her mind cleared. Katherine shut the door behind them, and Megan started down the stairs.

"Well," she said. "That was certainly illuminating."

"And a little frightening," Katherine added. "Please do not ever do that to me."

"I promise," Toni said. "I don't really want to do that to anyone. *Ever* again."

CHAPTER 15

$\mathcal{T}$oni drove home directly from interrogating Marissa. She was exhausted, a little nauseated, and a lot hungry. The last thing she expected to see was Henry's pickup truck in her driveway.

She pulled her Mustang into the barn and parked it next to the ancient blue truck she was fixing up in her spare time; then she walked out and past Henry's truck, where she heard a soft whine.

Earl popped his head up from the bed.

"Hey, buddy." She reached up and patted him. "What are you and your dad doing out here, huh?"

Your dad.

Henry was going to be a dad.

A dad of her kid.

It was still a head trip.

Toni released the tailgate on Henry's pickup and patted the edge. "Come on, Earl. You can get down."

Earl just lay down in the bed of the truck and sighed deeply.

"Huh." She closed the tailgate and walked up her front steps. The front door was open, but the screen door was keeping the bugs out. "Henry?"

"Hey!"

Toni walked in the house and saw him stick his head out from the kitchen doorway as she was taking off her boots. "What are you doing in my house?" She wasn't upset exactly. It was just out of character. Henry was usually overly polite and went out of his way not to intrude on her territory. "And why won't Earl get out of the truck?"

"He's not supposed to get down unless I let him. And I wanted to make you dinner and my kitchen is pathetic. I hope you don't mind I let myself in. I was trying to finish the pasta before you got home."

If it was any other night she probably would mind, but Toni was too relieved that she wouldn't have to cook. "It's fine. Call me next time, but I am exhausted and hungry and nauseated at the same time." She let herself collapse on the couch. Shelby immediately walked over and curled on her lap as she stretched her legs across the cushions.

"You're nauseated and hungry at the same time?" Henry asked. "Is that normal?"

"I have no idea." She laid her head on the back of the couch and felt her whole body start to relax as Shelby began purring under her hand. "I don't seem to get sick in the morning, it happens more at night. And I'm trying to avoid eating anything big for lunch because I don't want to get sleepy before the workday ends. But that means I'm hungry at night and then I eat a big meal and I get sick again. It's a vicious cycle."

Her eyes were still closed when she felt him sit on the

end of the couch and lift her feet into his lap. "I am very sorry that women get all the pregnancy symptoms and men get none. That's always seemed unfair to me." Henry started rubbing her feet. "The ziti is baking and there are steaks I can grill when we're done with the pasta."

She forced herself not to cry. His hands felt good and he was so thoughtful and she didn't want to cry. She was such a sap lately. The increased empathy was bad enough, and now she had hormones coursing through her body like a freaking estrogen flood.

"Thank you." She kept her eyes closed so they wouldn't leak. "That's really nice of you, and you give a great foot massage."

"I will do what I can to take the load off," he said. "Think about letting me cook for you since I'm around here at the end of the day. I don't mind, and you work longer hours most of the year."

"Not right now." She blinked and opened her eyes, watching him as he rubbed her sore feet. "I know you're working insane hours right now." It was crush season at the winery, which meant there were likely nights that Henry was crashing in the office. "Don't run yourself ragged."

"I won't. But when harvest is over, I'll have a much easier schedule, and I like cooking. I'm not trying to dictate your life —that's what you said, right? But I am worried that you're going to push yourself too hard and make yourself sick. Cooking is a thing I can do. Even if you need the night to yourself and you just want me to leave food for you, that's fine."

Toni opened her mouth. Closed it. "Don't be so logical," she muttered. "It's spoiling all my arguments."

He smiled and kept rubbing her feet. "You said you're getting tired in the afternoon? That's normal." He worked his large hands from her ankles up her calves. "You don't need to be eating less food so you don't get sleepy, you need to be taking a nap when you're tired. You have a couch in your office. Use it."

"How am I supposed to explain that to the guys?"

"At some point, they are going to start wondering why you're smuggling a basketball under your coveralls, Toni. You might have to tell them you're pregnant."

Since all her longtime employees were dads, she had a feeling it would be a mostly positive reaction.

Still. Very weird.

Toni was melting into a puddle. Her house smelled like cheese and baked pasta, Henry was rubbing her feet, and her cat was purring on her lap.

"I could get used to this," she murmured.

"So could I." He pressed his thumbs into the side of her ankles again. "I'm gonna show you, Antonia Luciana Dusi, that there are some very real benefits to being my girlfriend."

Her head popped up. "How did you find out my middle name?"

He smiled broadly. "I have my secrets."

"Did you call me your girlfriend?"

"Yes." He squeezed her ankles. "Before you start arguing with me, you need to look at the evidence and be logical. Are you romantically involved with anyone else?" His hands halted on her legs.

"Henry, of course not."

His hand started moving again. "Okay, good. Neither am

I. Do we spend regular time together?" He held up a finger. "Not go out on dates, but spend time together."

Saturdays in the garden. Home-improvement projects. Phone calls that turned into watching movies together that turned into something in the neighborhood of phone sex.

"Uh..."

"You know we do."

The cat, sensing an opportunity for more attention than Toni's half-hearted pets, decamped from her lap and headed toward Henry.

"We spend time together," he said. "We like talking and being together. I'd like to actually show my face in public with you and meet some of your friends since I've liked the ones I've met so far." He moved one hand to pet Shelby and kept rubbing Toni's legs with the other.

Betrayer cat. Toni would have to plot some petty revenge.

"And you know, just as an aside, we're also going to have a kid together," he said. "So there's that."

Toni opened her eyes and sat up straight. "See? This is what I was afraid of. Just because I'm pregnant does not mean that we have to change everything and commit to some kind of long-term—"

"Toni." He cut her off. "I was trying to have a committed relationship with you before the baby happened. It's not like this is some kind of one-night stand. We've been involved for almost a year. *I'm in.* Do you get that? I am in this."

She felt her heart racing. It wasn't that she didn't want Henry, it was just that no man in her life had ever been able to accept her—*all* of her—without trying to change who she was.

And Toni wasn't okay with that. She *liked* who she was.

She liked her life and her job and her crazy family that was constantly in her business. She wasn't going to change. No relationship was worth that.

"Do I want more of a commitment from you?" Henry continued. "Yes. I mean, that's not exactly a secret. But I can't force you. I know you well enough to know that if I push it, you're just going to dig in your heels."

She closed her mouth and sat back. "You make me sound like a child."

"You're not a child." His hand snuck up to her thigh. "But you do have a slightly overdeveloped need for independence."

"I don't like everyone knowing my personal life."

"Considering the size and closeness of your family, I get that. But can you just... consider letting me be your boyfriend and not keeping me a secret for the sake of our relationship and also possibly our future child?"

She slumped down. "I told Megan and Katherine about you."

"Which is great." Henry raised an eyebrow. "Is your mom aware that I exist?"

"How can you ask that? You've been to dinner at her house."

"Yes, as Nico's winemaker. And you didn't speak to me all night."

Okay, he maybe had a point. Toni took a deep breath. "Henry..."

"Yes?"

She said it quickly so she wouldn't lose her nerve. "Would you like to go with me to Sunday dinner at Frank and Jackie's this weekend?"

Both of Henry's eyebrows went up. "As your date?"

She nodded.

"Yes." He leaned over, grabbed her hand, and kissed her knuckles. "Antonia Luciana Dusi, I would like that very much."

"Okay." She wasn't panicking. Who was panicking? Not her. Probably the cat. Maybe she was panicking a little. She reached outward and searched for Henry's calm, centering presence.

"Toni."

"Mm-hmm?"

"Don't freak out about your parents. I like your parents."

She took a deep breath. "I mean, you think you like them because you met them as Nico's new winemaker, but you didn't meet them as my boyfriend, did you? Also, you like my parents, but do you like my brother, my sister, my nieces and nephews, my aunts and uncles, my forty-two cousins, and all their children?" She stared at him and his goofy smile. "You're stuck on the fact that I called you my boyfriend, aren't you?"

"Yeah." His smile was wide and... Yes, it was goofy. And adorable.

Toni sighed. "You need to understand something. When you dive into this pool, it's not the shallow end. There is no shallow end with my family, and they are not optional."

He nudged the cat—who had slowly taken over his lap— to the floor and pulled Toni's hand until she was nearly sitting on him.

"I know I'm diving into the deep end." He brushed a thumb over her cheek and examined her lips. "I know you don't come solo." He drew her across his lap so she was strad-dling him before he took her mouth in a long, lazy kiss.

Henry's hands worked their way from her shoulders, along her spine, and down to the curve of her bottom. His hands stroked her skin and the small of her back, teasing a shiver from her spine.

"Antonia." He whispered her name against her mouth.

Toni's eyes were closed and her head was swimming. "Uh-huh?"

"Are you going to let me feed you and stay the night?"

Nausea was a distant memory. "Yeah. That sounds good."

"Then I will take all the crazy family you throw at me." He scraped his teeth across her lower lip, which was swollen from his kisses. "Worth it."

***

HOURS LATER, Toni was barely hanging on to consciousness with a full stomach and a very relaxed body that Henry had teased and seduced to the point of spontaneous combustion before he put her out of her sexual misery.

He pulled on his boxer shorts and left the bedroom. She heard him walk to the door and whistle for Earl, who galloped into the house.

"Shhh," he whispered to the dog. "You have to be quiet, okay?"

The dog's excited paws tapped on her hardwood floor.

"Okay, go lie down. Stay."

Earl gave a low woof, and Shelby meowed from under the bed.

Toni poked her head over the side and saw the cat. "He's in the house now. What are you going to do with him?"

Shelby stared at her with narrowed eyes. *I could say the same thing about you, human.*

"Okay, we've let a dog and a large man into the house." She glanced at the clock. "It's after midnight, so I don't think—"

"Are you talking to the cat?" Henry leaned in the doorway, arms crossed over his bare chest, smiling in amusement.

"I am." *Deal with it.*

He climbed into the bed and immediately drew her into his arms, wrapping her up with blankets, a warm hug, and a contagious sense of calm. "Don't worry. Earl is sleeping by the fireplace." He yawned deeply. "He won't bother her in here."

"Oh. Okay." She snuggled back into his chest and was nearly asleep when she heard her phone buzzing.

"Is that you or me?" Henry asked.

"Me, I think." She opened her eyes and looked at the name flashing on her screen. "Nico?"

She sat up. He wouldn't be calling if it wasn't an emergency. Toni answered the phone. "What's wrong?"

"It's Marissa." Nico's voice broke. "She's at the hospital, Toni. Can you come? Someone broke into her house and beat her up pretty bad. The doctors aren't sure what her condition is yet, but they put her in a coma because there's a skull fracture and—"

"We're coming." She was already shoving Henry out of the bed. "We'll be there as soon as we can."

CHAPTER 16

The emergency room waiting area was filled with Dusis, Lópezes, and various members of Marissa's family by the time Toni and Henry arrived. They'd thrown on clothes and dropped Earl off at Henry's place before they raced down to the hospital in San Luis Obispo.

As soon as the doors opened, Nico's daughter, Beth, spotted them.

"Auntie Toni." She ran over and threw her arms around Toni.

"I'm here, kiddo." Toni pressed her hand to Beth's head and felt the girl nearly collapse as she started crying. "I got you."

Henry put his arm around both of them and guided them toward an empty set of chairs.

"She texted me last week, and I was such an asshole." Beth was crying and hiccuping as she tried to speak. "I'm so sorry. I hated her, but I didn't want anything—"

"Honey, of course you didn't." She stroked Beth's hair. "She knew that."

"She wanted me and Ethan to go over to her house this weekend, and I told her we had better things to do and now he's, like, really mad at me because I didn't tell him she texted, and he and Dad are, like, so angry and—"

"Bethy." She tried to calm the torrent of words. "Bethany." She drew away and patted the girl's cheek. "Honey, no one is angry with you. We all know you would never want something bad to happen to your mom. Where's your dad?"

She wiped her eyes. "Uh... I think he was talking with the doctor. They're still married, like, officially, so they want to talk to him and not Grandma and Grandpa Bianchi, so they're mad too, but I think that Grandma is really just upset."

"Of course she is." Toni scanned the crowded emergency room but couldn't spot Nico. "Beth, can you stay with Henry for a little while so I can figure out where your dad is? Or do you want to find Grandma Dusi?"

Beth blinked, suddenly realizing that Henry was sitting next to her. She wiped her eyes and looked between Toni and Henry. "Is Henry, like, your boyfriend or something?"

"Yeah. Henry's my... uh—"

"I'm her boyfriend," Henry said. "Do you need anything? Do you want some water or Kleenex or anything?"

"Wow." Beth looked at Toni. "Way to go, Auntie Toni."

"Why don't we focus on finding Grandma right now, okay?"

"Okay."

She rose with Toni as they walked back toward the fray of relatives, wading into the cacophony of people asking questions, speculating about what had happened, and fighting back tears.

Nico and Marissa might have split up, but she was still Beth and Ethan's mom. She was still family. And as Toni noticed the crowd of men gathering around Marissa's father, Toni's uncle, her father, her brother, and Nico's extended family, she realized that whoever had assaulted Marissa misunderstood their family on a very fundamental level.

Marissa might be annoying as shit, but she was still one of theirs.

"Toni!"

She turned toward her mother's voice. "Mom." She grabbed her mother in a swift embrace. "This is so awful."

"Can you believe this? What kind of world are we living in now? What is wrong with our town? First someone murdered and now someone breaks into Marissa's house and beats her? I just don't understand any of this."

"Did someone break in? Have the police said—"

"I mean, someone must have broken in, don't you think? They must have been going after a woman on her own. That's the only thing that makes sense. They must have thought she had some jewelry or something like that." Her mother pressed her hands to Toni's cheeks. "See why I worry about you living out there all on your own? If someone broke in—"

"Mom, can we not? This isn't about me. We need to think about the kids, okay?" She lowered her voice. "Did you know that Marissa and Whit Fairfield—"

"I don't know anything about any of that, so don't start. You know I don't listen to gossip, Toni Luciana. Saint James said the tongue is a fire and a world of evil, so I do not listen to gossip about my children." She must have spotted Henry over her shoulder. "Who is that?"

"That's Henry. You know, Nico's winemaker."

"And why is he with you in the middle of the night?"

"Can we talk about this later please?"

Rose Lanza Dusi narrowed her eyes. "I need to find Julia. The doctors are only talking to Nico, which is just ridiculous. Their daughter is in intensive care, and they haven't even seen her yet. They're talking about surgery, but they won't say on what."

"Okay, let's go find Nico." She ushered her mother toward the nurses' station where she could already see her cousin Leah fielding questions. Leah was a pediatric nurse, but someone would have called her as soon as anyone in the family landed in the hospital.

HOURS PASSED as they waited to find out what was happening with Marissa and the surgery that was supposed to happen. The last Toni had heard, there was swelling on her brain from the attack, and that was what the doctors were most worried about.

She was resting against Henry's arm, dozing as the hospital noise buzzed around her. Henry was out cold, his long legs stretching halfway across the waiting area. She saw Drew Bisset from the corner of her eye, talking with her cousin Max near the double glass doors of the emergency department.

She lifted her head and raised a hand, only realizing after she'd done so that she might be in very serious trouble.

Shit.

Oh Toni, you've stepped in it this time.

Of all the times for her to remember that she, Katherine, and Megan were probably the last people to see Marissa before she was attacked, this was a bad one.

"Hey." Drew sat across from her and kept his voice low. "This is pretty bad, huh? I talked to the guys who got the call and it was ugly. I hope she pulls through."

"Who called the police?"

"One of her neighbors. It was late, and the older lady downstairs heard arguing. Then a big thud and slamming doors. It was enough for her to call, and it's a good thing she did. The ambulance said she was touch and go with the head wound."

Toni took a deep breath, glanced at Henry, and decided to rip the bandage off. "Okay, so there's something I should probably tell you."

Drew sat back and narrowed his eyes. "Nothing that comes after a statement like that is ever good."

"We only went over to ask a couple of questions, and she was perfectly fine when we left, but if anyone dusts that house for prints, you will see me, Katherine, and Megan all over the place."

He crossed his arms over his chest. "Anything else?"

Toni glanced at Henry. "Uh... Whit Fairfield and Marissa were blackmailing Henry?"

"Oh, for fuck's sake!" He glared at her. "When were you going to tell me about this?"

"I only found out about it like three days ago, okay? I haven't exactly had a lot of time to process."

Drew rubbed a hand over his face. "Tell me you can alibi

the big-ass suspect sleeping next to you, who was being black-mailed by the murder victim and the lady who got beat up tonight."

"He was cooking pasta in my kitchen when I got back from Marissa's house last night, and he did not leave my place once until we got the call from Nico about her being in the hospital."

Drew nodded. "And Nico?"

She shrugged. "I have no idea."

"Okay." He shook his head. "The neighbor who called the cops said she heard a man and a woman arguing, but she couldn't hear them clearly. There's no way she could identify him."

"Security cameras?"

"We're pulling the footage, but I can tell you that condo complex doesn't have a great system. It's more for show than anything else."

"Because it's Moonstone Cove," Toni said. "Where's safer than the Cove?"

"Exactly." He tapped his fingers on his knee. "Dammit, Toni, I really want to get back to my quiet little beach community. You know what I mean?"

"A *Big Lebowski* reference at" —she looked at her watch — "two in the morning, Detective. That's impressive."

"I do what I can." Drew didn't crack a smile. "So Fairfield was blackmailing your man here?"

She sighed. "Okay, it's a long story and it doesn't exactly make Marissa very sympathetic, which feels wrong to talk about when she'd fighting for her life, but the short version is, Marissa tried something with Henry before she and Nico split, Henry never told Nico about it, Marissa and Fairfield used that incident—and Henry's failure to tell Nico—as leverage to try to get him to sabotage Nico's business."

"And did he?"

Toni shrugged. "Henry passed along some bullshit information, but mostly he kept trying to put Fairfield off. He doesn't know who was doing the sabotage at the winery like the tractor and stuff."

"You believe him?"

She nodded. "I do. He's an honest person, and he kind of spilled his guts. If he'd done anything to Nico, he would have told me."

"So Fairfield and Marissa were blackmailing Henry, who has an alibi for this attack."

Toni nodded. "And the reason I went over to talk to Marissa after work yesterday was to find out who else they might be blackmailing."

"In my admittedly limited experience with blackmailers, it's a fairly safe bet your man wasn't the only one." Drew raised an eyebrow. "But you thought Marissa was just going to tell you?"

Toni shrugged. "I can be pretty persuasive when I need to be, and Marissa isn't as smart as she thinks she is. She gave me a couple of names. And she said that Fairfield had a safe. Said he kept guns in it and a black book with his contacts."

"I knew about the firearms. He had them registered. Have not found any book like you're talking about."

"The gun that killed Fairfield? Was it his own?"

"Yeah." Drew nodded.

"Weird and horrible," she said softly.

Henry shifted and leaned toward her. Toni put her head

back on Henry's shoulder and he rested his head on top of hers.

Drew smiled. "You guys are cute."

"Don't get started, okay? This isn't exactly how I'd planned to introduce him to my crazy family."

"Ah, he's a good guy. Cynics like us can tell who the jerks are, and he's not one of them."

"I'm not a cynic."

"Of course you are." Drew crossed his arms over his chest and yawned. "Names?"

Toni was too tired to argue with him. "Of who? Blackmail targets?"

Drew nodded.

Toni lowered her voice even more. "I'm not positive, but she mentioned Marla Price at the Moonstone Cove Ledger. She mentioned Ruben Montenegro, who—according to Marissa—did not get along as well with his boss as he makes out. And she mentioned his accountant. I can't remember his name, but it was a guy. And one more person..." She closed her eyes. "Um, the lady at the club. At the country club. The social director?"

"Pamela something? Yeah, I'm pretty sure she had a relationship with Fairfield. That was an affair. Fairfield's fiancée knew about Marissa, but she didn't mention Pamela."

"Interesting." Toni took a deep breath. "That's it. Those are the only names I can remember."

"I wonder if Marissa knows who killed her boyfriend or if she simply suspected someone and confronted them. Maybe she thought she could continue Fairfield's blackmail operation."

"You think whoever killed Fairfield is the one who beat Marissa up?"

"Yes." He nodded. "I do."

She frowned. "That seems like a leap. If it was the same person, wouldn't they have killed her?"

"I'm starting to wonder whether Fairfield's death was intended. Before he was killed, the medical examiner says that Fairfield was beaten quite badly." Drew nodded at the hospital doors. "Not unlike your relative here. Cracked ribs. A busted jaw. Whoever beat Whit Fairfield up was a powerful person. Likely a man around six feet tall based on the injuries. Whit Fairfield might be the victim of a fight that got out of hand. A crime of passion, so to speak."

"A crime of passion against Whit Fairfield and Marissa by a powerful man around six feet tall?" Toni glanced at Henry, then at Nico. "So what you're saying is...?"

"Unless Nico has an ironclad alibi for last night, I still can't rule him out."

CHAPTER 17

"An alibi?" Nico rubbed two hands over his exhausted face. "It was Tuesday night. School night. I made the kids dinner, helped Ethan with some geometry homework, and went to bed." He frowned. "Watched a movie for a while. Fell asleep. That's it."

They were sitting in Nico's office at the winery, Drew and Toni in the chairs across from his desk and Henry leaning against the edge of it.

Marissa was stable but still unconscious. They had performed the surgery she needed the previous night and were keeping her in a medically induced coma for the first twenty-four hours to give her body the best chance to heal.

Nico had taken the kids home to sleep. He and Henry were trying to organize the harvest crews at the winery so they could run without him, leaving him free to shuttle the kids back and forth to the hospital if necessary.

Drew looked disappointed. "Mr. Dusi, I'm trying to help. Can you think of anything—?"

"Why the fuck would I beat up Marissa?" Nico was obviously exhausted. "She's Beth and Ethan's mother, for God's sake. You think I'd do that to my kids?"

"She is your soon-to-be ex-wife, involved in a messy divorce, and in a relationship with a man who repeatedly tried to sabotage your business." Drew spread his hands. "I can't ignore it even if I want to rule you out."

Henry looked at Drew. "Do you need me to make some kind of statement about what Marissa and Fairfield did? What they threatened me with? Nico didn't know about any of it."

"Until four days ago," Toni said. "And three days after Nico found out, Marissa was beaten up. So I don't know if that really helps."

Henry clamped his mouth shut.

"Thanks, Toni." Nico's sarcasm was tangible. "You're really helping this guy?"

"Katherine, Megan, and I went over to Marissa's yesterday to ask her about the blackmail stuff. She told me some more names, and then she was attacked. There has to be a connection between someone on that list and whoever did this. We're trying to help because I don't want a cloud of suspicion hanging over you. Just suck it up and accept the help."

"Who did she say they were blackmailing?" Nico asked. "Who else besides Henry?"

"Pamela Martin, for one. Or at least that was a name she mentioned."

Nico looked half-asleep, but he tapped both his hands on the edge of the desk. "You need to talk to Jackie maybe."

"Jackie, my sister-in-law Jackie?"

Nico nodded. "They were in school together, and I think

they're still pretty close. I'd be shocked if Pam and that guy were actually involved, but Jackie would be the one to ask."

"Okay." Toni glanced at Drew. "I guess I'll call Jackie then."

Drew pursed his lips. "What makes me think I'm not invited to this meeting?"

"Do you want actual information from this woman?" Toni asked. "She'll talk to other women. She's not gonna talk to a police officer. Not without knowing what it is you want from her."

Drew took a deep breath. "This town is so damn insular it drives me absolutely nuts sometimes."

"Just be glad you have me on your team," Toni said. "Me and my sister-in-law."

———

THE NEXT DAY, Megan picked Toni up at the garage so they could meet Toni's sister-in-law for lunch. They met Jackie at a South Beach bistro that looked over the pier and backed up to tasteful boutiques just a block away from the boardwalk.

Jackie had grown up in a ranching family farther down the coast. She was the privileged oldest daughter of two successful parents and had a keen financial mind that had taken Frank Dusi's vegetable business national and then international.

Jackie also knew *everyone.*

"Hey." She stood and kissed Toni's cheek. "How's Nico?" She turned to Megan. "You must be Megan. I've heard a lot about you, and I adore that bag."

Megan held up a mustard-yellow leather tote bag that

complemented her rose-colored blouse. "Thanks. I was just looking at yours."

"It's my favorite, and you can't get them anymore because the shop went out of business. Isn't that the worst?"

"I hate that."

"Wow," Toni said. "Yeah. Purses. And stuff..."

Jackie smirked. "Toni will never admit to caring anything about fashion, and yet she always manages to look amazing and completely her own style. As long as she's out of her work coveralls, obviously."

"I have no idea what you're talking about." Toni knew she stood out in the pale, sun-washed dining room decorated with tasteful coastal influences and driftwood. She was wearing a slim pair of dark blue denim jeans, her favorite Merle Haggard concert T-shirt, and a brown leather jacket. "You asked about Nico."

"Yeah." Jackie's expression turned hard. "This whole thing with Marissa? It's bullshit. Anyone who knows Nico—knows our family at all—knows that we will come down like a ton of bricks on anyone who hurts one of ours."

Megan said, "So you had a good relationship with Marissa? Because most of what I'm hearing is—"

Jackie lowered her voice. "Oh, don't get me wrong. I think she's a complete bitch."

Megan blinked. "Oh."

"But she's a bitch. She didn't abuse her children. She didn't murder anyone. She fucked around on Nico—I'm pretty sure—and she was never satisfied with the life they had, but she's gonna regret those things eventually. She's still Beth and Ethan's mom. And she adores her kids. She's a selfish little shit about it, but I know she loves them."

Toni said, "Her parents were at the hospital. Did you see them?"

Jackie nodded. "Marissa is gonna end up straightening up her life after this. She was going through some kind of midlife crisis, but she's got a good family, and she'll figure it out. Whoever beat her up like that?" Jackie shook her perfectly coiffed head. "They better pray the police arrest them before Frank and the boys find out who it was."

Toni looked around the small restaurant. "So Pamela Martin is going to meet us here?"

Jackie kept her voice low. "I told her to meet me about fifteen minutes after I told you so we have a little time to talk. You think Pam knows something?"

"I think she was involved with Whit Fairfield," Toni said. "That's what Drew said. Marissa thought they were sleeping together."

Jackie wrinkled her nose. "No accounting for taste, but it wouldn't be her worst. I like Pam a lot, but she tends to have horrible judgment when it comes to men. Of course, it wouldn't be a bad move for her professionally."

"Why?"

Jackie kept her voice barely over a murmur. "Everyone knew he was expanding his place. What did Nico call it that one time? The Disneyland of wine? He's not far off. Fairfield wanted to build a hotel, a spa, a restaurant. Rumor was he even wanted a golf course attached to it."

"That's ambitious," Toni said.

"Yep. But land is still cheap here compared to up north. He wanted to put Moonstone Cove on the tourist map and buy up as much property as he could before everyone discovered it."

"He was looking at development?"

"Oh yeah. He picked up some acreage over in the hills above North Beach. Got another stretch farther south, closer to my parents' place. And there was that piece he wanted to buy from Nico, of course."

"Do you have any idea why?"

"I think it's just proximity. Fairfield's tasting room and operations look over the creek right into that little corner of Nico's land. If Fairfield had it, he could build a bridge and expand a little. It seems minor, but if Whit got it into his head? I can see him being a massive asshole until he got what he wanted."

"But why was it good for Pamela to hook up with him?" Megan asked. "She's got a steady position at the country club."

"A club that would have a lot less appeal if Whit Fairfield created a hotel, spa, and golf course smack in the heart of wine country," Jackie said. "The country club is already seeing things die off in the events department. Younger people are wanting the more 'rustic wine country' look for events and not the 'polished country club' thing."

"So Pamela may have been looking for work," Megan said. "Looking for the next big opportunity."

"She'd have it with Fairfield." Jackie had started to scan the restaurant. "Because I don't know who's in charge of that whole estate now, but from what I hear, they're not letting up on their plans for Moonstone Cove."

"There she is," Megan said.

"And you're looking to get into events too, right?" Jackie sipped a glass of ice water. "That's the reason I'm introducing you?"

Megan nodded. "I had a very successful event-planning company in Atlanta before I moved, but I'm starting from scratch here. Honestly, it really is a favor for me to meet her."

"No problem." Jackie rose and stretched out her hands, pulling Pam into a hug. "Hey, you! It's been too long."

"So nice to see you." Pamela was smiling. "And your sister-in-law, right? It's Toni, isn't it?"

"Yes." Toni shook Pamela's outstretched hand. "And this is a good friend of mine, Megan Carpenter. She moved here a little over a year ago from Atlanta."

"It's so nice to meet you," Megan said. "I think we were introduced at the club months ago, but it was at a big party."

Pamela narrowed her eyes. "Yes. I remember. You do look familiar, and I remember your adorable accent."

Toni bit her lip and tried not to snort at the "adorable accent" comment. Her friend just loved it when people patronized her because of her native Atlanta sound.

Megan cocked her head and gave Pamela a dimple-inducing smile. "Well bless your heart, you probably meet so many people in your line of work, I don't know how you'd keep any of them straight!"

"Yes." Pamela's smile faltered for only a second. "What brings you to Moonstone Cove?"

"Well, my husband was transferred out here for work" — Megan laid the accent on thick— "so I packed up the kids and closed my event-planning business in Atlanta so we could come out west for a new adventure, only to find out he's been dippin' his brisket in someone else's sauce if you know what I mean."

Pamela's jaw dropped.

"Oh, not you." Megan took a sip of water. "I think she

was a cocktail waitress or whatever you call those little girls who pour wine at the wineries." She waved a hand. "So I kicked him out. Now I'm looking to start up an events business again. I'm really looking forward to a new challenge. I hate being bored."

"I imagine." Pamela didn't know quite how to react to Megan. "What kind of events did you throw in Atlanta?"

"Oh, the usual. Weddings. Birthday parties. Bar mitzvahs. Corporate conventions. Book signings and film openings. Stuff like that."

Pamela perked up when she heard *film openings*. "Really? That's a pretty impressive résumé."

"Yes, I've had a few former clients offer to fly me out to coordinate events for them, but honestly I've had so much going on here that I just haven't been able to accommodate them. Plus I'm looking to build a more local clientele. I don't want to have to be flying cross-country to keep busy, you know?"

Jackie waved the server over. "Megan and I are tossing around ideas for Frank's company party the end of next month. She's so creative."

They were? Toni smiled. That was news to her and probably Megan too. She had to hand it to her sister-in-law—it did not take much to get Jackie up to speed.

Jackie ordered a bottle of white for the table and a bruschetta appetizer that had Toni's stomach sounding off. "Anyone object to those?"

"Not me," Toni said.

"Sounds amazing."

"Thanks, Jackie."

"So Pam," Jackie started. "What a shock about Whit and Marissa, right?"

Pamela nearly did a spit take, but she caught herself. "It's..." She cleared her throat. "It's so shocking. How is Marissa doing?"

"Looking like she'll pull through one hundred percent," Toni said. "Thank goodness."

"When I heard about Whit..." Pamela genuinely looked stricken. "I know not everyone liked him, but he was kind to me."

"Kind how?" Megan's eyes were wide. "Was he a client?"

"No. Well, not yet." Pamela shrugged. "I don't think it's that big a secret that he was looking for an events coordinator, and we were talking about the position."

"I hadn't heard that," Toni said. "He's not too far from me. Do you really think people would have booked events there?"

Pamela smiled. "With his plans? Absolutely."

"So he was really talking about expanding the place, huh?"

"The level that he was talking about was just..." Her face nearly glowed. "It was so beyond anything offered in Moonstone Cove currently. Right now we're kind of a quirky beachside town. Whit's plans would have put us on some lists. The kind that Silicon Valley money would have eaten up."

"He thought there was that much potential in the area, huh?"

"Whit had big plans," Pamela said. "But he had the money and drive to follow through with them. There were just a few obstacles that he had to smooth out, and then the sky was the limit." Something about Pamela's mouth turned bitter. "I suppose it might just come to nothing now. It'll all depend on what his fiancée decides."

That brought Toni up short. "Sorry, what?"

Megan asked, "Did you say his fiancée was in control of the estate now?"

"I didn't know he was engaged." Toni played innocent. "Are you sure?"

"Oh yeah. He told me when it happened." She wrinkled her forehead. "Honestly, it seemed more like a business merger than a marriage. Angela Calvo was an equal partner in the investment company with Whit. That was the deal." She looked a little uncomfortable. "I know people speculated about me and Whit, but it honestly wasn't like that. He thought it was funny to insinuate we were sleeping together."

"Seriously?" Toni could feel the woman's embarrassment and deep-seated shame. "That's messed up. What a shitty thing for him to do."

Pamela shrugged, but Toni could tell it bothered her. "I'm not like that." She turned to Jackie. "You know me. I'm not. I may not have the best track record, but I steer clear of married men. Engaged ones too."

Jackie reached across the table as the server appeared with her wine. "I know that."

"Besides" —Pamela held out her glass as Jackie poured the wine— "I met Angela Calvo once, and trust me, I would never try to poach on that woman's fiancé. Crossing her seemed like a good way to ruin your life."

CHAPTER 18

*M*egan, Katherine, and Baxter followed Toni at a polite distance as they walked up the gravel driveway toward her brother's sprawling ranch house on top of the hill overlooking the dunes and the Pacific Ocean.

"Your brother's property is beautiful," Baxter said. "Has he lived here a long time?"

"It's a family house," Toni said. "This is actually where I grew up."

She'd been a country kid, running on dirt roads, playing in the creek, and rolling down hills on her bike when she was barely old enough to walk. Her parents had been old-fashioned: little to no TV and don't bother Mom in the kitchen unless you were helping cook.

Toni had run wild on the hill and the small family farm her father and uncles managed, munching on figs and tomatoes in the garden and learning from her uncle Martin how to take apart an engine when she was only ten years old. She'd hated school but had been utterly fascinated with how mechanical things worked.

Within a few years, she was taking apart anything her mother didn't nail down, and Rose Lanza Dusi begged her husband to take the little girl with the freckles and the dark brown curls to the car shop they ran in town.

At fifteen, Toni rebuilt her first engine. At eighteen, she started working for her dad and her uncle. And at twenty-one, she stood at the front of the church as her brother married her sister-in-law, Jackie, and Toni got to breathe a sigh of relief.

Jackie was awesome, and even better from Toni's perspective, she wanted a bunch of kids, she wanted to be a stay-at-home mom, and she wanted to host all the holidays at her house.

Which let Toni off the hook.

Jackie and Frank moved into the house a few years later, Luna and Toni having little to no interest in it, and promptly started filling it with numerous small Dusi grandchildren. Rose and Bobby moved into town, closer to the beach and the bocce ball club where they liked to hang out with their friends.

"So" —Toni finished a short summary of the house just as they reached the driveway— "it was kind of understood that whoever had kids first got the house if they wanted it. Which we were all fine with. Luna and her husband Rani always lived in Monterey, so it was just me and Frank, and he has four kids so..." Toni shrugged. "There're a couple of extra little houses on the property. Like guest cottages, you know? If anyone in the family needs a place to stay, they stay here."

"That's so lovely," Katherine said. "I think large families like yours are fascinating."

"I can't lie," Megan said. "It makes me miss all my cousins back east."

"And I can't lie." Toni turned and paused before they walked in. "With my empathy, big parties like this are getting harder and harder for me to do. So we may not be able to stay long. Jackie said she managed to get Fairfield's accountant here as a guest, so our priority is questioning him and seeing what he knows about Fairfield's death, the blackmail stuff, and why Fairfield was so determined to screw with Nico."

"Understood." Katherine looked around. "Is Henry coming?"

"Yes. He was working today so Nico and the kids could help Marissa move to the rehab center." Marissa was better, but according to doctors, she had a long road in front of her. "He'll be done in another hour or so. I told him to meet us here." And that could be the other reason that they weren't staying long.

Did Toni want to introduce Henry as her... boyfriend / significant-other-type person?

Yes.

Did she want to stick around for questions?

Most decidedly no.

Just as they were about to walk into the backyard, Jackie rushed out of the house with a giant smile on her face.

"Hi!" She jumped over and hugged Megan. "So great to see you." She stuck her hand out to Katherine and Baxter. "You must be Toni's professor friends from the university, Katherine and..."

"Baxter." Baxter shook her hand. "You have a beautiful home, Mrs. Dusi. Thank you so much—"

"Yep. I am going to chat with all of you, but first" —she turned to Toni— "please don't kill me."

"What did you do?" Alarm bells were going off in her head. Jackie could be dramatic. But this time she looked genuinely panicked.

"So!" She took a deep breath. "Okay, the guy you need to talk to is Ron Withers and he was Whit's accountant and I guess he's also a customer of yours because he was *really* excited when I told him you were my sister-in-law and he thinks you're really cute and he kind of thinks this is a blind date. I am so sorry—it was the only way I could get him to come to the barbecue."

Toni had to rerun it three times in her head. "Sorry, you *what*?"

"You wanted to question him about the stuff for Nico, but it was the only way I could get him here, okay? I'm so sorry."

"You... you told him you'd set me up with him? On a date?" Toni looked around in a panic. "Jackie, the week that I told Henry I would introduce him to my family *as my boyfriend*, you set me up on a fake date so I could interrogate someone about a murder?"

Jackie made a high, whining noise. "I'm so sorry! I didn't know about Henry, and it was the only way he'd agree to come!"

Baxter leaned over and spoke quietly to Katherine. "It really is like watching a television drama, isn't it?"

Toni was panicking. "Oh my God, Jackie!"

"I'm sorry!"

"What am I supposed to do? Henry will be here in an hour!"

"Okay, well just... interrogate Ron fast?"

Megan grabbed Toni's arm and hooked it around hers. "We can do this. Jackie, you take care of Katherine and Baxter for us, point us in the direction of the accountant, and we'll handle it."

Toni's mind was racing, but Megan's calm presence steadied her. "Do you know what you're doing?"

"Sadly, I have had to pretend to be interested in more than my fair share of boring men over the years." She patted Toni's arm. "We got this. I'll be your wingwoman."

"He's a little older, like midfifties, and he's got a white beard and he's completely bald otherwise. Pretty fit, but he dresses like a dad." Jackie looked at Megan. "You got it?"

"I got it."

Toni could feel her panic start to rise with every step she took into the maelstrom of her big brother's backyard. She felt a low burning anger start to simmer. She was trying to exonerate her cousin. Did men have to put up with faking interest in women to get information about murderers? Did men have to play dumb in order to—

"Okay, you're gonna want to tamp down on that."

Toni took a sharp breath. "Can you feel it?"

"It's just rolling off you in waves, honey. I'm surprised no one around us has thrown a punch yet."

"What do you want me to do?"

"Imagine I'm Henry, okay?"

She could do that. Henry was calm. Cool. Steady. Toni took a deep breath and tried to imagine Henry was holding her arm. "Do you see him?"

"I think so? Oh. Don't look up. He's at three o'clock and he's by the buffet table. We're going over to get a drink."

"How do you know it's him?" Bald with a white beard

and dressed like a dad could be any number of Frank's friends.

"He's staring straight at you."

"Pretend you don't see him."

"I'm gonna wave."

"Don't wave!"

"Waving." Megan's voice went a little higher. "Okay, look up. Act interested."

"I cannot do this."

"You are a supernatural feelings wizard, Toni Dusi. You telling me you can't bullshit a man for a half an hour to get some answers?" She squeezed Toni's arm. "Look up and smile."

Her head shot up, and she plastered a smile onto her face. "I am not used to this."

"I realize that, but it won't kill you."

"No, but I might kill someone else."

"Have I told you that you look fantastic today? You do. The ripped concert-tee thing with the long vest is kick-ass, and those boots make your legs amazing."

"Yeah, well, I thought I was being cute for Henry." Oh, she'd spotted him now. Dammit. She knew who he was. He owned a recent-model BMW 4-Series that he drove like crap. Everett had already had to rebuild his clutch.

"I like Henry so much," Megan chirped. "I want you two to get married and have, like, three more babies."

Toni nearly ran for her car. "Are you kidding me?" she asked under her breath. "Have you forgotten that I'm going to be forty-two when this one pops out?" They walked through the crowd, and Toni kept the plastic smile glued to her face. "One is already more than I planned for."

"Pfft." Megan waved and laughed at nothing in particular. "Age is just a number."

"Biologically speaking, it really isn't. Hi!"

"Hi." They'd arrived at the accountant. "What was that?"

Megan stuck her hand out. "I was saying that age is just a number."

"Agreed!" Ron Withers's face was flushed a bright red, and his head looked a little sunburned. "I'm Ron." He turned his smile on Toni. "And you're Toni. Jackie said you'd be here. I don't know if you remember me, but—"

"Grey BMW," she blurted out. "Four series. Needed transmission work." She nodded quickly.

The man appeared flattered. "You have a good memory."

"For cars."

Megan's elbow dug into her side.

"And people," she added. "People too. I remember them. And cars."

"Nice to meet you outside the garage." Ron held up his glass of wine. "Can I get you a drink?"

"Just water for me." She touched her throat. "I'm parched."

"Water for me too," Megan said. "But sparkling. Maybe with a slice or two of lime?" She laughed. "Am I being a pest?"

"Not at all." Ron Withers's attention was split as if he couldn't believe his luck. Two women were waiting for his attention. "Give me a minute."

He walked away, and Toni carefully kept the smile pasted on her face. "He looks like he's about to spontaneously combust in the sun."

"That is a pale, pale man," Megan murmured. "Maybe

let's move to the shade." She sidled over to a quieter corner of the yard under a canvas shade cover and away from the grill.

Toni immediately felt calmer. The press of people and emotions in the middle of the party was just too intense. Now that she had a little distance, she could think more clearly.

"Do you see him?" Toni asked.

"Yep." Megan lifted her hand and waved. "On his way back."

"Goodie." She glanced at her watch. It had already been fifteen minutes just finding the man and exchanging small talk. How was she supposed to interrogate him with so little time? "I think I'm going to have to resort to the woo-woo feelings-wizard-stuff."

"Are you sure that's a good idea in a crowd?" Megan was looking around the backyard. "Are you actually related to all these people?"

"Most of them, yes."

Ron returned with three drinks balanced in his hands. Toni felt slightly guilty. The man was laboring under the delusion that she might be interested in him romantically, and he'd been very polite.

He was also the accountant for a very sneaky murder victim, and she needed to clear her cousin's name.

"Thanks." She quickly took the drinks and set them down on the small picnic table. "Care to sit? This sun is pretty intense, right?"

Ron wiped his forehead. "Yes. I'm from San Francisco originally, so this heat..."

"It can be pretty intense when you're not right on the ocean." Toni felt like fanning him; his face was so flushed. She reached over and tapped his hand slightly, pushing a little bit of calm toward him. The last thing she wanted was for Ron the accountant to pass out.

"Thanks." His color immediately evened out. "So Toni, I know you have your garage. Megan, what do you do?"

"I'm an event coordinator," she said. "I was in Atlanta for most of my career. I just recently relocated to Moonstone Cove."

Ron's eyes lit up. "It's an exciting area, isn't it?"

Megan leaned toward him and lowered her voice, creating a sense of conspiratorial flirting. Ron was into it; Toni could tell.

"You know," Megan said. "I heard a rumor that they were going to be building this big wine-country-estate kind of thing around here. Winery, event venue, restaurant, private club. The *works*. No idea where they'd put that though."

Toni knew immediately what she needed to do. If there was one thing men adored, it was correcting women. "I don't know," she said. "I've lived here my whole life, and I just don't think anyone would put money into something like that. That would be a *lot* of cash, and it's still really a farming town."

"Oh, I don't know." Ron took the bait. "I have a few clients that... I think you'd be surprised by the plans they have for the town. Moonstone Cove is on the rise."

"Really?" Megan leaned her chin on her palm and cocked her head at him. "Well, that's good news for the event-planning business, isn't it?"

"I'm just saying," Toni said. "Moonstone Cove is small. It's not really a *destination* like Napa or Sonoma. I don't really see anyone coming all this way off the highway to get here."

"Napa and Sonoma aren't on major highways either," Ron said. "I think the seclusion is part of the charm."

She needed to give in to keep him interested. "I guess. I mean, I live just off Ferraro Creek, and I love how quiet it is. It's incredibly beautiful in that area."

"I've heard that area is really desirable." A hint of a smile teased his mouth. "I'd hang on to any property around there if I were you."

"Is that so?" Toni leaned forward to touch his arm. "Any other insider tips you want to share?" She pushed him just a little. She didn't want him to notice anything was going on.

"I may have heard that..." He blinked slowly. "There's a big developer—someone from up north—who's looking to buy in that area. Not sure when, of course." He sipped his wine. "It might be just a rumor."

"Mmmm." Toni smiled at him and kept her fingers on his skin, stroking the inside of his wrist provocatively. "I've heard developers can be... a little pushy."

"Pfft." Ron shrugged. "You know, I deal with a lot of these companies in the course of my business—"

"And what do you do?" Megan played dumb.

"I'm an accountant and tax consultant," Ron said. "I also do some estate planning."

"Oh!" Toni's eyes went wide, and she kept her fingers on Ron's arm. "Did you know that poor man who had the winery next to my cousin? Whit Fairfield?"

Ron frowned, and for a minute he looked very confused. Toni pushed a little more calm into him to assuage his suspicions. "I... Yeah. I know that estate. In fact, his fiancée... I can't really—"

"I didn't know he was getting married." Megan was all

sympathy. "That poor woman. She must be devastated. Were they starting the winery together? God, I think I'd just sell everything if it were me. I'd never want to look at it again, you know?"

"A crushed dream," Toni added, giving a little hitch in her throat. "I feel for her."

"Heh!" Ron looked a little drunk, and Toni decided to back off on the ease she was pushing, but she kept her hand on his wrist.

"I..." He stumbled a little over his words. "I'd not... I wouldn't feel sorry for her. I think she's very... Uh, she's in finance. She knows her business. So I think she just sees everything as an investment, you know?"

"Oh, that's so brave." Megan blinked hard and actually managed to produce a few tears. "Just carrying on to fulfill their dream on her own. She's still going to build that club and expand the winery and everything?"

"She's determined." Ron leaned forward. "Maybe even more than before. I warned her... he was gonna shoot his foot off with the tricks and th-the sheeeh..." He slapped his palm on his cheek. "What's the word I'm looking for?" He started to laugh. "What did Frank put in this wine, am I right?"

"Shenanigans?"

"Yes!" Ron laughed hard. "I tell you, that one listens about as well as Whit did."

"Well, you're smart," Megan said. "I'm sure you'll get your point across to her eventually. You just have to keep telling her..." Megan gestured toward Ron.

"You can't buy too fast. That's just... common... It's common—"

"Sense." Toni squeezed his arm. "It's common sense. Obviously."

"She acts like that one piece of land is the only place they could build a cave in that area and it's just... it's not the case. The geologist said so."

"Really?" Toni nodded. "I mean, I don't know about you, but I trust science, you know?"

"Yes." He slapped his hands together, breaking their connection. "Exactly. Trust science."

"I trust science too." Megan looked past Ron and her eyes went wide. "My Lord, I need to pee. We should go, Toni."

Toni had been reaching toward Ron again, trying to reconnect and get more information. "What?" She looked up.

"Toni, don't..." Megan reached out, then pulled her hand back.

She looked past Ron and saw Henry standing a little distance away, watching the two of them flirt with Ron Withers.

Toni stood up, her eyes locked on Henry. "Oh. Hey."

Shit. Shit! She'd been leaning into Ron, nearly in the man's lap trying to get information from him. She could only imagine how it looked.

Henry was freshly showered and his dark hair was still damp. He wore a pair of fitted blue jeans and a crisp button-down shirt in a light grayish blue. There was a slight flush on the top of his cheekbones, and it wasn't because of the heat. The heat didn't bother Henry.

He was pissed. This was Henry quietly furious, and it was somehow far more devastating than the explosive feelings she'd grown up around.

"So..." He looked around at the party. "Guess I was a little late, huh?"

Toni opened her mouth. Closed it. She couldn't speak. Her heart was in her throat. She'd never understood that saying before that moment, but it suddenly made sense.

She couldn't speak if she tried.

Megan rose and stood next to her. "Henry, it's not—"

"It's fine." He turned. "Whatever. I'm gonna go. I'll see you later."

He walked through the mass of people, past Jackie, Katherine, and Baxter, and down the driveway where his truck was probably parked.

And all Toni could think of was his excitement when she'd first invited him.

"Would you like to go with me to Sunday dinner at Frank's ranch this weekend?"

"As your date?"

Yes.

Yes! She only wanted him.

"Antonia Luciana Dusi, I would like that very much."

Toni started to run. "Henry!"

CHAPTER 19

She caught up with him as he reached his truck.

"Just don't bother, okay?" He yanked his door open.

"Henry, it's not what it looks like, okay? Jackie set it up. That guy's name is Ron Withers, and he's the accountant for—"

"You were all over him." Henry slammed his door shut and spun toward her. "I mean... *really*? I can barely get you to acknowledge I'm alive when we're in public, much less get you to do something crazy like *hold my hand*, but Jackie sets you up with some friend of hers and all of a sudden—"

"I was interrogating him, okay?" She looked around, making sure no one was in earshot. "He's Fairfield's accountant!"

Henry froze midrant. "Fairfield's accountant?"

"Yes. Megan and I were trying to find out—"

"That does not explain why you had your hands all over him."

"I was touching his arm." *Please don't do this here. Please don't do this here.* "That's hardly having my hands all over him."

Henry stood and crossed his arms over his chest. "For you, that's practically groping."

"It wasn't..." She let out a breath. Shit. "It's just a thing that..."

Just tell him. It's Henry. You know you want him. If he's going to be part of your life, he needs to know what he's in for.

"It's called empathy." She stared at the cab of his truck. "Can we go somewhere private to talk about this?"

"I know what empathy is, Toni. And it doesn't require you getting touchy-feely with some guy to— What are you doing?"

Toni walked over, reached both hands up, and pressed her palms against his lightly stubbled jaw.

Shhhhhh. She pulled the anger out of him and she did it quickly, dramatically, and thoroughly. Toni sucked Henry's anger up like an emotional vacuum, which left her sick to her stomach and really, really pissed off.

"Who are *you* to tell me that I'm groping someone?" She pointed at the party. "You come in, make one snap decision, and decide to just throw away all my feelings for you?" She stood on her toes. "Screw you, Henry!"

Henry's jaw was hanging open. "What the hell was that?"

"That's fucking empathy! And if you don't know what that means by now—"

"That is not..." He grabbed her arm and opened the truck door. "Okay, we're not doing this in front of your family."

"Fuck you!" She tried to yank her arm away, but his grip

was firm and she didn't really want him to let go. She was just annoyed. Really, extremely annoyed.

Henry muttered, "Like locking myself in a cardboard box with a bobcat." He nudged her into the truck cab. "Don't argue, Toni."

"Fucking men and their fucking high-handed—"

He slammed the door shut.

Toni watched him walk around the front of the truck, his eyes locked on her. "You think you know what's going on? You have no idea!"

He opened the truck door. "Stop yelling."

"I don't have to!"

"Why are you yelling?" He slammed the door closed. "What did you do to me?"

"You were fucking furious!" She felt like hitting something. Anything. "So I grabbed that, and I haven't ever done anything that extreme before, and now *I'm* fucking furious and I have no idea how to calm down!"

"For Pete's sake." He started the truck. "I don't know what the hell is going on here. Is this some kind of pregnancy symptom I've never read about?"

"Oh, of *course* you're reading books about pregnancy. Of *course* you are!" She sat back in her seat and didn't argue when Henry reached across and buckled her in. "That is exactly something you would do."

"Why are you pissed off about me reading pregnancy books?"

"Just drive me somewhere I can yell really loud, okay?" She felt like her skin was crawling over her body. "I am never doing that again."

Henry started driving down the hill, his face a grim mask. "What did you do, Toni?"

"I. Have. Empathy. Okay? Not the usual kind. I can literally feel people's feelings. And sometimes—like *now!*—I can even influence them. You were furious at the party, so I calmed you down." She crossed her arms. "And I probably miscalculated just how mad you were."

"Apparently." His face was grim. "At the risk of starting a massive argument, why were your hands all over that accountant?"

"Because I was questioning him!" She felt a headache coming on, a gripping tension headache that was building at the back of her scalp. "It's the same way I got Marissa to talk to me. If I kept skin contact with him, I could make him calm. I didn't grab his emotions; I let him feel mine. Or what I wanted him to feel—*I'm still learning how all this works, okay!*"

"Okay." Henry's voice was tuned low. "That is... very weird. If you make them calm, they'll answer your questions?"

"Exactly."

"Have you done that to me before?"

"No! The most I've done is absorb your mellow. If I'm upset or stressed, you're like a living fucking meditation aid. All I have to do is touch you and I chill out."

Why was she so angry? Toni felt like she was having an out-of-body experience. Purposely absorbing all of Henry's anger had been an absolutely idiotic thing to do.

"Huh." His face was oddly blank. "Is that why you like me? Because I'm calm?"

"I fucking liked you before all this shit happened to me at

the gym, okay? Don't make this about that. I already knew you were fucking sexy as hell and our chemistry was off the fucking charts, Henry! I fell in *love* with you when I could literally feel how honest and genuinely good you are, okay? I am *not* going to apologize for that."

Toni, what the hell are you doing—you just told Henry you love him!

His smile was luminous. "You love me, huh?"

Take it back. Tell him you were in an altered state.

"Of course I fucking love you!"

Ahhhhhh! This was a disaster! She was so angry she'd turned into a truth-spewing harpy!

Henry chuckled. "I think I like this."

"Don't ask me anything else, okay? Just take me somewhere that I can punch something!"

"We're going back to my place."

"Fucking hell, Henry, take me home!"

"I have a punching bag in my garage." He turned north on the highway and headed into town. "You can work out your mad on that."

"Good! And for the record" —she pointed at herself— "this is *your* mad, not mine!"

For the love of red wine, this was far longer lasting than anything she'd experienced before. Which was probably good to know. When Henry got really angry, he held on to it. Probably a useful reference for the future.

"So tell me more about how you fell in love with me," Henry said. "I'm really curious about this. Was it before or after you got pregnant?"

Shut up. Just shut up and— "It was after you pulled that really nasty redwood splinter out of my hand."

Henry blinked and turned toward his house. "That was six months ago."

"I've been in denial a long time, okay? Not all of us are emotional geniuses or whatever."

"Hey." He rubbed her thigh. "Look at that. You didn't yell. I think you're calming down."

"Don't touch me!"

"Or maybe not."

Toni woke with a head full of cobwebs and hands that ached. She sat up and realized she was in a strange bed and a familiar jowly dog stood next to her, his head resting on the edge of the mattress.

"Earl." She reached out to pet him and let out a low groan. "What the hell happened to my hands?"

Just then she heard footsteps coming down the hall. Henry opened the door, holding a tray of tea and two towels. "There you are. I thought I heard your voice."

He was shirtless, wearing only a pair of grey sweatpants, and Toni saw four long scratches on his left shoulder.

She wanted to die. "Did I do that?"

Henry set down the tray, glanced at his shoulder, and reached for the towel. "Uh, yeah. You did. I didn't really realize at the time. That was... pretty intense."

Memories came flooding back, and Toni covered her face with both hands and fell back on the pillows. "Oh my God."

He reached over, took her right hand, and folded it into a cotton towel filled with ice. "So the punching bag kind of worked for a while, but then you lost interest in that and got *very* interested in something else."

"Oh my God." She wanted to literally be absorbed into Henry's too-small bed and disappear.

He let out a small laugh and pulled her left hand from her face. "Do you hear me complaining? Come here. Do you need some aspirin? You were complaining about a headache earlier."

"I want aspirin, but I also don't want to move."

He kept her right hand wrapped in the ice-filled towel and pulled her over his bare chest, draping her left arm across him as he reached over and rubbed her temple. "So the thing at the gym, huh? You told me as little as possible about that whole thing. That's what triggered all this?"

The rhythmic touch soothed her. "Yes. Katherine tackled the man with the gun, and then I jumped on him, held him down and... I just knew that more than anything in the world, he needed to calm down. So I made him calm. I don't know how it happened."

"And after that is when you got to be good friends with Megan and Katherine, right?"

"Yeah." Her eyes drifted closed. What the hell? They wouldn't mind. It was Henry. "Katherine is a seer. I think that's what they call it. She has visions, but they usually only happen minutes before the event. Makes it hard to do much about them, but it is an early-warning system."

"And Megan?"

Her ear was against his heart, and she felt the slow steady thump through her whole body. "She has telekinesis. She doesn't always find it very useful, but she's trying to work on it.

Focus her energy better, maybe? I don't know. We know a few other psychics up in Glimmer Lake, but other than that, it's hard to tell what's good information and what's bullshit, you know?"

"Uh-huh."

"You can't believe everything you read online."

"I've heard that."

"And there's a lot we don't know. Like, I've never tried to purposely absorb someone's emotions before like I did with you."

"That was weird. I'm not going to lie about that. Very weird experience."

"But I was just trying to get info about the Fairfield estate. For the record, I was really pissed at Jackie for setting it up like that. I don't think she knew I invited you."

"As your boyfriend?"

"Yeah." Her eyes were closing again. "Why am I so tired?"

"Probably because it's nearly midnight."

"This day has been really strange."

"I don't disagree with that."

She felt unfinished somehow, like there was something hanging over her head. Flashes of the afternoon started coming back to her.

I fell in love with you when I could literally feel how honest and genuinely good you are, okay?

Oh. Right. *Kill me now.*

"Henry?"

"Yes?"

"I told you I was in love with you earlier, didn't I?"

"Yes, you did." The hand stroking her temple moved

down to stroke her back. "Don't try to take it back. I know you weren't lying."

"Right." That was it? That was all she was getting. She'd bared her soul in an anger-induced bout of emotional clarity and all she got was "don't take it back"?

"I love you too," he said. "And since you can feel my emotions, you don't have to wonder if it's true."

Toni's heart raced in wild panic until Henry's hand stroked down her back again. She took a deep breath, listened to the steady thump of his heart, and settled into the warm glow.

Because now that he'd named it, she knew it was what she'd been feeling for months. Not infatuation. Not sexual compatibility. Far more than affection.

Love. She'd been feeling love.

CHAPTER 20

"So you spilled the beans, huh?" Megan sipped her coffee as they sat on her porch Monday morning.

Katherine had called to check on Toni after she drove off with Henry, and Megan had gone to her house. She placated both of them by taking the day off work and chilling out at the house since she was emotionally exhausted.

Katherine had to work, but Megan came to check on her and steal her sweet, sweet caffeine.

"Yeah, I kind of told him everything," Toni said. "He was so pissed and I didn't know how to explain anything, so I thought I'd show him. Remember your stupid pistachio trick with Baxter?"

"So you figuratively floated a pistachio in front of Henry's face?"

"More accurately, I sucked all his anger out and absorbed it, which turned me into a pissed-off psychic with more emotions than brains."

Megan cackled. "I so wish I could have seen that."

"I was frighteningly honest," Toni said. "I told him about

me, about you and Katherine, about what I was doing to Ron Withers. Then I told him I was in love with him. So that happened." She stared at her barn. Did it need paint? Probably it needed paint. And a new door.

"Back up—you told Henry you love him?"

"I did." She stared at the barn. Yep, it definitely needed a new door. "I did do that."

"Okay." Megan stared at her. "And how was that?"

"Very awkward. And then very not awkward because he told me he loved me too. And it was very nice. Very... reassuring. I'm ninety percent sure these feelings have nothing to do with the pregnancy."

"Okay."

"But now I'm questioning everything," she said. "Also, I need a new barn door."

"You need a new...? Toni!" Megan shook her head. "Don't. Don't question it, okay? It's been obvious to both me and Katherine that you love him for weeks now. Honestly, I think you've probably loved him for a while and you were just getting caught up in all the reasons that you shouldn't love him or it wouldn't work for your life. Just go with it. Don't make it so complicated."

"That's the problem though. It is complicated. It doesn't work for my life. What do you think is going to happen? Henry's going to move in here with his giant dog and shack up with me and we're going to be some happy little nuclear family with a dog and a cat and a baby and... stuff?"

Megan shrugged. "That sounds perfectly reasonable. You have all the things you like about your life, just with a wonderful guy and a kid added to it."

"I never wanted a dog."

"You love dogs. Don't be weird."

The problem, as Toni saw it, was that she was getting all the things she didn't realize she wanted, and it just seemed... way too easy. "Life just doesn't fall into place like this, Atlanta. Haven't you learned that? Nothing is this easy."

Megan turned to her with a frown settled between her eyes. "Listen. I did all the things in the order I was supposed to, exactly when the world told me I was supposed to. Went to college, had a profession I loved. Married a man with a solid job and a nice family. Had three kids. Did all the things a working mom is supposed to do with a healthy bank account and a team of support staff. Then I moved out here and it all fell apart." She threw up fingers as she counted. "No husband. No business. No support system. All gone."

"Are you thinking of moving back to Atlanta?"

"No." She shook her head firmly. "I'm starting over. And for some reason, I have this ridiculous confidence that everything is going to work out. Fate just had something completely unexpected set up for me, and I'm determined that it's going to be great."

"So you're saying that fate has something equally unexpected for me, and I just need to go with it?"

"What's not to go with?" Megan spread her arms. "You're living in your own home that you bought and are fixing up. You're taking a day off from the business you've dedicated your life to for over twenty years. And you know you can do that because you're a kick-ass businesswoman who knows how to delegate. You're going to have a baby." Megan smiled. "How ridiculously beautiful and crazy is that? A *baby*. And you have this wonderful man who loves you and wants it all. You. The baby. The life in the country. The whole plate."

Toni rubbed her temple. "Why am I overthinking this? Why can't I just be happy?"

"Because you're a problem solver and you're always on the lookout for a new thing you need to solve. And do not worry, my friend, there will be things to solve. But for now, with all the craziness going on in your family and in town, just chill and enjoy this part." Megan sat back, kicked her feet up on the porch railing, and sipped her coffee. "Henry loves you and you love him and y'all are going to have a baby. It doesn't have to be more complicated than that."

"Okay."

Megan nodded. "Okay." She glanced at Toni's hands. "I'd maybe think twice about taking up boxing though."

"You're telling me."

———

MEGAN AND TONI decided to walk up to the winery after they'd had their morning coffee. They'd never really made it all the way up the trail on the day they found Whit Fairfield's body, but Toni was determined not to let the memory of that day stain the beautiful scenery around her house.

"I know nothing about wine," Megan said. "Other than that I like it. How do you learn what good wine is? To be honest, I go by the label and the price tag. I've got no idea how to pick."

"My dad always had a really simple way to tell if something was a good wine."

"Oh?"

"Do you like it?"

Megan laughed.

"I'm serious." Toni stopped to pick a bunch of dark purple grapes from the cabernet vines that butted up to the path. "Do you like it? Then it's a good wine. What's a good wine anyway, right? I mean, you can say something is more complex or better blended or what have you, but at the end of the day, if you like it…"

"It's a good wine. I'll go with that." Megan reached over and picked a grape, popped it in her mouth, and made a face. "It's so seedy."

"Yep. Thick skin too." She ate one, sucked out the juice, then spit the seeds and the skin into the dirt. "Still sweet though."

"Yep."

The day was warming up. Though it was fall and the leaves were starting to turn, the sun was getting higher and the fog from the ocean had burned off the top of the hills. As they walked up to Nico's winery, Toni heard footsteps behind her.

She stopped and turned.

"What is it?" Megan asked.

Toni shook her head. "I thought I heard someone."

They turned and started walking again, past the turn of the creek where Fairfield's body was found. Past the rocky hill where an old oak towered over a broken-down tractor. They walked over the hill and down into a small hollow where a flock of wild turkeys took flight, surprised by their arrival.

"Wow! Does anyone hunt them?" Megan watched the group of birds take flight over the creek.

"Nico and the guys try, but the turkeys always seem to disappear as soon as the season starts."

"They're no dummies."

In the distance, past the vines and across a dip in the terrain, another flock took to the air, drawing Toni's attention.

Footsteps and startled birds weren't just her imagination.

Megan kept her voice low. "Is someone following us?"

"I think so."

"We keep going?"

"No choice."

Toni and Megan kept walking through the vines and toward Nico's place. As they drew closer, they could hear voices in the distance. A harvesting crew was singing along with the radio. The footsteps behind them got louder.

Megan and Toni started walking faster.

"You hear it too?"

"Yeah."

Just as Toni was about to break into a run, someone popped up from between the rows. Toni turned, shoved Megan behind her, and braced herself. "Hey!"

Only to see Danny Barba waving behind them. "Hey Toni!"

She released her breath. "Danny."

"Gorgeous day for a walk, huh?" He slung a backpack over his shoulder. "You headed up to the office?"

"Yeah."

Danny nodded. "I think Nico and Henry are meeting Ruben right now, but they'll probably be finished pretty soon."

"You get that tractor running?"

Danny grinned. "The old one on the hill? That thing's a relic."

"No, the one that had the wires cut." She was slowly

walking backward, moving steadily down the hill. "The one where I found the finger."

"Oh right. The finger." Danny paled. "Yeah, I just had to fix the safety cable. Haven't had a problem since."

Toni nudged Megan. "Danny is Nico's foreman. He keeps the whole place running, and he's a far better diesel mechanic than I am."

"I try." The man smiled. "Hard to keep track of all the moving pieces sometimes, you know?"

"I'm sure." Megan scanned the vineyards. "It's a big place."

"It is." Danny tugged on the end of his baseball cap. "You ladies have a great day." He walked in the direction of the harvesting crew, back into the vines.

Megan kept her voice low. "Was he the one...?"

"I have no idea. Are we being paranoid?"

"Maybe." Megan slid her sunglasses back on. "But let's not forget a man was murdered about half a mile from where we're standing."

"Good point."

⎯⎯⎯⎯⎯⎯

Nico, Henry, and Ruben Montenegro were sitting on the back patio behind Nico's office, three open beers on the table in front of them.

Nico raised his hand when he saw her. "Toni!"

Henry didn't say anything, but his smile felt secret and warmed Toni down to her toes.

"You're blushing," Megan said. "Just a little. It's pretty cute."

"I'm not blushing, I'm hot. From the hike."

"Okay, sure." Megan pressed her lips together. "Whatever you say." She grabbed her phone from her pocket and took a quick picture. "I cannot lie, I am seeing the benefits of California-wine-country life more and more every day."

Toni narrowed her eyes. "You mean the three tall, dark, and handsome, slightly sweaty men sitting around a wooden table in the middle of a vineyard drinking cold beers?"

"I'm just saying, if you wanted to promote Moonstone Cove in an advertising campaign, you should definitely mention the handsome sweaty men that come included with the beautiful scenery."

Seeing as Toni had grown up with Nico harassing her like the annoying little shit he'd been, she was always slightly surprised when women found him attractive. She knew he was; it was just hard to forget the swirlies.

"Have you actually met my cousin before?"

"Nope." Megan pressed her lips together. "I've only heard stories." She lifted her sunglasses for a second, then lowered them. "Which right now I'm really hoping are true."

"Ew." Toni shook her head and kept walking. "Don't lust after my cousin. That's just weird."

"I think you mean understandable." Megan put on her thousand-watt smile. "Good afternoon, gentlemen. Y'all have another beer hiding around here?"

Toni watched Megan proceed to make two men jump for her attention while the third only had eyes for her.

Henry rose and walked over to Toni, slid his arm around her waist, and leaned down to her. "Gonna kiss you now."

"Okay."

He pulled back. "That's it? No lecture about public displays of affection or keeping our business to ourselves?"

Toni shrugged. "I think after last Sunday, the secret is out. Everyone heard me screaming at you, which in my crazy family is as good as a declaration of love."

"If only I'd known months ago."

She rose onto her toes and drew him into a sweet and lingering kiss. "Plus it's Monday, I'm taking the day off, hanging out with my friend, and I can't even have a beer. You're my only vice left."

He smiled. "Feel free to take advantage of me whenever you like."

"I'll remember that." She nodded toward Ruben and Nico, who were standing by the fridge outside Nico's office. "What's Ruben here for?"

Henry shrugged. "Nothing too big. Hopefully a little bridge. I wanted some cabernet franc grapes to blend in the Heritage Red this year, and Danny told me that he'd heard Fairfield had some. I convinced Nico that it might be friendly to reach out."

"No point keeping the winery as an enemy if Fairfield is gone, right?"

"It was never something Nico and I wanted anyway. It's always better to be on good terms with your neighbors. Ruben's a good guy. He and Nico have known each other for years, so as long as he's running things down the road, there's no reason to feed any kind of rivalry, you know?"

Nico and Ruben were laughing at something Megan said, both men watching the pretty blond woman intently.

Lovely. This was shaping up to be more than slightly predictable.

"Of course." Toni kept her eye on the trio. "Ruben and Nico being on good terms means that two of the most competitive men I know will suddenly decide *not* to compete over something else."

Henry added, "And the likelihood of that is pretty small."

"Yep." She turned to him. "Ruben ever give up why Fairfield wanted those five acres over by the creek so badly?"

"I was trying to work my way around to asking that when you ladies showed up."

"Then why don't we stay for a drink?" Toni turned on her most charming smile. "We can see if any interesting information pops up."

CHAPTER 21

"I'm telling you," Ruben said with a broad smile, "you ladies need to come up to the winery for a tasting. We'll treat you like queens." He cast a look at Nico. "Unlike this guy."

"Just because we go for a more rustic experience—"

"Your tasting room is in a barn, man."

Ruben and Henry laughed while Nico shrugged a little. "We're getting there, okay? Not all of us have Bay Area bank accounts to play with."

"Well, that I can't argue with." Ruben raised his beer. "And you've still got more productive acreage than me, so I should probably shut up."

"Any word on what's going to happen?" Toni asked. "I heard through the rumor mill that Fairfield's fiancée is in charge of the estate now. Any truth to that?"

Ruben nodded slowly. "I think so. She's supposed to come down this weekend and take a look at the place. I guess the memorial was last week. They were holding off because the coroner still hadn't released the body, but then his parents insisted."

"So horrible what happened to him." Megan's expression was tragic. "I met him a few times, and he was just so polite. Had so many big plans."

"Huh." Nico rolled his eyes. "I shouldn't say anything. Everyone knows how I felt about the man."

"That's all in the past now," Ruben said. "Now I can be the one to convince you to sell that five acres."

Nico and Henry laughed, and Ruben gave Toni a rueful smile.

"I had to try." He shrugged. "Hoping the new boss won't be quite as obsessed as the old boss."

"I know your plans are just going to be amazing." Megan leaned toward Ruben. "Do you have anything drawn up? I'm so curious."

Ruben looked triumphant. "I do. I mean, I have what Whit and I were working on. I know it'll change, but if you wanted to come over to the winery this week—"

"Ooh!" Megan clapped her hands. "I think we could do Wednesday, don't you think, Toni? Grab Katherine and go over to Fairfield's for a tasting on Wednesday?"

Nico looked like he'd bitten into a lemon.

Toni glanced at him and then Megan. "Sure. I'm game for that."

"That's right." Henry rubbed Toni's back. "Wine Wednesdays."

"It's tradition." One that Toni would have to work around in a tasting room. "I'm in if Katherine is."

"Sounds like fun." Megan beamed at Ruben. "Can't wait to see it."

"Why do we want to see this place?" Katherine was leaning forward from the center seat in the back of the car. "I thought we didn't trust the Fairfield people."

"We don't." Toni was driving down the twisting road to Fairfield Family Wines since she couldn't drink. "Not even a little bit. But Ruben brought up buying that strip of land again yesterday, which makes me curious about why they want it. I'm hoping if we can see the plans they've drawn up—"

"Didn't Ron the accountant say something about that? Something about a wine cave?" Megan asked. "Do you think he was right?"

"The acreage he's talking about buying is a thin strip of land right along the creek that butts up to a rocky hill that's completely undeveloped. There's no good reason to dig a wine cave out there," Toni said.

"Why would you dig a wine cave at all?" Katherine asked. "Is it a tourist gimmick?"

"Oh no. They serve a few different purposes, and if you can afford one—or if you buy an old vineyard that already has one—they're really valuable. Personally, I think more wineries are going to start digging them because it saves you a lot of energy aging wine underground. You don't have to pay for the warehousing, and the underground is always the perfect temperature and humidity. It's a classic for a reason."

Megan said, "Something like a wine cave—if you created an event space—would be super popular. People always want a unique experience, and that sort of thing would feel very exclusive."

"So it's a sound business decision and good for marketing," Katherine said. "Why don't all wineries have caves?"

"Because they're expensive as hell to dig," Toni said. "A good-size cave with all the necessary plumbing and air circulation could easily run you in the tens of millions to build from scratch. That is if you even had the right kind of land to build it."

"So we need to find out if that land is the right kind to dig under," Katherine said. "I have a few friends in the geology department who could find out."

"Didn't Ron the accountant mention a geologist too?" Megan said. "Fairfield might have already consulted with one."

Katherine nodded. "I'll ask around. A number of the geologists at Central Coast do outside work. They would be the most local."

"Cool." Toni saw the alley of oaks that led to the winery and turned. "For now, let's focus on some good old snooping at the victim's place."

"And wine," Megan said. "After all, if we're being sneaky, we might as well enjoy ourselves."

THE TASTING room at Fairfield Family Wines really was more like a club than a room. Built on the edge of Ferraro Creek, under a stand of sprawling oak trees, the entire back wall of the winery was made up of giant glass doors that opened to a French-style garden with classical sculptures, scattered tables, and pea-gravel paths leading between the planting beds.

In the distance, Toni saw a raised stage for live music events along with a large built-in barbecue pit and long stone tables.

"This is amazing," Megan said. "Purely professionally, I completely understand why Pamela was interested."

Toni tried not to be overly critical. "I guess you can make really pretty stuff when you have endless funds." The Fairfield winery made her feel small. Nico's operation was family-run and casual. Visitors could grab a sandwich or tacos from the food trucks in the Cove and have a picnic with a bottle of wine or spend some time inside, tasting the new vintages in the refurbished barn.

They didn't have sculptures in the garden; they had old farm equipment. Their servers weren't wearing crisp white shirts and black pants; they wore blue jeans with flannel button-downs over their Drink Dusi T-shirts.

They also didn't have dozens of visitors in the middle of a Wednesday afternoon, buying wine and souvenirs from the gift shop.

"Good afternoon." An immaculately dressed server greeted them. "Did you have a reservation?"

"We don't," Megan said. "Not really. But Ruben invited us yesterday."

The young woman smiled. "Of course. Let me call him."

"Sounds good."

Katherine strolled along the walls of wine that led to a large gift shop. "I love these tablecloths."

"The colors are gorgeous." Megan picked up the edge of a waxed cotton tablecloth with a traditional French pattern on it. "Toni, this would look so cute on your patio outside."

"That's okay." Toni wasn't buying anything at this place. Not a single, blessed cracker or cork. "I'm good."

"Maybe I'll get it for you as a house-warming present." Megan was looking at the label. "I never got you—"

"Really." Toni put a hand on the tablecloth and pushed it back to the table. "I'd really rather you didn't. Not here."

Megan's eyes widened. "Got it."

"Thanks."

"Ladies?" The server stood a polite distance away. "Ruben has a table set for you in our members' room."

"Thank you," Katherine said. "That sounds very exclusive."

The server smiled. "If you'll just follow me."

She led them toward a small glass-enclosed room with a gorgeous view of the creek and a small footbridge that led from Fairfield's side of the creek to Nico's. Unlike the main tasting room where visitors stood at a long bar, in this room servers visited small tables, filling wineglasses, clearing glasses, and bringing plates of fruit and cheese with the wine.

Toni's stomach flipped and she realized she'd forgotten to eat lunch again. "Well, at least I won't go hungry."

The server motioned toward a table with four wine-glasses. "If you'll wait here, I'll send Marius right over."

"Marius?" Toni muttered. "No, thanks. No vampire servers for me."

Katherine cackled, and Megan looked confused.

"What?"

Toni shook her head. "Never mind." She was being petty. It was nice that Fairfield had built this beautiful place. Nicer that it was close to Nico's winery. If her cousin put up a better sign, he could probably capture a lot of the traffic from here.

After all, not everyone wanted stuffy servers and immaculate aprons. Some people liked to kick back. Some people preferred Linda Perry on the sound system instead of Vivaldi.

Toni was those people.

She felt underdressed. She felt like everyone was looking at her.

Hey! she wanted to yell. *I was drinking wine when you people were sneaking your parents' awful, watery beer.*

No, that just made her sound like an alcoholic.

The man at the next table was saying something about "fragrant tobacco" and "racy acidity."

Give me a break.

"Megan!" Ruben entered the members' room, wearing a black polo shirt with Fairfield Family Wines on the pocket. The dark color set off the silver at his temples and the near-black color of his hair. He really was a great-looking guy.

The image of Ruben and Megan flashed in her mind. They were all dressed up, being fancy, and they looked stunning together.

"Weird," she muttered.

"What?" Ruben looked at her.

"Sorry!" Toni shook her head. "My mind was drifting to something at work. Ignore me." She plastered on a smile and motioned toward the windows. "Ruben, this place is stunning."

"Thanks." He sat with them. "I'd love to take credit for the tasting room, but that's all the architect and designer. Ross, Taylor, and Associates in San Francisco."

Toni nodded like that made any sense to her at all. "Cool."

"The way the building just blends with the landscape," Megan said. "It's just stunning."

Ruben nodded at their glasses. "And what do you think of the wine?"

Megan smiled, and Toni nearly bit her lip to keep from laughing.

"So nice," Megan said. "It fits the setting perfectly."

Toni could feel Megan from across the table. She was lying through her teeth. Well, not pants-on-fire lying, but definitely a polite gesture.

Ruben looked at Toni and Katherine. "And what do you ladies think?"

Katherine frowned. "It's very... subtle." She glanced at Toni. "I think that's the word I'm looking for. It's subtle. I agree with Megan; very pleasant."

Pleasant? Toni pressed her lips together and sipped the ice water the server had placed on the table. *Pleasant* was the very definition of damning with faint praise. *Pleasant* was what you took to a party when you didn't like the host or didn't really know them. You took *Pleasant* to the office holiday party and didn't really mind when it was left there at the end of the night.

"Thank you." If Ruben was offended, he didn't show it. "Do you ladies drink much wine?" He scoffed. "I mean, other than Toni of course."

"Way to make me sound like an alcoholic, dude."

He grinned. "You know what I mean."

"I do drink wine," Katherine said. "Quite a lot of it. I like local wines mostly. Have you tried Toni's cousin's wine? It's very good."

"I have." Ruben didn't seem to know what to do with Katherine. "It's a solid offering. A little fruit-forward for my taste, but they know what their customers like."

Oh, fuck you. Toni plastered on a smile. "We were hoping we could get a tour of the place," she said. "Do you have time? We're so curious to hear about the plans."

"Sure." Ruben looked around the room, then pulled out his phone. "Let me just text my foreman and he'll take care of things for me."

He looked up after sending the text. "Ladies, I'm all yours."

CHAPTER 22

"So what we're trying to do long term is a type of neural interface for use with prosthetics that mimics the biological systems seen in cephalopods." Katherine stayed close to Ruben as they moved across the grounds. "It's all quite fascinating."

"I'd say so." Ruben was completely confused.

To be fair, Toni often had the same reaction when Katherine started talking about her work. Her professor friend was so enthusiastic that she sometimes forgot that not all her friends had multiple PhDs in a broad range of subjects.

"And this is where we make the wine." Ruben opened a metal door to a cavernous tank room with stainless steel tanks rising up from the floor. Workers in white coveralls were shouting from walkways that ran along the outside of the building and around each tank. A man on the far side of the building sprayed down the concrete.

Ruben leaned toward Megan. "I'm sure most of this is

218

familiar to Toni, but do either you or Katherine have any questions?"

Before Megan could even open her mouth, Katherine started.

"How long does the fermentation process take? Do you use wild yeast or manufactured?" She charged into the tank room, pointing at the complicated array of valves and sensors at the bottom of the tank. "Can you tell me more about the temperature? I was assuming it was more like beer, which I've studied extensively, but..."

As Katherine occupied Ruben, Megan and Toni hung back.

"We need to find his office," Toni said.

"Will it be in the winery or in this building?"

"Ruben's will be here, but I'm betting Fairfield's office is in the main building. The pretty one."

"Do you want to look for Ruben's office or Fairfield's?"

"I'd stick out like a sore thumb in the fancy building. You go snoop over there, and I'll try to find Ruben's office here."

"Sounds like a plan." Megan nodded decisively. "Now to create a distraction."

Toni stood back and surveyed their surroundings. Megan, with her magnetic charm, blond hair, blue eyes, and tele-kinetic power was pretty much distraction personified.

"How disastrous do we want to go?" she asked.

"No one gets hurt," Toni said. "Other than that?" She spotted a line that ran from the crush machine to the fermen-tation tanks. "Okay, you see that giant red hose with the silver fitting that runs from the crusher to the top of that tank?"

"Yeah."

"How far away can you use your telekinesis?"

Megan's eyes went wide. "This could be a challenge."

Toni, Katherine, and Megan were leaning toward Ruben, listening to him explain how the red wine was pressed, when they heard the first shout.

Toni's senses went wide when the first splash of wine hit the concrete floor of the fermentation room. Within a second, her senses were overwhelmed.

"Boss!"

All the workers started yelling at once as gallons and gallons of crushed grapes, along with the skins and seeds, splashed to the floor, spraying everything within fifty feet.

"What's happening?" Megan yelled. "Oh my Lord!"

"Allen!" Ruben yelled. "What the hell?" He turned to them. "Ladies, I'm so sorry, but I'm going to need you to exit—"

"Ruben, I can't shut it off! It's stuck!"

Toni patted his shoulder. "We'll find our way back! You go deal with this."

"Thanks, Toni." Ruben ran off, leaving Katherine, Megan, and Toni standing to the side of the fermentation room, their backs to the office, watching the chaos that Megan had wrought.

A mess of juice, grape skins, and seeds rained down around them, and the air was starting to feel sticky.

"How many hoses did you unhook?" Toni asked as they backed away.

"I think I maybe did all of them? It's kind of hard to

distinguish a single valve when they all look alike and I'm so far away."

"That is a lot of crushed grapes." Katherine was staring. "What a waste."

"Come on." Toni tugged her arm. "Megan, you good?"

She nodded. "I was scoping out the building when we walked in earlier. Pretty sure I know where the executive office will be."

"Katherine and I will look at Ruben's." Toni walked into a dark hall, the winery a hive of chaos as they disappeared through the metal door.

As soon as they left, Toni turned and started peeking in the windows of the doors they passed. "He's not going to be down here, I don't think."

Katherine said, "No. Look at the tone of his skin. He likes the sun."

"Agreed." Toni ran up a set of stairs and onto the second floor that looked over the top of the tank room. She paused at the top. Which side of the building would Ruben pick for his office? "Sunrise or sunset?"

Katherine thought for only a second. "Sunrise—he's a farmer."

"Agreed." She ran to the right, headed toward the east end of the warehouse. They passed one person on the walkway who barely glanced at them as he rushed toward the stairs.

Looking in the rooms, Toni saw familiar activities. There was what looked like break room, one gal entering something on the computer with a set of headphones blocking the noise, and another office with two women chatting over manila folders.

At the end of the walkway, Toni saw his name on the door.

RUBEN MONTENEGRO, GENERAL MANAGER.

She pushed open the door, which wasn't locked, and walked straight to his desk.

"Okay, where would you put those plans?" she muttered. Toni sat in his seat and pulled out the top shelf directly to her left.

It jammed.

She tugged on each of the drawers in turn, hoping to trigger the catch for the top left drawer while Katherine moved to the standing file drawers across the room.

"I'd say the plans are probably on the computer, but that seems to be the one thing that people still want paper for," Katherine said. "If I go to the geology department, I always see massive pieces of paper the size of old maps spread out on every table."

"Spread out." Of course they wouldn't be stuffed in a drawer. That would crumple them. She scanned the office for anywhere that large pieces of paper could be hidden.

"Anything?"

Katherine was pulling files out. She shook her head. "Nothing."

"Keep looking. Keep your eyes out for anything that looks like it doesn't belong either."

Katherine turned her head. "Like Whit Fairfield's will?"

Toni blinked. "Uh, yeah. Why would Ruben have a copy of that?"

"I have no idea." She took it out and pulled out her phone. "I'm going to scan it quickly."

"Still no luck on these plans. Maybe they're in Fairfield's

office and not—" Her elbow bumped the calendar blotter on Ruben's desk, shoving the plastic-edged blotter to the side and revealing a curled edge of paper.

Toni stared. "Of course."

She stood, lifted the blotter up, and spotted what looked like blueprints underneath Ruben's desk. The difference was, there weren't two set of plans drawn on most architectural plans.

"Katherine, I found them. I think."

The professor shoved the last will and testament up her blouse before she walked over to Toni. "We don't have time for me to scan all these. I'll be here for an hour."

"I think he was trying to alter these." Toni pointed to faint lines that contradicted some of the diagrams on the blueprints. "Do you see?"

"I do." Katherine glanced at the door. "We can't take these. He could go weeks without knowing the will is gone. These? He'll notice."

"What do we do?"

"Pictures," she said. "It's the best we can do. Just be fast."

Toni snapped a series of photos, trying not to leave anything out of the frame. Then she carefully positioned the calendar blotter over the blueprints and straightened it on Ruben's desk. "We better go."

"I feel so daring!" Katherine said. "Baxter will completely overreact to this."

"I think Henry might do the same." Toni started for the door and paused before she opened it to listen to the warehouse.

She didn't hear any voices close by, so she cracked the

door open, glanced outside, then opened it wide enough for her and Katherine to slip out.

"Is this technically considered industrial sabotage?" Katherine whispered.

"I'm not sure." There was a set of narrow stairs at the east end of the building. Toni started down them. "Why?"

"Because there's a clause in my contract with the university about industrial sabotage, and I wouldn't want to break it."

"Since you don't have a personal stake in any of Ruben's competitors, I think you're in the clear."

"That's good."

They reached the bottom of the stairs. The panicked yelling from down the hall was far quieter, but people were still shouting about cleaning up and repairing hoses.

"I think we made it." She shoved her way out the double doors at the end of the warehouse, only to run smack into the barrel chest of Danny Barba.

Toni looked up with wide eyes. "Danny!"

"Toni?" He was frowning. "What are you doing here?"

"We... Uh."

Katherine said, "Ruben was giving us a tour of the fermentation tanks when something broke on the second story and grape juice came pouring down. It was a very big mess."

"Yeah. We were looking for a bathroom because I got some on my jeans." Toni looked down. "We couldn't find one." She pointed at the tasting room building. "Maybe over in the main building?"

"I think so." Danny still looked confused.

"What are you doing over here?" Toni asked. "Something about those grapes Henry wanted to buy?"

Danny opened his mouth, then closed it. "Um. Yeah, the grapes. The, uh, the pinot grapes he wanted to buy from Ruben." The corner of his mouth turned up. "Sure hope that wasn't what ended up on the floor of the tank room."

"You and Henry both." Toni laughed. "Okay, tell Ruben we said bye. We're gonna find a bathroom and get out of here. We shouldn't take up more of his time."

"Okay. See you." Danny walked in the warehouse and Toni and Katherine kept walking straight toward the car. "Are you texting Megan?"

"Yes." Katherine nearly tripped as she tried to read her phone. "She says she's at the car too."

"Good." Toni was desperate to get out of there. She felt like at any moment, someone was going to run out and tackle Katherine to grab the will from under her shirt. And then Toni would have to explain to Baxter why Katherine had been tackled and why she had a murder victim's will up her shirt.

She saw Megan in the distance, leaning against her Mustang and checking her phone as if she didn't have a care in the world.

"Hey."

"Hey!" She tipped her sunglasses down her nose. "You two found something."

"You could say that."

"Good." She pointed to her white purse, which was splashed with purple wine must. "Then I didn't ruin this beauty for nothing."

MEGAN WORE her reading glasses as she paged through the living trust that detailed the extent and disbursement of Whit Fairfield's assets. They were sitting on Katherine's back deck, which seemed like the least likely place for a thief to search should anyone suspect them. Also, there was Archie. He was sweet as sugar, but he did make a lot of noise.

Of the three of them, Megan had been the one reading the most legal documents lately, so she was probably their best bet at understanding them without a lawyer.

"Can I tell you? I'm surprised by how straightforward this is." She looked up and slid off her glasses. "He didn't have any children, so that simplifies it. He had two main asset streams, what he'd inherited from his family and grown—that's mostly real estate investments—and what he developed on his own, which consists of quite a lot of stocks, mostly in technology, and also shares in various businesses, most of which he shared with Angela Calvo, who is designated here as his fiancée and primary beneficiary. For the most part, anything that came from his family he left to his younger brother, and anything of his own he left to Angela. There's some mention of a reciprocal agreement in her own living trust, so it's not surprising. It sounds like they've been working jointly for a few years now. At least financially."

"Anything about the winery in general?" Toni asked. "Anything that mentions anyone here in town? Marissa? Ruben? Anyone?"

"Not that I can see." Megan shrugged. "He didn't even designate personal items to individuals. This man seemed to have no friends, no loyal employee that he wanted to benefit. Just his fiancée and his brother. That's it."

"That's strange," Katherine said. "What an isolated existence."

"Single-minded." Toni stared at the will. "It fits."

"What about the blueprints?"

Katherine pointed inside. "Baxter was very interested in them, but he said they're too small to really examine, of course. He's trying to piece them together from the pictures I took; then he said he has a friend at the university in the engineering department who can print them out full size. This professor also specializes in seismic design, so he's very knowledgeable about geology as well as engineering."

Toni felt like she was about to fall asleep. "I may have to take off soon. Even with Baxter's tea, I'm starting to fade."

"Should you call Henry?"

Toni's immediate reaction was to brush off the suggestion and fight her way back to awareness long enough to drive home.

Then again, he had asked Toni to let him help. "Yeah, that might be a good idea."

"Look at you." Megan smiled and patted her shoulder. "It's like you're in a grown-up relationship after all."

"Don't test me, Atlanta. If I wanted to, I could make myself throw up on you with very little encouragement."

CHAPTER 23

*T*oni felt a kiss brush across her temple. "Toni."

"Mmmm."

"Going to work."

"'Kay." She blinked through the foggy veil of sleep. "You get coffee?"

Henry was sitting on the side of the bed. "I made some. And there's hot water for tea if you want it. You want me to make a cup for you?"

She rolled over and blinked at him. "You're very nice to have around."

His eyes crinkled in the corners when he smiled. "I like being around. I need to go get Earl though. I'm sure he's feeling left out."

"Bring him anytime." She snuggled farther down in the pillows. "He's sweet too."

"Look at you." He ran his fingers through her short curly mop. "Not even a hint of salt this morning. What did you do with my girlfriend?"

Girlfriend. *Girlfriend?*

Whatever. She could be a girlfriend.

"I blame you." She closed her eyes and snuggled closer when Henry started rubbing her back. "It's the empathy. I'm hanging out with you so much, your sweet is rubbing off on me and dampening the salty."

"Better be careful. You don't want to lose your edge."

"I'm sure someone will come along soon enough and piss me off," she muttered.

"Okay." He rubbed small circles on her hip. "If you haven't kicked any doors or told off anyone by the time I finish work today, I'm going to take you to the doctor to get you checked out."

She reached over and patted his arm. "It's good you realize that I'm not going to change."

He chuckled, leaned over, and placed a line of kisses across the back of her neck that left her shivering. "Have a good day, cougar." Henry ducked out of the way, laughing as she tried to pinch his ear.

"Get," she said. "I'm going to drink my tea and then go work on Bubba. I've been neglecting him."

"Bubba?" He stood and walked to the door. "The truck?"

"He's a '64 Ford pickup. He can only be called Bubba."

Henry winked at her and headed out. "Say hi to Bubba then. I'll text you later."

"Cool." Toni lay in bed, listening to Henry putter in the kitchen for a second. He whistled a little before he paused at the door, opened it, and headed out of the house.

What is happening to you, Toni? You're such a sap.

"Stupid hormones." She sat up, pulled on a pair of sweatpants, and walked to the kitchen to see a mug of tea already steeping on the counter.

Tea. On the counter. Waiting for her.

She hadn't asked him. He'd just made it because he knew she'd wake up and feel a little queasy. Toni's phone rang in her pocket as she balanced on the edge of bursting into tears.

"Hello?"

"Toni?" It was Katherine. "Are you all right? I just had a vision of you sobbing uncontrollably. Are you okay? Is the baby okay? Did something happen?"

Okay, it wasn't uncontrollable sobbing, but tears had started leaking down her face. "Henry made me tea."

"Okay and...?"

"He just left for work and he must have made a mug right before he left." She walked over, sniffing. "There's honey beside it."

"And?"

"Nothing." She reached for a paper towel to blow her nose. "That's all. He made me tea."

"But why are you crying?"

"I don't know!" She blew her nose loudly, set the phone on speaker, and put it on the counter. "When he's around, I feel normal and steady—though admittedly a little less hostile to the general population than I'm used to."

"That's not a bad thing."

"Yes, but then he leaves and I'm a disaster! Emotional and messy." She took the tea bag from the mug and dumped it in the sink. "I swing from being worried to being angry to being unreasonably happy for no reason. What is wrong with me?" She upended the squeeze bottle of honey and poured a direct stream into the ginger tea. "Am I getting addicted to him or something? This is not normal!"

"I'm guessing this is completely normal for an empath who is newly pregnant and also recently realized she's in love with the father of her baby."

Toni hiccuped a cry.

"What's wrong now?" Katherine asked.

"I forgot I'm in love with him!" She grabbed her phone. "What am I supposed to do with that? Just be in love with someone for the rest of my life?"

"Um... yes? Ideally, that's how it works."

"What if we end up making each other miserable and codependent?"

"I'm in a happy relationship. Do I look miserable or code-pendent?"

"No." She wiped her eyes with another paper towel. "But you're you."

"I don't know what that means, but I think a good rule of thumb—I can check with a psychologist if you really want me to—is that when you fall in love with a nice person who is healthy and brings out the best in you... don't fight it."

She sniffed. "I'm kind of used to fighting everything."

"I have discovered that about you. But for now, consider *not* fighting this. Just thank the universe for putting that person in your path and appreciate that you're going to live life together instead of separately."

Toni wiped her eyes. "That seems way too simple."

"I have little doubt that as you're living life, problems will arise. Just plan on dealing with those later. Did I tell you that I never planned to get married?"

"No." Toni had always planned to get married. Kind of. It

was in the back of her mind. She was just a little too busy to meet anyone.

"Yes, I was quite determined that I would remain single forever. Which is an excellent path for people who enjoy their own company, which I think you do. But then I met Baxter! And I was surprised by my own feelings, and also I liked who I was when I was around him. And he made me coffee and added a great deal of good things to my life. So despite my own parents' miserable marriage, I decided that Baxter and I were different and we could get married."

Toni sniffed. "How long did it take for you to say yes when Baxter asked you to marry him?"

"It wasn't a traditional proposal. We agreed after several discussions that took place over the course of four months."

"So it took him four months to put enough equations on the whiteboard to convince you that it was a good idea to marry him?"

"How did you know there was a whiteboard involved?" Katherine sounded delighted.

Toni sniffed and smiled a little. "Just figured it was a pretty solid guess for you two."

"What I would suggest is that you simply live as you are now, with significantly more time spent together to determine if you're truly compatible as a couple. He can stay over at your place. You can stay over at his. Don't change anything more than that until after the baby arrives. Isolate the variables."

"Right." It sounded so logical when Katherine explained it. "And if I want him to move in with his big scary-looking dog because someone was murdered at the creek behind my house?"

"Yes, there is the murderer variable. Henry moving in wouldn't be a bad idea. Baxter and I live together and have a dog. Megan lives with her three children up in the hills."

"And I live with a chickenshit cat about a half mile from where Whit Fairfield was murdered. With a gun in the safe, but still."

"So reconsidering initial parameters, perhaps Henry and his large canine might be two variables that should be more constant."

"Are you and Baxter coming over later with the plans?"

"Yes. He went over to the university to see Chimezie, his engineering friend, this morning, but it sounded like he wanted to take a look at the area in person if that was possible."

"It's about a ten-minute walk from my house, just down the creek. Easy."

"Then we'll see you this afternoon."

It was late morning and the radio was blaring Bruce Springsteen as Toni tinkered under Bubba's hood. She'd bought the old Ford a few years before, and one of the primary reasons she'd bought the cottage was the large barn that could house her project cars and her personal tools.

She'd replaced essential parts of the fuel line a few weeks ago and was contemplating the carburetor when she heard a car coming down the gravel drive from the main road.

Toni walked out, slipped her sunglasses on, and watched as Drew Bisset climbed out of his car.

He looked around and nodded. "I understand why you want to live here. Even with the murder and stuff."

"Yeah, it's not bad." She waved him into the barn. "I'm messing around with my truck. Come on in."

Drew walked into the barn just as Toni jumped back up on the stool that propped her short ass up. She often wished she was taller, but then it would just make getting under cars more complicated.

She asked, "So what's up with you?"

"Did Marissa's formal interview this morning."

She glanced up. "Yeah? How did that go? Was Nico there?"

"He's a suspect, Toni. He can't be there."

She rolled her eyes. "Fine. Whatever. What did she say when you interviewed her?"

Drew glanced at her from the corner of his eye. "She says she doesn't remember."

Toni looked up. "She doesn't remember who she argued with? She doesn't remember getting beat up?"

"I actually asked a neurologist about it, and he said it would be consistent with the kind of brain injury Marissa had. It's usually short-term memory loss, but sometimes when a trauma happens, the memory never comes back. The doc said it happens in attacks but also in stuff like car crashes. Documented thing."

"Amnesia, it's not just for soap operas anymore?"

"Apparently not. Marissa said the last thing she remembers is you and your friends coming to her apartment."

"Huh." Toni had nearly forgotten about that. "It's been nearly two weeks. She's got nothing?"

Drew shrugged. "Like the doc said. Maybe it'll come back, maybe it won't."

"Do you think she's lying?"

Drew took a deep breath. "Possibly. She might lie to protect the father of her children."

"Come on. That doesn't make any sense. Nico is helping her out in rehab, bringing the kids around, running errands for her, even though it's his busiest season. If she could get her memory back at any time and accuse him, why would he do that?"

"Unless he's hanging around so he can know for sure if any of her memory has returned."

"Drew, you know Nico. That's a level of diabolical he just doesn't have in him."

"Right now I don't *know* anything. I've got about four different suspects bouncing around in my head, and that includes your cousin."

Four?

"So Nico and who else?" She narrowed her eyes. "The fiancée?"

"Angela Calvo has the most motive by far. I can't eliminate her, even though by all accounts she has an alibi for Fairfield's death, and she's set foot in Moonstone Cove a grand total of three times in her life."

"She could have hired someone."

"Very possible, which is why I can't rule her out."

Toni reached for a wire brush. Bubba was gonna need a new battery. Stat. "Nico, the fiancée, and who else?" She tossed ideas around in her head. "Ruben, yeah? Fairfield's foreman? He and his boss didn't get along."

"True, but he also didn't have much incentive to kill his boss. He's poured a lot of time and personal attention into that winery. There's no reason to think that the fiancée is going to keep him on. He was way more secure with Fairfield."

"True."

"Added to those three, there are two women at the country club who cheated on their husbands with the man."

"Ew." She curled her lip. "What was the attraction? I do not get it."

"You may not get it, but he did." Drew shrugged. "Money, I guess? Anyway, there's more than one angry husband who might have wanted to kill him. Then there's Pamela at the country club."

"Pamela Martin?" Toni popped her head up. "What did she have against Fairfield? She was talking with him about a job, wasn't she?"

Drew looked around, then back at Toni. "Strictly between us?"

"Who am I going to tell?"

"Katherine and Megan."

"Fair point. I would totally tell them."

"So keep this between us." Drew walked closer and leaned on Bubba's fender. "I interviewed Pamela a couple of times because something wasn't adding up for me with her. It was just a feeling."

"And?" Toni focused on brushing sediment away from the top of the carburetor.

"Fairfield offered her a job, but it came with conditions. And those conditions weren't anything she was willing to consider." Drew shrugged. "At least, not according to her. But it didn't help that he was spreading rumors they were already having an affair."

"Gross." She fumbled the brush and nearly scraped her hand. "Whit Fairfield was *such* an asshole. She had every reason to hate him."

"Plus she doesn't have an alibi for the night he died."

Toni looked up. "You know what I'm discovering about crimes and stuff since I got to know you, Drew?"

"What's that?"

"Normal people don't have alibis for much."

He started to laugh.

"It's true!" She pointed the wire brush at him. "Know what I do every night? Hang out at my house, watching TV or working on this truck or cooking. And you know who can verify that?"

"Absolutely no one?"

"Exactly." She threw up her hands. "I mean, no wonder rich people get away with all the crimes, right? They have household staff who can give them alibis."

Drew's eyes were dancing. "I can't lie, sometimes when someone has an ironclad alibi that doesn't involve hanging out at a bar, I get suspicious."

"Of course you would. Because normal people don't have alibis for ninety percent of their life."

Drew smiled. "You would have made a great detective, Toni."

"I don't think so." She wrinkled her nose. "Interacting with the public is never going to be my strong suit."

He narrowed his eyes. "Fair point."

"Question."

"I might answer."

Toni set the wire brush to the side. "You keep asking about the *night* Fairfield died. Why are you assuming he died at night? He was out there for like a week and a half, right? Can autopsies be that precise?"

"In this case, we have his watch." Drew tapped his wrist. "Old-fashioned fancy brand. Swiss-made something or other. I told you he was beat up, right? We think he must have fallen to the ground at some point and the crystal was smashed on a rock. The watch face completely shattered, and the watch was stuck at two in the morning."

"Weird." Two in the morning? "No one is wandering around at two in the morning for a good reason."

"You sound like my mom."

"Ha ha." She picked up a wrench and put it down. What was she doing? "I'm telling you, you're barking up the wrong tree looking at my cousin."

"You saying Marissa wouldn't cover for him?"

"I'm saying it's more likely she's covering for someone else."

"Why?"

"She had some deal going with Fairfield, right? The blackmail thing with Henry? Maybe she knows more about that than she's letting on. Maybe she's trying to salvage that business since Fairfield is gone and her sugar daddy won't be around. Maybe whoever else Fairfield was blackmailing is the same person who killed him and beat Marissa up?"

"Henry was the only one we know for sure they were blackmailing, and thankfully for him, he has an alibi for Marissa's attack."

"But Marissa also said she thought Fairfield was blackmailing other people too."

Drew leaned against the truck. "Who else would Whit Fairfield have been blackmailing? Who would he have leverage over?" Drew drummed his fingers on the side of the truck, then looked over at Toni. "Didn't you say there'd been some sabotage over at Nico's winery?"

Toni nodded. "Yeah. Henry said there was stuff missing. A tank got turned off. There was the tractor thing."

"Well then," Drew said. "It sounds like I need to take a trip up the hill."

CHAPTER 24

*W*hen they got to the winery, Nico was shouting at a crew sorting and loading grapes into the de-stemmer and crusher. There were three men in long sleeves tossing grapes in and throwing others into bins on a raised trailer that had been pulled up to the back of the tank house.

"You know," Drew said, "I like wine, but I had no idea how complicated it was before I moved here."

"It's a lot of manual labor," she said. "Unlike a lot of crops, everything still has to be picked by hand and sorted by hand. There's only so much you can automate."

"What are they doing there?" Drew pointed to the men Nico was yelling at.

"I think those are cabernet grapes." She nodded at the large white bins of harvested fruit. "Which means they're making red wine. So right now they're sorting the grapes, and then they're going to go through the wash and into the crusher."

"No stomping feet?"

"Sadly, that part *is* automated now."

Drew pointed at the long metal machines that jutted out from the back of the building. "So the crusher takes the juice out?"

"Nope. It takes the stems off and then it literally crushes them. All the skins and seeds and pulp and everything are going to go right in those giant tanks inside. The yeast is going to be added and then it's all going to ferment together. That's why someone messing with the temperature controls is a big deal."

"How long do they ferment?"

"Depends on the grape variety and what Henry wants. See Henry" —she pointed to her boyfriend, who was talking with Danny by the doors of the tank house— "Henry is the one who actually makes the wine. Nico grows the grapes and sells the finished product, but Henry is the one who decides how long things are going to ferment, decides how long before the must—that's the mixture with the juice and the skins and the seeds and everything—when all that is going to be pressed. And then he tastes all the new wine—which is really not as tasty as it sounds—and he has to imagine how everything is going to age, which wines will blend together well. All that stuff."

Henry and Danny finished their conversation. Then Henry tossed Danny some keys, and the younger man walked off toward Henry's truck.

"Lot of moving parts," Toni said. "Lots of people."

Drew nodded. "This is actually really helpful. So over at Fairfield's place, does Ruben do all that winemaking stuff?"

"No. Ruben is like Nico. He grows the grapes and oversees the vineyards. I think Fairfield hired a fancy winemaker from up north and then another person to sell and market the wine. I've never met any of those people. Henry might have."

Nico spotted Toni and waved. Toni pointed toward Nico's office, and he gave her an exaggerated thumbs-up sign and held up five fingers.

"Five minutes?" Toni asked.

"Works for me."

Drew and Toni started toward Nico's office.

"So" —Drew kept his voice low— "does your cousin know you're pregnant?"

Toni froze. She turned to Drew with wide eyes. "How did you—?"

"Father of two." He pointed to himself. "You're not drinking. Taking things easier, according to the guys at your garage. More mood swings than normal." He leaned back. "Plus there's just this..."

"If you say I have a fucking glow, I will punch your face."

Drew's face split with a grin. "I was going to say you're a little fuller around your cheeks."

"You saying my face is fat?"

"Yeah. That's definitely what I'm going to tell the scary pregnant woman. That her face is fat. Do I look like an idiot?"

"Fuck you, Detective Bisset."

"I'm going to put that aggression down to hormones. So Henry, huh?"

"What about him?" She crossed her arms over her chest, only to realize that her boobs were both swollen *and* staging a revolt. Owwwwwww.

Drew laughed a little. "Okay."

Toni pulled open the door to Nico's ranch office. "Do you enjoy being a nosy asshole?"

"I'm a police detective. It's kind of my job." He sat in one of two clear chairs. "I think it's nice. You'll make a great mom."

"It's still very early, so..."

"My lips are sealed." He looked around. "This looks more like a geologist's office than a farmer if you ask me."

"It's all about the soil." Toni shoved part of the small couch clear and sat down, putting her feet on the coffee table. "That reminds me." She pulled out her phone. "Baxter was showing the plans we found for those five acres to his engineering friend at the university. I should tell them to just come here."

"You found plans?" Drew raised an eyebrow. "For what?"

"We... happened across some plans related to that five-acre stretch that Fairfield kept pressuring Nico to sell. It's not particularly valuable land—that we know of—which is why Nico always wondered why Fairfield wanted it so bad."

"But this is Dusi land, correct? And Fairfield had plans about it?"

"Yeah. Nico and his dad got it at auction about twenty years ago when the previous owner passed with no will. It's a really beautiful stretch of land with a unique microclimate, and the cabernet vines that grow there are a big part of the Dusi house red now. He's never been tempted to sell."

"That seems suspicious." Drew narrowed his eyes. "And you just... happened to come across these plans?"

"I think someone gave them to Megan." Toni's face was carefully innocent. "You'd have to ask her."

"Really? Is she coming today?"

"Don't think so. Lunch with her kids." Toni nodded. "Family time."

"Yeah, I think I've heard of it." Drew pursed his lips. "That reminds me. I heard there was some kind of commotion at Fairfield's winery last week. Some hoses that mysteriously busted. No one could figure out what happened. They just... came apart. All by themselves."

Toni made her eyes wide and guileless. "That's so weird."

He folded his hands carefully and stared at her. "The world is full of mysteries, isn't it?"

"Hmmm." She took out her phone and texted Katherine. "I'm just telling Katherine that she and Baxter should meet us up here." She held up her phone a moment later. "They're on their way."

"Great."

It was far more than five minutes later that Nico walked in. "Hey. Sorry about that."

"No worries," Toni said. "Thanks for taking a break. I know it's crazy out there."

Nico sat behind his desk and pulled out a Coke from the small fridge beside it. "I keep telling myself two more weeks and it'll slow down. A little." He held up the soda. "You guys want one?"

"I'm good."

Drew said, "I'll take one."

"Sure thing." Nico reached down and grabbed a second soft drink. "So, Detective. Please don't tell me anyone else died or was beat up last night, because I got home late and crashed and I do not have any kind of alibi."

The corner of Drew's mouth turned up. "I'm not here

about that. Toni was telling me about the sabotage you were dealing with a few weeks ago. Wanted to question you about that."

Nico let out a long breath. "Damn. I nearly forgot about that; it seems so long ago."

"It's only been a few weeks," Toni said.

"I know. But since the tractor, we haven't had another incident. Not even a minor one that I just kind of wondered about. Whoever was messing with us stopped. Right around the time that Whit Fairfield went missing."

"But not before he was dead," Drew said.

"Oh right." Toni realized where he was going. "The tractor happened after Fairfield was killed, but before he was found. So it couldn't have been Fairfield behind the sabotage."

Drew said, "But it's possible someone wanted you to think that it was."

"Okay, I see where you're going." Nico frowned. "Speaking of the tractor, did you ever figure out if that finger was...?"

"Oh yeah," Drew said. "The finger belonged to the victim. Prints confirmed."

"But how did it get all the way over—"

"It had cat teeth marking it," Drew said quietly. "So... we have a pretty good idea of what happened."

Oh. Ewwwwww.

Please don't let it be Enzo. Please don't let it be Enzo.

"So the finger was Fairfield's but the sabotage wasn't," Nico said. "Because the sabotage happened on a particular night, and Fairfield was already dead."

"Correct."

Toni said, "What if it was someone Fairfield paid who didn't realize he was dead?"

"That's a possibility I can't rule it out." Drew turned his attention to Nico. "Do you have any idea who it could be?"

"No." Nico shrugged. "Honestly, I thought it was Fairfield or one of his guys sneaking over. I hate to think it's anyone I hired, but how much do you ever really know a person? I can't think of anyone on our staff who's having money problems or anything like that. Not that they've shared anyway."

"And these were things that happened in the tank house?"

"There were a few different things. The tractor you know about." Nico tapped his finger. "The next most serious thing was a fermentation tank that had been reset and would have spoiled if Henry hadn't caught it. Even though Henry saved it, the added heat will affect the quality. I'd say that at best, it'll be a blending wine," Nico said. "So we did lose money on that one. Then there was the labor contractor someone called, pretending to be from the winery here, and canceled all our crews for a week. That put us way behind."

"Damn," Drew said. "That can mess you up, can't it?"

"It can, but it's not going to ruin us," Nico said. "It would take something more than that to really run us out of business. It was, at best, a half-hearted attempt. We managed to fix everything."

There was a tap at the door, and Baxter poked his head in. "Perhaps the goal wasn't to run you out of business," the professor said. "But rather to put enough pressure on you to sell some land."

"Hey." Nico waved them in. "It's not out of the question. Not ideal, but not unheard of."

"I highly suggest," Baxter said, "that you do not sell this parcel."

Baxter and Katherine walked in the office, and Katherine bent down to spread a large set of plans on the coffee table where Toni had propped her feet.

"It's clear that Whit Fairfield had plans for your property." Katherine looked up at Nico. "And we think we know what they were."

"Looking at these" —Baxter spread his hands over the blueprints— "the reason he wanted the land becomes evident. It's not what is *on* the land, but what is *under* it."

Nico brought a chair over. "What is it? Oil? Natural gas? Some mineral or something?"

"Nothing like that. I admit, that's what I expected at first, but my engineering friend Professor Njoku made it quite clear that because of the topography of the land, any valuable mineral or mining rights were unlikely to be the motive."

"Okay." Nico looked over the spread-out papers. "But you do know why he wanted it?"

Baxter continued, "When I finally pieced these plans together and Chimezie and I printed them out, we thought we were looking at a brand-new structure Whit Fairfield had commissioned from scratch."

Toni looked at what appeared to be an Italianate facade with elaborate columns that almost looked like a temple. "What is this?"

"I believe it's a facade for a portal site," Baxter said. "It would be built into the hill overlooking the creek across from the current Fairfield winery. This portion is purely aesthetic."

"A facade for what?" Nico asked.

"For an elaborate wine-cave complex dug into the hill." Katherine flipped the top plan up to reveal a more detailed and technical one underneath. "See? The cave goes back into the hill, which is made from a soft volcanic rock that would be very good for tunneling. The ornate facade faces the Fairfield winery, but there are actually two portals. See? It's like a stretched horseshoe shape. The second portal is very near the road that runs by Toni's house."

Nico sat back. "So Fairfield wanted to buy that land because it'd make a good wine cave?"

"It makes sense when you consider his own property situation," Baxter said. "I took the liberty of looking up his holdings. His acreage isn't consolidated. It's spread out and scattered. In addition to that, looking at the topographic and geologic maps available publicly, it would be much more complicated to find as suitable a site that would also be accessible to his existing facilities." Baxter tapped the spread blueprints. "But for this wine cave, all he would have had to do is build a pleasing facade on the front portal and a sturdy bridge across the creek."

Nico snorted. "And a freaking *wine cave.* I mean, it's a hell of a thing to have on your winery, but caves cost millions to dig."

Baxter placed a hand on a corner of the plans. "They do indeed. Of course, if the wine cave had already been dug and all the landowner had to do was improve the infrastructure and create a grand entrance, the cost would be far less."

Toni's eyes went wide. "What?"

Nico looked confused. "Are you saying—?"

"I'm saying you need to look more closely at the plans."

Baxter pointed to the blueprints. "What Professor Njoku noted are these large studs."

"Aren't those just part of the support?"

"No. They are seismic retrofitting. Earthquake retrofitting would only be done on older structures, particularly those built prior to 1980."

"We didn't own that land in the 80s," Toni said. "It still belonged to the old Hungarian guy."

Nico sat back in his chair. "Are you saying that that weird little strip of land my dad and I bought at auction has a wine cave dug into it?"

Baxter smiled. "I believe that is the case, yes."

"Holy shit." Nico's eyes were wide as saucers. "Toni, are you hearing this?"

"I'm hearing this." She looked at Drew. "That certainly explains why Fairfield wanted to buy it."

"Holy shit." Nico seemed to be frozen in shock. "It's just been sitting there empty for thirty years?"

"Perhaps even longer," Baxter said. "And if these plans are recent—which they appear to be—with a moderate investment to update the structure, you could have functional wine storage caves with very little trouble."

There was a rapid knock at Nico's door.

"Come in!"

Henry opened the door, frowning when he saw the crowd gathered in Nico's office. "Hey... sorry. So many people." He seemed scattered.

Nico said, "What's up?"

Henry turned to Nico. "I'm sorry if I'm interrupting, but I need you to see something."

Nico stood. "What is it?"

"Nothing's wrong with the guys or the equipment." He shook his head. "Danny and I had to trade trucks, and I found something in his that I... I don't know what to think."

CHAPTER 25

The blood-covered shirt was balled up and creased; the spatters were dark brown and smeared over the previously white cotton button-down. It was sitting on the floor behind the driver's seat in Danny Barba's pickup truck.

Henry stood with his arms crossed at the open truck door. "Danny needed to borrow my truck because it has a trailer hitch. I forgot that I'd ordered some new lines that were supposed to be in today. The store just called, so I figured I'd borrow his truck to go pick them up. We've traded trucks before. I'm a lot taller than Danny, so I tried to move the seat back and it made a ripping noise."

Drew returned to the half circle that had formed around Danny's truck with a large evidence bag. "Did you touch it?"

"Yeah. I reached under the seat—figured it was just a T-shirt or a rag or something—but when I pulled that out, I dropped it on the floor there."

"Okay." Drew pulled on gloves and lifted the shirt from

the floor into the large plastic bag. "I may need a DNA sample to rule you out, but we'll see what the lab has to say."

"Okay."

Toni stood next to Henry, and he had his arm around her, rubbing her shoulder. She could feel his emotions; they were everywhere. He was angry, confused, and worried all at once. Layered over all that was a blanket of guilt.

She tugged on his shirt, and he leaned down to her. "You did the right thing."

"I can't believe Danny would be involved in anything violent," Henry said quietly. "He's my friend."

"I know, and maybe that shirt means nothing." She rubbed her thumb over his cheek. "Maybe it's all a misunderstanding. Or maybe something did happen that he got involved in and he doesn't know how to come forward."

Henry looked skeptical. "Maybe."

"However that shirt got in his truck, you did the right thing, okay?" She kissed his cheek. "Don't question yourself."

Nico was standing on her other side, staring at the truck and the shirt while Drew searched the rest of the vehicle. The detective had already called for backup.

"I can't believe Danny would get involved in any of this," he said.

Toni looked up at her big cousin. "You and Henry both."

"I have to admit though..." Nico sighed. "Someone might be able to convince him. He's not a ringleader, but he can be a follower."

"Do you think he was responsible for the sabotage?" Toni asked.

Nico shrugged. "It's possible. Maybe it's even likely. He

had access to all the equipment. Hell, no one would think twice of him working on a tractor or messing with one of the tanks. That's his job."

"But why?" Henry ran his hands through his hair. "Danny's been here longer than me. I thought he was loyal."

"I thought he was too." Nico shook his head. "I don't want to keep guessing. Did you call him?"

Henry nodded, and the wave of guilt nearly knocked Toni over. "Yeah. I didn't say anything, just asked when he would be back."

"Okay." Nico walked over and leaned against the barn. "Then we wait."

Nico and Henry went back to work, so Toni and Drew went to Nico's office to wait. Toni stretched out on Nico's couch and leaned against a threadbare pillow that smelled a little dusty. She didn't care. It was nearly three o'clock, and she was about to pass out from exhaustion.

"Your symptoms getting worse?" Drew asked, eying her from the easy chair next to the desk.

"They're not too bad so far." She yawned. "Exhaustion is the most obvious one. I get morning sick at night, so sometimes I have to force myself to eat. Uh…"

"Your hips hurt?"

She nodded. "Yeah! What is that about?"

Drew shrugged. "Something about your joints loosening up. My wife hated that part."

"I don't blame her." Toni shuddered. "Was it worse with twins? Probably, right?"

"Oh yeah. Everything is real… extreme. It's, like, extreme pregnancy, all-star edition or something."

"Well, this one only has one heartbeat," Toni said. "So I think I'm in the clear for that."

"Probably a good thing." Drew smothered a smile.

"What?"

"Nothin'." He shook his head.

"No, not nothin'. I can see you've got some smart-ass comment or something you're just dying to—"

"I was gonna say at least Henry will have someone to watch *Sesame Street* with now."

Toni snorted. "Good one."

"Mister Rogers probably."

"I can't even argue with any of these. He probably loves all those shows. He's very…"

"Wholesome?" Drew asked.

"Like a Midwestern dairy product." Toni nodded. "And that's good. At least one of this kid's parents is going to be up for the task."

"Oh, you'll do fine. Just remind Henry—when he gives you shit about letting the kid listen to the Sex Pistols—that you don't have to worry about toddlers repeating song lyrics for about two, maybe three years."

"I'll tuck that bit of wisdom away," Toni said. "Thanks, Drew."

"I'm full of fatherly advice." He stretched his legs out. "Wish I knew more about this Danny Barba guy though."

"Well, you wouldn't know about Danny because he's a very normal, very noncriminal person. I do not know what is going on here, but I guarantee it didn't start with him."

DANNY STARED at the bloody shirt for a long time, not saying a word.

"Mr. Barba?" Drew snapped his fingers in front of Danny's face. "I understand your confusion, but if you could answer the question for me—"

"I don't know whose it is." His face hardly moved when he spoke.

Toni and Henry were watching from the couch. Drew was in the chair across from Danny, and Nico was sitting on the edge of his desk.

"Danny, whatever is going on—"

"I'm serious, boss." Danny turned to Nico. "I didn't hurt anyone. I don't know whose blood that is."

Drew glanced at Toni.

"You're lying," she said, leaning her elbows on her knees to get closer to Danny, trying to sort out the confusing mix of emotions coming off him in jagged, panicked bursts. "You're telling the truth, but you're lying too. You believe you didn't hurt anyone. You really believe that."

Danny's eyes darted to the bloody shirt; then he looked away.

"But you know—or you think you know—who that shirt belongs to. You know whose blood is on it."

He snorted and looked at Toni from the corner of his eye. "What are you? Psychic or something? You don't know shit."

Drew said, "I may not be psychic, but I know that this shirt looks like it belongs to someone who beat the shit out of another human being. And I know there's more than enough blood on it to get a match. So whose is it, Danny? It'll be better if you tell me yourself. Whit Fairfield or Marissa Dusi?"

Danny went pale. "I'd never beat a woman."

"So you're admitting you killed Fairfield then?" Drew nodded. "I mean, everyone said he was an asshole, right? Probably better that he's dead. Who's gonna miss him?"

"I never said I killed that Fairfield guy!"

"It's either Fairfield's blood or Marissa's, Danny." Drew scooted closer. "Nothing else makes sense."

"That's bullshit." Danny was on the verge of panic. "I want a lawyer," he said. "Right the hell now."

Toni tried to sort through the emotions. There was too much. Drew's calm focus was the easiest to ignore, but Nico and Henry were both tense and intent on Danny.

"You." She pointed to Henry. "And you." She pointed to Nico. "Leave me and Drew alone with Danny."

Drew sat up straight. "Excuse me?"

"Tell them to go out and wait with the other police." The pressure was so great, she felt like her ears would pop. "Just do it."

Henry stood and motioned for Nico to go with him. He cast one more look at Toni before he left the room.

She turned to Danny. "Breathe."

He took a deep breath. Let it out. The pressure in the room began to dissipate. Danny began to calm down, and she could sort through his feelings more clearly.

Worry. Anger. Guilt. A lot of guilt, but anger too.

"You're angry with someone," Toni said. "None of this was your idea. Someone pulled you in."

Danny refused to look at her.

"You didn't kill anyone," she said. "But you know more than you're telling Drew. You need to come clean."

Danny shook his head over and over. "I'm not gonna say another—"

"You want to talk," she said. "I can feel it. You want to tell him because you feel guilty. You know it was wrong. You know..." Toni blinked. "You're the one who cut the tractor wires, aren't you?"

Danny froze.

"You never meant for it to go this far." She wanted to reach out and take his hand, but she knew she shouldn't. Whatever he confessed to, Drew needed it to come from Danny, free and clear.

Toni remembered what Henry had said. *...it's like that asshole crept into my head and knew everything. He played on every single thing I was most afraid of.*

"He pushed all your buttons, didn't he, Danny? You needed the money for a good reason, and it was there. It wasn't anything too big, right? Calling off a work crew. Fiddling with a tank. Cutting the switch on a tractor. No one was going to get hurt. Nico would be fine."

Danny started to nod. "Yeah." His voice was broken. "No one was going to get hurt."

"Because you're not that kind of person," she said. "I know that. Henry knows that. He's your friend. We know you wouldn't hurt anyone on purpose."

The young man's face fell and his eyes grew glassy. "I don't know what to do."

"You need to tell Drew the truth."

"I can't. I honestly don't know whose blood is on that shirt."

Toni blinked. "You're telling the truth."

"He's what?" Drew sat up. "What now?"

"I don't know whose blood it is." Danny spoke quickly. "I was the one who tampered with the equipment, okay? That was me. Fairfield told me to do it. My dad needs a knee replacement, and I'm trying to save up money for the copayment. So I needed the money, and Fairfield wanted stuff done. Not big stuff, okay? Nobody was going to get hurt. He just needed Nico to lose enough this season so that he'd sell that land, okay? I don't know any more than that."

"Whose shirt is it?" Drew asked.

"I don't know whose blood is on it." Danny pleaded with him. "Please don't arrest me. I've never been arrested in my life. Please."

"How did it get in your car?" Drew asked. "Danny, I need more."

"I don't know." Tears rolled down his face. "I can't tell you that. I didn't beat anyone up."

"Truth." Toni rubbed her temple. "But also a lie." A headache was starting to pound.

Drew went back to his first question. "Whose blood is on that shirt, Danny? We're gonna find out soon enough. It's already at the lab."

"I don't know!"

"Truth." Toni frowned. What was going on here?

"Tell me who the shirt belongs to." Drew was insistent. "Tell me how it got in your truck."

"I'm telling you..." Danny heaved out a breath, trying to control his crying. "I don't know."

"Lie." Toni's eyes went wide. "You do know whose shirt it is, but you don't know whose blood it is."

Danny looked at her. "I can't tell you."

Anger. Pain. Guilt. Frustration. Shame.

Toni shook her head. "I can't tell. There's too much."

"Okay." Drew stood and reached for Danny's arm. "Danny Barba, you're under arrest for charges I am going to have to sort out down at the station because I know your ass is lying." He shot a look at Toni. "Stay here. I'll tell Henry to come get you. You're about a minute from passing out."

CHAPTER 26

She fell asleep in Nico's office, minutes after Drew took Danny out the door in handcuffs. She had no idea how long she slept, but when she woke, the sun was beaming in through the west-facing window and her body was stiff from sleeping so hard on Nico's couch. She sat up and stretched carefully, taking a drink from the bottle of water someone had set on the coffee table in front of her.

The door cracked open and Toni looked over, rubbing her eyes.

"Hey you." It was Megan. "You ready to go?"

"Where?"

"Your cousin is down at the police station, trying to talk to Danny. He's got a lawyer in there, but he agreed to talk to Nico. Then I guess Nico came out and asked for you. We told them you weren't feeling okay, but we'd call when you were awake."

Toni blinked. "So I need to go talk to Danny at the police station? And he has a lawyer, but he wants to talk to me?"

"Yes. Baxter and Katherine went home—we're gonna

260

have to treasure hunt another day—but Henry and I stayed here to make sure you were okay."

Was she still sleeping? "Treasure hunt?"

Megan cleared her throat. "I hear tell there's caves in them there hills."

Toni felt like her face would crack when she smiled. "Right. The caves. Did Katherine and Baxter fill you in?

"Yes. So wild, right? So after Nico went down to the police station to give his statement, it was just Katherine and me, Baxter, and Henry. It's kind of cute actually. Baxter was very gently interrogating Henry for around an hour, and I don't think Henry had any idea."

"It wouldn't occur to him that Baxter was being anything but polite."

"I know. That's what makes Henry so adorable." Megan walked over, held out a hand, and took Toni's. "How are you feeling?"

She stood and realized that she actually felt better. Then she immediately felt guilty for sleeping in the middle of the day. "What day is it?"

"Saturday."

"Oh good. I'm not missing work."

"You're going to have to reconfigure that in your brain, little mama. You are growing a human in that body. When it wants to sleep, you're gonna have to let it sleep."

"Henry said something similar, and I've been trying to ignore him." She covered her mouth when a giant yawn hit her.

"Don't make me ask Katherine to look up the scientific literature on this topic, because you know I will and you know she will." Megan guided Toni through the office and out to the loggia that led to Nico's lavish home. "I love this place, don't you?"

"It's a very cool house," Toni said. "His parents built it in the 1960s, but they wanted it to feel Italian. Nico's dad is like mine is, and I don't know how many generations in the US, but his mom grew up outside Salerno, so she wanted to make the house feel like home."

"It's amazing. I feel like I'm on vacation just walking around the gardens."

"That's why everyone wants to have weddings and baptisms and everything here." She spotted her niece Beth and Henry on the patio outside the kitchen. "Is Beth helping you out?"

"Yeah, Nico put her in charge while he was gone."

"She's a good kid. Smart as a whip too."

"You're telling me. She was wondering about you. Noticed the sleepiness, the mood swings. So she asked Henry—"

"Noooo." Toni froze. "He totally told her about the baby, didn't he?"

"Oh yeah. Foooooolded like a cheap suit. That man cannot keep a secret. You're gonna have to be careful leaving him unattended around your mother."

Toni tried to quash the rising panic. "At least Beth can probably be quiet about it."

"I might have stressed to her that it was still very early and you did not want a lot of people knowing."

She patted Megan's shoulder. "Thank you."

They walked to the patio, and Toni hooked her arm around Beth's shoulders. "Hey, sweetie. Did you talk to your mom today?"

"Yeah." The seventeen-year-old girl was statuesque and gorgeous like her mother but with her father's dramatic dark hair and eyes. "She's doing okay, I guess. Is it bad that I'm suspicious? I felt so horrible after she was attacked, but now she's, like, immediately pivoting to get something out of Dad." Beth rolled her eyes. "I just can't. She makes me tired."

"Try not to stress about it, okay? Maybe your dad can make her see sense."

"I just want her to, like, get a boyfriend—a real one—and move on already. This sucks so hard for Dad."

"Well, your dad's got you and your brother," Megan said. "So speaking from experience, he got the better end of the deal."

Beth gave her a small smile. "Thanks." Her smile widened when she looked back at Toni. "And congratulations, Auntie Toni!" She whispered, "You're going to be, like, the coolest mom ever. I promise I won't tell anyone, okay?"

She squeezed Beth's shoulders. "I know you won't because you want to borrow my Mustang for prom."

"Not *just* that, but definitely that." Beth pointed at Henry. "He's the one who told me."

Toni looked at Henry, who only grinned.

"I'm allowed to be excited about our baby."

"Can you maybe be more *quietly* excited?"

It was useless. He was so adorable she had a hard time mustering up the annoyance she knew he deserved. She walked over, and Henry stood and opened his arms.

"You're not to be trusted." Toni leaned forward, rested her head on his chest, and allowed herself to melt as he rubbed her back and shoulders. "I don't want to go to the police station."

"Then we'll take you home."

"But I need to go," she said. "If Danny wants to talk to me, I need to find out what he wants to say."

Megan jingled her keys. "I'll drive. You relax. Let's get you a cold drink and get this over with."

It was dark when they finally rolled into the Moonstone Cove police station, and Toni saw Drew's car in the parking lot along with some black-and-white cruisers.

"I wonder where Nico is?"

Megan shrugged. "Maybe he just wanted to get home."

They walked inside, and Toni walked up to the front counter. "Hey, Sharon."

"Toni, how you doing? You here to see Max?" The receptionist at the police department was a sweet older woman named Sharon who'd worked in the high school office when Toni was a student there.

High school to police department. Toni imagined the police department was probably a little calmer.

"No, I'm not here to see Max." Her younger cousin was probably at home with his new wife and baby daughter. "I was told that one of Drew's suspects wanted to talk to me."

"Let me call him." She lifted the phone and dialed a couple of numbers. "Detective Bisset, Toni Dusi is here." She nodded. "Uh-huh." She frowned. "You sit tight; I'll bring her back." She hung up the phone and pointed to Toni. "Okay, you he wants in the conference room—I'll walk you back— and anyone with you" —she turned her attention to Megan and Henry— "needs to stay out here. You got that?"

Henry squeezed Toni's shoulder. "Megan and I can hang in the front."

"Take your time," Megan said.

"No idea what Danny wants to tell me that he couldn't say earlier," Toni said. "Sharon, lead the way."

She walked back through a maze of cubicles to the small break room with glass walls where she could see Danny Barba eating something out of a white Styrofoam container. Drew spotted them through the glass and waved her in.

"Thanks, Sharon." He pulled out a chair for Toni as Sharon shut the door. "Our man here has consulted with his lawyer" —Drew gestured to the whip-thin woman with tightly curled hair and flawless red lipstick— "and Ms. Aguilar has advised him to speak with us about his associates. Thank you, Ms. Aguilar."

"I've already spoken with the DA, and my client is prepared to be forthcoming about his role in all this. We are hoping to avoid jail time due to my client's perfectly clear record." She turned her eyes to Toni. "I honestly don't know why he wanted you here, Ms. Dusi, but thank you for coming."

"No one was supposed to get hurt." Danny shoved his to-go container to the side and leaned toward Toni. "You can tell them that. You know when I'm lying. You're like a psychic or like one of those smart people on the TV who read people real well, right?"

Toni glanced at Drew, then back at Danny. "Uh... something like that."

"So you'll know. You'll be able to tell Detective Bisset here that I'm not lying about this."

Toni could already feel the tension in the room building.

Danny's lawyer did not want him talking to Toni. Drew really didn't want her in the room at all, and Danny's wild, desperate hope weighed on her like a lead backpack.

"Danny, I can tell him if you're lying or not, but you need to just tell him the complete truth. Don't try to hide—"

"Is Miss Marissa at the hospital still?" Danny asked Drew. "I heard you had a guard and stuff with her at the hospital."

"She's at a rehab center," Toni said. "Why?"

"The rehab center?" Danny asked. "Do they have guards for that?"

"I honestly don't know," Drew said. "What are you trying to say, Danny? Is someone going to go after Marissa?"

"I don't know. Not for sure." Danny squirmed in his seat.

"Truth," Toni said. "But there's something else."

"I don't know for sure," he said. "I just, I mean I'm wondering if..." His voice dropped to near-imperceptible levels. "...maybe my cousin knows something. About Marissa, I mean. He knew about me and Fairfield. I think maybe he even told Fairfield about me. How I needed money and all."

"Your cousin?" Drew asked. "Who's your cousin, Danny?"

"Ruben Montenegro," Toni said. She didn't know how she'd forgotten. Maybe she just didn't put it together because Ruben was so much older than Danny. They were nowhere close in school. Ruben was Nico's age, and Danny was in his twenties. "Your mom and Ruben's mom are sisters, right?"

"Oldest and youngest." Danny traced circles on the table. "Our moms don't really get along, but when I wanted to get in the wine business, I went to talk to Ruben and he told me to go talk to Nico. Said Nico might give me a job or something."

Was it Ruben all along?

Had Ruben killed Fairfield? Why?

Had Ruben beat up Marissa? How had he kept her quiet?

Drew was taking furious notes. "Did Ruben beat up Marissa Dusi?"

"I don't know for sure."

Drew glanced at Toni.

"That's the truth," Toni said. "But I'm getting all sorts of doubt all over the place. He's not sure of much right now."

All this was making Danny's lawyer very nervous. Her emotional signature was like a pinball. "Detective Bisset, I don't know who your consultant is, but I'd like to pause this interview to speak with my client—"

"No, I need to tell them." Danny wasn't finished talking. "I don't know... I mean, he might go after her at this other place, you know?"

Drew turned to the uniformed officer in the room. "Get over to Hillside Rehab, and call the front desk right now. Tell them their security needs to be on alert. Park a cruiser in front until I can get there."

"You got it." The officer hightailed it out of the room, but Danny had more to say.

"See, I don't know if Nico knows, but there's a thing on that land that Ruben's boss wanted to buy. And Ruben's dad, he knew about it because he helped that weird old man build it."

"We know about the caves," Toni said.

"Okay." Danny nodded. "So the story is, our grandpa was

a bricklayer, and he helped build it and he told Ruben about it. He was already dead when I was born, so I didn't hear it, but after Fairfield hired me to... you know."

"Sabotage the Dusi winery?" Drew offered.

"Yeah." Danny shrugged. "After he called me, I went to Ruben because I knew the guy was Ruben's boss and all." Danny kept his eyes on the table. "And Ruben told me about it, and he said that his boss needed that land and we were gonna help him get it, and if we did that, he'd have a better job for me at Fairfield's place. Something with the wine and not just, like, fixing the tractors and keeping the equipment going, you know? I'd really learn about making wine."

"So Ruben told Fairfield about the caves in the creekside land," Toni said. "Then Ruben told Fairfield you needed fast cash." What a dick! Who would hang their younger cousin out to dry for a piece of shit like Whit Fairfield?

Drew said, "And Fairfield hired you to sabotage Nico's winery so he'd lose money."

"Not like the whole winery, you know?" Danny said. "Just enough that Fairfield could offer him a bunch of money at the end of the season and he'd sell that piece of land. No one was supposed to get hurt. I told Ruben and Fairfield that I wouldn't do anything that would hurt someone."

"Did Ruben kill Fairfield?" Drew asked. "Is that where the blood came from? Whit Fairfield was beat up pretty bad before he was shot."

"I don't know. I mean, I don't know what to think." Danny gripped a handful of his hair. "Did he borrow my truck? Yes."

Toni and Drew exchanged a look. "Okay, when?"

"Ruben's not that kind of guy," Danny said. "Sure, he has

a temper, but that's why he doesn't have a gun. He's never owned one. He used to joke about it. Joke about how he'd end up in jail with his temper if he ever bought a gun."

Toni's gauges were swinging back and forth like a pendulum. Danny didn't want to believe Ruben was guilty, but there was something giving the man a walloping sense of guilt.

"There's something that's making you think Ruben might have been involved though," Toni said. "More than just the shirt. You don't want to believe it, but you suspect him anyway. Why?"

Danny shook his head. "It's like you can see right into my brain. How the hell can you do that?"

"Just answer the question," Drew said. "What makes you suspect that your cousin killed Whit Fairfield?"

"Because Ruben's the one who told me to stop." Danny's voice was barely over a whisper. "After the tractor thing happened. After I cut the wires. He called me that night, and he told me I didn't need to do any of that stuff to sabotage Nico anymore. That the job was done."

It took Toni a second to realize the implications. "Ruben knew he was dead."

Danny nodded.

"Fairfield's body wasn't found for a week and a half," Toni said. "When you cut the wires, he was still considered missing."

"But Ruben knew to call you off," Drew said. "Ruben already knew that Whit Fairfield was dead."

CHAPTER 27

*H*enry and Megan followed Toni as she and Drew raced to Hillside Rehab Center.

"If Ruben knew Fairfield was dead, then he killed him," Drew said. "Or he knows who did."

"But why? You said it yourself, he was better off with Fairfield. He had information the man wanted and job security."

"Maybe he grew a conscience and didn't want to cover for the man. Maybe he got impatient and suspected Fairfield would cut him out. Maybe Fairfield took it a step too far and threatened *him*."

"Maybe." Toni still felt like, even with Danny's confession, there was a lot they weren't seeing. "Are your guys already at the rehab center?"

"Yeah. You call your cousin?"

Toni nodded. "He's already there. Going to take Marissa to her parents' place in Santa Cruz tonight."

"Good. I'll call the police up there, but I have a hard time imagining that Ruben Montenegro has hardened criminal connections." Drew's mouth was set in a grim line. "I have a feeling that this was a 'brilliant plan' that spiraled way out of control."

They arrived in silence at the Hillside Rehab Center and parked between the patrol car and Nico's work truck. Toni hopped out of the car and walked straight toward the glass double doors.

"Miss." The receptionist stood. "I'm afraid you can't—"

"I'm consulting with the police." She pointed back to Drew. "Need to speak with the witness before she leaves."

"But the officer said—"

"She's fine." Drew walked in behind her, holding out his badge. "I'm Detective Bisset. Are you Isabelle?"

Toni ignored the voices behind her and listened for Marissa.

"...still trying to tell me how to live my life."

"...not going to argue with you about this. Do you know what it would do to Beth and Ethan if something happened to you?"

"They don't care about me." Marissa sulked. Her head shot up when she saw Toni walk through the cracked-open door. "Oh. You."

"Great to see you too." She turned to Nico. "Are you driving her up to her parents'?"

"Yeah. The police are even going to escort us, I think? Which is weird."

Toni turned to Marissa. "Rumor has it, you were trying to get something out of Nico to sign the divorce papers. What was it?"

Marissa didn't look well. Her rich, olive-toned complexion was wan and dull. She'd lost weight, and her cheeks were hollow. Her expression hardly changed. "I don't know what you're talking about. And even if I did, it's none of your business, Toni."

"Sure you do," Nico said. "You brought up the Ferraro Creek acreage about two and a half weeks ago, right before you got beaten up."

She blinked rapidly. "What creek land?"

Toni exchanged a look with Nico. "Okay, so I'm going to get her to tell us the truth. Save your questions for later."

Nico looked confused. "What?"

"Just go with it." She grabbed Marissa's hand and held it firmly between her palms, letting a creeping sense of calm settle over the woman. Marissa's eyes went wide, then unfocused.

"Hey." She blinked slowly.

"Hey. Did you know about the wine caves on the creek land?"

"Yup." She popped her lips together on the *p* sound. "I did know that. And so did Whit."

"Who told you?"

"Ruben of course." She scrunched up her face. "He told me all kinds of stuff. He was real angry at Whit."

"About what?"

"Supposed to be partial owner. Whit told Ruben he was gonna be a partial owner of the whooooole place. But then Whit told *me* he wasn't really gonna do that."

"And you told Ruben?"

"I mean..."

Toni felt an unexpected wave of emotion from Marissa. Something between shame and embarrassment.

"It wasn't right." Marissa looked to the side. "Ruben told

him all that. And Nico didn't even know that shit, but Ruben just told him because he was loyal. And then Whit decided to cut him out."

Nico walked over. "Fairfield was gonna get the creek land and then cut Ruben out?"

"Yeah. So I told Ruben. And Ruben..." Marissa's mouth turned up at the corner. "He's smart. He's smarter than Whit. He just doesn't have the money."

"What did you and Ruben plan?" Toni kept a firm hand on Marissa.

"He told me to get the land from Nico. Use the divorce. Then we could set the price and sell to Whit. Ruben would convince Whit that he couldn't get a better price for it; then I'd give him half and I'd keep half. Whit really fucking wanted those caves. It was all he talked about for weeks."

Toni let go of Marissa's hand and turned to Nico. "So Ruben needed Fairfield to buy that land. Why would he kill him? It makes no sense."

Marissa was coming back to consciousness. "What the fuck just happened? Toni, what did you do to me?"

Nico had taken out his phone and was dialing. "Change of plans, Marissa. Jackie is gonna take you up to your folks'."

"What?"

"Jackie or your brother." He looked at her. "Your choice."

Marissa slumped in her seat and glared at him. "Jackie."

"That's what I thought." Nico looked at Toni. "Tell Drew that I'm not going up to Santa Cruz and send the cruiser with Jackie and Marissa."

"What are you going to do?"

"I'm gonna fucking talk to Ruben Montenegro," Nico said. "Then we're gonna find those fucking caves."

THE ONLY PROBLEM with Nico's plan?

"Where the hell is this guy?" Nico stomped back to the truck, opened the door, got inside, and slammed it shut.

Drew strolled back to his car from Ruben's front porch. Toni was waiting on the sidewalk.

"So he's not happy," Toni said. "And you don't look much better."

"No one's answering, and I can't get a search warrant until Monday because of the judge. I put an alert out for Ruben Montenegro. At this point, while we're waiting for the shirt to come back from testing, he's only wanted for questioning. Hopefully we can avoid any more violence."

Toni was about ready to collapse. "It's Saturday night. This was very far from how I thought my weekend was going to go, and right now I just want to go home."

"Nico gonna take you?"

Toni nodded. "Henry just texted me. He and his big dog are staying at my house tonight, so I won't be alone."

"Good. I don't think Ruben would go after you—he doesn't have a reason to—but I'd rather you weren't all alone out there."

"I won't be. Nico is just up the hill too."

Drew hooked his thumbs in his front jeans pockets. "You all going out to try to find those caves tomorrow?"

"It'll probably depend on Baxter and Katherine. They're the ones most likely to be able to find it with the plans and stuff."

"Got it. That area have cell reception at all?"

"Nothing. That's a complete dead zone."

"Right."

She patted his shoulder. "But it's not far from my house. We'll call you from there if we find anything."

"All right." Drew still looked unsure. "I just have a feeling that you need to be careful."

"What are you, psychic?" Toni couldn't stop the smile.

"That's funny." Drew pointed at her. "I see you, Dusi. Very funny."

"I don't know what you're talking about."

"I bet you don't." He opened his car door. "Drive safe."

Toni walked back to Nico's truck and climbed in, every cell of her body aching. "Take me home or I will pull my weird psychic shit on you too."

Nico started the truck. "Are you gonna tell me what that is or what?"

"Or what." She leaned against the door and closed her eyes. "You don't want to know."

"Is this why you always win at horseshoes?"

She snorted. "It doesn't work that way."

"Are you sure?"

"Nico, just drive."

SHE WAS HALF-ASLEEP when Nico drove up to the house. Henry was at the truck, arms out when it came to a stop.

"I can walk."

Earl woofed and Henry helped her out of the car. "If you say so."

"I'm just tired. When did you and Megan get back?"

"She dropped me at my house after you and the detective

stormed out of the station and didn't tell us where you were going."

Toni blinked. "Oh. Oops."

"We both figured you'd gotten a lead on something, but we couldn't get through to your phone."

She pulled it out of her pocket. "It died during my talk with Danny. Let me take a quick shower and I'll fill you in."

Henry waved at Nico from the front porch as he drove away; then he helped Toni into the shower and went to make her some food.

It smelled like spaghetti and red sauce by the time she rinsed off and wrapped herself in her favorite fluffy robe. She looked at her face in the mirror and noted the dark circles under her eyes, along with her lips, which looked fuller.

Her belly was starting to get firm and her hips ached. She wasn't even going to mention her boobs, which were suddenly everything she'd wanted as a thirteen-year-old only somehow far more painful than anything she could have imagined.

She was nearly twelve weeks pregnant, and her next doctor's appointment was less than a week away. Henry wanted to go to that appointment. By her calculations and her doctor's reassurances, the chances of miscarriage were getting less likely by the day. The knot in her chest starting to ease, and the reality of the future was starting to become clear.

A baby. She was going to be a mom. At forty-two. When the kid graduated from high school, she'd be sixty. Sixty?

What was she thinking? She couldn't do this! Who decided that women could have babies in their forties? That was *such* bad planning.

"Toni?" Henry called from the kitchen. "You okay?"

Okay. Deep breaths. *You can do this.* Wasn't Jamie Lee Curtis sixty? Emma Thompson was too. Or something like that. They weren't old. She could do this.

And she had Henry. Henry would only be... fifty-three when the kid graduated high school. That wasn't old at all.

"Toni?" He tapped on the door. "Are you okay?"

She pulled it open and steam rushed out, making Henry blink. "I can do this, right?"

His eyes fell right to her boobs. "Do what?"

"Have a baby. At my age."

He raised an eyebrow and brought his eyes up to hers. "You *are* doing it."

"I know that, but you know what I mean."

"Will you be able to handle being a mother to an infant? Baby-proofing your house? Breastfeeding?"

"Stop thinking about my boobs, Henry."

The corner of his mouth turned up. "I can't help it. They are absolutely incredible right now, and you told me they were hands-off. I'm only human."

Toni cracked a smile. "All of the above. I have never taken care of a small human before. Not full time."

"And while I won't be able to do some of the things, like breastfeeding, I am planning to do half of all the other stuff, so you're not going to be on your own with all this, okay?" He hooked his finger through the belt on her robe and pulled her toward him. "We'll figure it out. And we have lots of friends and family who can help."

Toni took a deep breath. "Okay."

"Kids are fun. And also a pain in the butt, but they're fun. And I always wanted one, and I honestly cannot think of a cooler person to do this with." Henry pulled her closer. "You're going to be the fiercest, badass-est—"

"I don't think that's a word."

"I think it is because you are." He kissed her temple. Then her cheekbone. "You're going to be a really good mom, Toni Dusi. And I'm going to be the best dad I can be."

"Just don't..." She lost her train of thought when he started kissing her neck. "Um..."

"What's that?" His hands were skimming along the outside of her robe, raising goose bumps all over her body as the material brushed against her skin.

"I... don't remember."

"Don't remember what you were worried about?"

"Nope."

"Good." He reached down and lifted her up so she was sitting on the edge of the counter. Then he nudged her knees apart and angled his hips between her legs.

The sensation of denim along her inner thighs made every nerve in her body go on alert.

Henry teased his fingers along the collar of her robe. "I like being your boyfriend. It gives me all kinds of ideas about how to distract you."

"When I get mental?"

"Hey," he said. "You're a psychic. I'm guessing it comes with the territory."

"Okay." If Henry wanted to distract her, she wasn't going to complain.

Not even a little bit.

CHAPTER 28

It was Sunday morning and Toni was in the middle of explaining to her mother why she wouldn't be at mass that morning when Katherine and Baxter rolled up in their sensible compact car, followed shortly by Megan and her three kids in their SUV.

Katherine got out of the car, and Archie came bounding after her. The large goldendoodle puppy loved chasing the rabbits at Toni's house, but he stopped and froze when he saw Earl, who was standing on the porch.

"Uh-oh." Henry walked out on the deck. "Are we gonna have a standoff?"

Baxter leaned against the car and observed. "This should be interesting."

Earl stood from sitting and slowly walked down the steps toward Archie.

"He's very well-trained," Henry said. "So don't worry—Earl!"

The big dog bounded over to Archie and laid a massive

lick right across the smaller dog's face. Then the two of them took off into the brush without a single look back.

"So they're friends." Katherine nodded. "I suspected they would be. They're both neutered males, so hormonally charged disagreements about territory shouldn't be an issue."

"Okay then." Henry sipped his coffee with a smile playing around the corners of his mouth. "Katherine, I can see why Toni likes you so much."

"I see why she likes you too." Katherine opened her mouth to say more, but Toni cut her off.

"Yep. Dogs." Toni nodded. "So... doggy. Gotta love those dogs."

Toni needed to change the subject before Katherine could launch into some interesting but distracting lecture about symmetrical features or hormone dominance or whatever it was that caused Toni to want to climb Henry like a tree.

Marissa wasn't wrong on that. Toni didn't like the woman, but she wasn't wrong. Henry was very sexy and also very cute. And climbable.

Stop thinking about sex, Toni.

She saw Nico's pickup truck rolling down the hill past the barn, and she clapped her hands together to grab everyone's attention. "Okay, who wants to ride in the back of the pickup and who wants to walk?"

Megan's three kids all raised their hands immediately. "Truck!"

Henry said, "I can take my truck down too. If Megan rides with Nico and puts the kids in the back, then Katherine and Baxter can come with us."

"Should we put the dogs in the barn?"

"Probably. Hopefully Enzo won't harass them while we're gone." Henry whistled for Earl and got the canines settled while Toni went to talk to Katherine, Megan, and Baxter.

"Okay," Toni said. "I have a feeling that we may need Megan's skills today, so we're going to have to come up with some ways to distract Nico and the kids when the time comes."

"I'll keep an eye on them," Katherine said. "Hopefully there will be enough going on that I won't have to do too much. I don't think we're going to need a seer to find the caves."

"I imagine not," Baxter said. "But I'm glad the antihistamines are working anyway."

"Seriously?" Megan asked. "Your hay fever was blocking your visions?"

"Apparently." Katherine shrugged. "Psychic powers are strange and unpredictable."

Toni agreed, but luckily the emotional mood of the group that morning was excited and optimistic, especially if she stayed close to Megan, Henry, and Baxter. She hopped in the back of the truck and let Baxter sit in front with the plans. Then they followed Nico's vehicle down the road toward the picturesque bend in Ferraro Creek that had been such a topic of interest.

Baxter pointed to the creek. "Since the creek is most prominent in the site plan, we should find a good place to park along it. We ought to be able to find the two cave portals from there."

"Cool." Henry pulled out his phone and called Nico.

"Baxter said we should park by that big oak between the two sycamores."

"Got it."

Toni saw Nico's truck veer off the gravel road and toward a clear patch of dirt where a spraying rig and an old wagon sat under a stand of trees.

Henry parked next to him and shut off the truck; then they all began unloading shovels and hedge trimmers from the back of the pickups.

"If we haven't spotted it already," Nico said, "then it's camouflaged in some way. So maybe look for areas of dense brush that don't really belong. Rocks that seems to have been placed deliberately."

Baxter walked to the creek and turned in circles, trying to orient himself with the site plan. "Does anyone have a compass? The one on my phone isn't working."

"This place is a complete dead zone." Nico tossed a compact compass toward Baxter. Then he squinted and shaded his eyes from the sun. "I can see Fairfield's place across the creek. It really is close."

"Perhaps that would be a better approach," Baxter said. "Since the plans were drawn from that side of the hill."

They walked along the path with the oak-covered hill rising along the left and the creek and rows of cabernet vines running along their right.

Nico reached out and pinched off a bunch of dark purple grapes and tossed them in his mouth. "We're close on these. End of next week, I think."

Henry reached over and grabbed a handful for himself. "Yeah. End of next week or beginning of the week after."

"Depends on the weather."

They walked in silence, and Toni tried to imagine what they might find.

Would the caves be as neat as what they'd seen on the plans? Would they be like her house? Basically sturdy but in need of some TLC?

"If these wine caves are nice," Nico said, "then I may be looking to move my entire tasting room facility down the hill."

"And out of the barn?" Toni grinned. "It's like you're listening to your mom or something."

"Ha ha."

Megan said, "Putting the tasting room closer to the creek and the caves makes sense though. You're pretty far back from the main road where you are. You'd snag a lot more of the traffic off the main road with good signage and a nice building."

"As much as I object to people in general," Toni said, "I can't argue with Megan's logic."

Trina, Megan's oldest daughter, was a year out of high school and already attending Central Coast State. She sidled up to Nico and said, "You should listen to my mom. She's really good at advertising and marketing."

Nico looked amused. "Is she now?"

"Oh yeah. When we lived in Atlanta, having her working for you was a really big deal. She even worked with film studios and stuff."

Toni tried hard to control her smile. Was Megan's oldest daughter selling Nico on her mom?

"I'll have to keep that in mind." Nico, to his credit, knew not to dismiss teenage girls. "What kind of brand development experience does she have on her résumé?"

"I don't know exactly what you mean by that, but there was a real big rum company that had a relaunch of their product in Atlanta, and she did the whole thing. Her team designed the labels. They planned the party. They got celebrities and everything there. It was totally in the newspaper."

"Trina!" Megan called from the front where she was walking next to Baxter. "What are you talking about?"

"Nothing!" Trina winked at Nico and kept her voice low. "Just saying. Her business is gonna take off in a matter of months. You don't want to sleep on that if you know what's good for you."

The corner of Nico's mouth turned up, showing off the dimple that had charmed half of Moonstone Cove. "Thanks for the tip."

Henry grabbed Toni's hand and swung his shovel over his shoulder. "It's a good idea, but we need to make sure the structure is sound."

"Such a realist." Toni squeezed his hand. "I appreciate that."

FINDING the entrance to a cave wasn't nearly as easy as Toni had thought it would be. After all, it was a door. Into the ground. But what she realized after three hours of searching was that as large as doors were, they were not larger than hills.

It wasn't until Adam, Megan's son, was randomly swinging a pick into a pile of rocks that they found a clue.

The thunk rang loud across the late morning air.

"Mom!"

Everyone stopped searching in the brush and ran over to the sixteen-year-old boy.

"Look!" He pointed at the pile of rocks and swung the pick again.

Thunk.

"That's wood."

Nico and Henry bent down to roll away the stones covering the wooden structure, only to find a sturdy set of doors with two horseshoes bent into handles.

"Okay, let's pop 'em up."

Nico and Henry both pulled up and out, exposing not a set of stairs but a storage area with many of the same tools they were already carrying.

"This isn't a portal." Katherine started scanning the brush. "But I bet it's close."

"Why else would you keep supplies here?" Toni asked.

They focused their attention on the area directly to the right and left of the wooden storage area, and within minutes they'd found the entrance, stacked with rocks, draped with old vines that fell down the hill, and with a menacing tangle of barbed wire mixed in with the brush.

Henry took a pickax and pulled the barbed wire away; then Nico and Megan pushed the rocks to the side.

"You're strong." Nico grinned at Megan. "You must work out."

Megan's smile was bright. "As often as possible." She was also a telekinetic who could use her ability to enhance her strength, but there was no need to share that part with poor, unsuspecting Nico.

"Did your ex-wife get up to Santa Cruz okay?" Megan asked.

"Yeah. Jackie called me around two in the morning. They made it up there, got out to her parents' ranch, and she'll stay put until they can find Ruben."

"Did Drew call anyone this morning?" Toni asked.

"No." Nico rolled the last stone away. "We'll probably be waiting until next week to hear anything from the crime lab."

"Fair point." Toni moved forward when she saw a rusted metal door appear. "There it is."

Baxter stood in front of it, faced the creek, then turned back to the door. "Yes. The degree is more than a little bit off on the plans, but that might have been intentional."

"Can we get it open?" Nico pulled on the handle, only to hear nothing as the door swung open.

Not a squeak. Not a creak.

"Someone's oiled the hinges." He ducked his head and turned on the large flashlight Baxter handed him. "Okay, folks, let's see what we've got."

One by one, they disappeared past the door, and then it was only Henry and Toni bringing up the rear.

"Is it bad that part of me really does not want you to go in there until I check it out?" Henry asked. "Seeing as you're the mother of my unborn child and all."

"I appreciate the protective instincts more than I expected, but seeing as we can already hear Megan's kids trying out the echo factor in the caves, it's probably unnecessary."

It was true. Toni could already detect the whoops and hollers from the kids as they ran around underground.

"Come on." Toni grabbed Henry's hand. "What an adventure, right?"

"Yeah." He walked through the doorway first, never letting her hand leave his.

The minute they walked into the cave, Toni felt the air temperature drop. She breathed in the scent of soft, slightly damp air, earth, and metal.

"The temperature and humidity are nearly perfect," Henry muttered. "A little more ventilation to get the humidity down and that's it. That's all we'd have to do."

"What are we walking on?" She pointed her flashlight down at the gently sloping floor. "It's all brick."

"Oh my God, Toni, are you seeing this?" Henry pointed his flashlight up. "It's so beautiful."

Toni followed the light and saw an intricate pattern of dark and light brick in an arching pattern that mirrored the lines of the barrel-roofed ceiling. He shined his flashlight along the walls, and she saw the flash of bright green and red mosaic tiles placed in a pattern that formed an alley of tall cedars.

Toni swung her flashlight around the larger room they entered where Megan's kids, along with Katherine and Baxter, were trying out the limits of the echoes. She heard Baxter exclaiming every now and then about some structural detail or referring to the plans.

The cave itself was narrow and looped around in a kind of stretched horseshoe with a central room at the apex of the arch where the children were shouting. The entire structure was lined in brick and tile with small alcoves built into the tunnels on alternating sides where barrels could be racked and stored.

Toni looked up at Henry, who looked like a kid on the most overwhelming Christmas morning ever. "You okay?"

"Our wine is going to be so much better." He looked like he was nearly crying. "And we won't have to pay for air-conditioning."

She looked for Nico, who was leaning against a pillar, staring up at the center of the main room where a two-barred cross was inlaid with red and white brick.

"There it is." He pointed to the giant cross. "There's the new logo. Branding done. This is... beyond."

"Yeah." She walked over to him. "This is very cool."

He looked back at her, blinking. "I feel like a complete idiot. This has been sitting here for thirty years. It's priceless. This isn't just a cave, it's a work of art."

"Mom?" Adam's voice rang through the darkness. "I found something weird."

"What is it?" Megan called. "Where are you, honey?"

Toni heard the sound of a gun cocking in the darkness, and a voice came from behind her.

"You know," Ruben said. "You people really picked the wrong day to go exploring."

CHAPTER 29

*H*enry stepped in front of Toni. "Ruben, what the hell are you doing?"

Nico turned carefully and looked at the man. "I thought we were friends."

"Are we?" Ruben kept the gun trained on Nico. "Do friends steal architectural plans, Nico? Do they sabotage your winery and get you in trouble with the new owners?"

Nico was the picture of confusion. "What are you talking about?"

Toni tapped Henry on the shoulder. "Um, I might be able to explain that one." Anytime Toni tried to get out from behind Henry, he moved in front of her. "Henry, let me—"

"I think Nico and I could be asking the same thing of you," Henry said. "Aren't you behind the sabotage at our place?"

"That wasn't me; that was Danny and Fairfield. *I* don't want to hurt anyone." Ruben carefully positioned himself, blocking the exit. His face was rough, and he looked like he hadn't slept in about three days. "I have been living with this shit hanging over me for years now. I just want to finish it."

"So let's get out of here and sort things out," Nico said. "There are kids down here and you have a gun. There's no reason for anyone to get hurt."

Ruben let out a strangled laugh. "I keep trying to make that happen, and every time I try to make it work, someone else gets hurt. So I don't know what to do now."

"Ruben—" Megan stepped forward, and Ruben swung the gun toward her. In the background, one of the girls screamed. "Hey. Hi. It's Megan; remember me? My kids are down here, Ruben. I have three kids. Can you let my kids go with Baxter and Katherine? The rest of us will stay down here and help you sort things out, but please let my kids go."

"With the professors? Oh yeah, sure." Ruben snorted. "So they can run to Toni's house and call the cops? I don't think so."

"Why don't you want us to call the cops?" Toni asked. "They just want to ask you some questions."

"Do you think I'm an idiot?" Ruben shouted into the darkness. "I know Marissa told them. I know Danny's been talking. I know what's going to happen if I go to the police!"

Toni stepped to Henry's side and grabbed his hand. "Ruben, let us help you."

He snarled at Nico. "If you hadn't been so goddamn stubborn, none of this would have had to happen. No one would have gotten hurt."

"So this is my fault?" Nico was getting heated. "Whit Fairfield dead. Marissa beat within an inch of her life. That's all *my* fault?"

"If you'd sold the land—"

"It's not my land to sell." Nico's voice was hard. "You pulled my family into this. You pulled your own flesh and blood into this. For what? Money?"

"My grandfather built this!" Ruben shouted. "All of this! It's his work. Did you know that? His blood, sweat, and tears went into this place. He spent years working on it after he finished his day job. It was supposed to be his retirement money. Years of laying bricks in the dark. Years of switching from one plan to another because that old man changed his mind over and over and over again. And do you know how much that cheap bastard gave him for all this work? Ten grand. That's it. A third of what my grandfather was promised. And then he shut it up! Didn't even show it to anyone or give my granddad credit for the build."

"That's horrible," Nico said. "That shouldn't have happened to him."

"Then years later, I find out Whit Fairfield was trying to cheat me. Just like my grandfather was cheated." Ruben shook his head. "Not this time. Not this man. I don't think so."

Toni watched Ruben, trying to find a way to get a hand on the man. If she could tackle him and get her hands on him, she could calm him down like she had with Justin McCabe. She could make him cooperate.

But unlike the gym, they didn't have the element of surprise. Ruben had a firm hold on the gun, and any attempt to rush him could end in tragedy.

Nico spread his hands out. "So what are you gonna do, Ruben? Kill us? Hide our bodies down here? Someone is bound to come looking. The police detective knows about the caves."

"I'm not gonna kill you. We're all gonna leave together as soon as I finish setting these charges. Then we're walking out of there, and I'm gonna blow these tunnels to hell." Ruben flashed his light over at a different pillar, and Toni saw dynamite strapped to it with duct tape.

Her heart sank, and she quickly exchanged glances with Katherine and Megan. Both of them looked as lost as she felt.

"Ruben," she said. "I know you don't want to do that. You're conflicted. You love this place."

"Yeah. You're right, Toni. I do. But here's the thing—" Ruben moved toward the pillar, keeping his gun trained on Nico. "I tried to make a good deal. I tried to get a little back for my family. If Whit Fairfield would have been *decent*, there would have been no problems. Nico would have eventually sold him the land, I'd have ownership in the winery, and all this would have been partly mine. Finally the Montenegros would have a little portion—just a fraction—of their own hard work."

Nico growled, "But I'm not going to sell, so no one can have it? That makes no sense."

"Sure it does. I'm blowing the tunnels, Nico. You didn't even know they were here to begin with. The land stays yours. It probably won't even hurt your precious vines. But you don't get" —his voice rose— "to profit off of my family being cheated."

Toni was getting hard swings from Ruben, from frightened and conflicted to wildly angry and murderous. She wondered if he was drunk or high. "Ruben, if you're going to blow up the caves, why not let us go?"

"I do not want anyone stopping me." He pointed at her. "And I know you're friends with that detective."

"These tunnels are beautiful," Megan said. "Ruben, these are works of art. Look at the love and pride your grandfather poured into them. You're just going to destroy all that?"

"Don't you think I tried to save them?" He shook the gun in her direction. "Do you have any idea how I tried? I even got Danny involved. Danny!"

"We're trying to help Danny," Toni said. "I talked to him, Ruben. He knows you're not the kind of person to murder your boss in cold blood. He knew there had to be an explanation. Just like I know there has to be a way to resolve this."

"But I did kill Fairfield." Ruben started laughing, and it was nearly a manic scream in Toni's mind. He was breaking. Something about the man felt like it was breaking in half. "I went out there to meet with Danny that night, and Fairfield insisted on coming along. He said we needed to up the ante. That's what he said. 'Up the ante.' Like it was a game or something. He wanted Danny to arrange an accident during harvest."

Megan gasped.

"Yeah." Ruben's lips were twisted in a grimace. "I told him about my cousin, and he wanted to make Danny responsible for something like that? I told him no way. Danny was out of it. No more."

Grim satisfaction was all she was getting from Ruben now. "You don't feel a bit sorry for killing him, do you?"

"He brought that fucking gun to threaten me and my cousin that night." Ruben pointed at the pillar. "I'd already talked to Marissa about using the divorce to get the land from Nico, but Fairfield told me he was on to us. He knew what Marissa and I were up to, and it wasn't going to work."

"Did he threaten to fire you?" Katherine asked.

"He did fire me!" Ruben barked a laugh. "Do you believe that shit? All my time, all my attention, all the extra hours worked? Gone. Like I was nothing. He fired me and then still expected me to convince Danny to cause an accident." His face was twisted with hate. "Said he'd ruin me if I went to the cops or told anyone."

"So you beat him up?" Nico asked.

"Yep." Ruben managed to get another charge taped to a pillar, even while the gun stayed trained on Nico. "I figured I'd teach him a lesson for firing me. And for messing with Danny. For scheming with fucking Marissa. For fucking with everyone and not *ever* paying the price." Ruben's face grew red. "That's really what it was, a big fuck-you from all the little guys to all the big guys. We do all the work, and they make all the money."

"If he attacked you, then it was self-defense," Toni said. "Why don't you turn yourself in and tell Drew everything? You're right. No one liked Fairfield. No one thought he was a good guy. If you tell Drew he threatened you with the gun—"

"Too late." Ruben's face was bleak. "Maybe I stay out of prison for that, but not for..."

"Marissa." Nico clenched his hands. "It *was* you who beat her up. You beat her so badly her brain just shut off."

"She's a backstabber." Ruben choked out the words. "I tried to talk to her, and she was so... smug. So confident that she'd be able to get everything for herself. She must have told Fairfield we were planning to cut him out. I guess she thought it would give her leverage? I don't know. But she told him our plan. She told him everything."

"So you beat her?" Henry said. "She nearly died, Ruben."

"I struck back at a *snake!*" Ruben waved the gun in Henry's face. "She wasn't a woman, she was a snake."

A heavy, terrible feeling swelled in Toni when she saw the gun inches from Henry's face, and something in her chest shuddered and clenched hard. She needed to get out of the cave. Something in her was breaking along with the last of Ruben's self-control.

"Let me go," she choked out. "Ruben, you need to let me go."

"The air." Henry put an arm around Toni's shoulders. "She's pregnant, okay? Take her phone if you want, but let her go. By the time she walks out—"

"Pregnant?" Ruben laughed. "Oh, that's rich. Just what this town needs. Another Dusi spawn. Probably another lying woman." He shook his head and backed toward another pillar. "I'd be doing Moonstone Cove a favor if I got rid of a few pests, but I'm not like that."

A few pests?

Was he talking about her and the baby? About Toni, Katherine, and Megan?

Rage built in her, and the quickly mounting waves grew bigger and bigger until Toni felt like the whole of her body and mind was centered on Ruben Montenegro.

She clenched her fist and felt like her skin would burst. "Ruben, you better let me out."

"Or what?" He laughed a little as he reached down for another stick of dynamite and a roll of duct tape hanging on his belt. "I'm not going to do that."

Toni felt the emotional signatures of everyone around her. Henry, strong and resolved. Nico, growing steadily more furious. Baxter and Katherine somehow melded together, both calculating and detached. Both splitting their attention between the terrified children they guarded and the violent man with the gun.

And Megan.

Megan was... not afraid. Not even a little bit.

Feeling Megan's calm centered Toni. *What do you have up your sleeve, Atlanta?*

Megan stepped toward Ruben, holding up her hands.

He saw her approaching. "Listen, princess, I'm going to need you to step back."

"I just want to tell you I understand. I understand all of it. How it feels when someone takes all your work, all your devotion and energy and love. And then just... spits on it, you know? Just treats all that devotion like it's nothing."

Ruben pointed the gun directly at Megan and yelled, "Do I look like I need a fucking therapist?"

Toni kept her eyes on Ruben. She pictured reaching out. She pictured taking his hand and making him sleepy. She pictured making him cry. She pictured making his head explode between her clenched hands.

Megan didn't stop inching toward Ruben. "I know how that feels, Ruben." Her voice was low and soothing. "I know what it feels like to be unappreciated. Taken for granted."

She was standing a few feet away.

Ruben said, "If you understand, then you know that you need to back the hell up."

Megan smiled sweetly. "I also know what it's like when the people you love more than life itself are threatened by a disturbed asshole who cares more about some fucking useless holes in the ground than the safety of three children." She lifted her hands, and Toni saw dust rise when a slew of loose bricks hurtled through the air and took aim at Ruben Montenegro.

The bricks hit Ruben directly in the chest, knocking him to the ground.

Megan lunged for the gun and screamed, "Katherine, run!"

As if on cue, all the lights they'd been holding were doused in darkness, and Katherine, Baxter, and the three teenagers were swallowed in shadows.

Toni jumped on Ruben, who was lying dazed at the base of a dynamite-clad pillar. She didn't think. She didn't hesitate. She put both her hands on his neck and sucked every bit of anger out of him, just like she had with Henry. Only Ruben was a lot angrier and a lot more disturbed.

His eyes crossed and he jerked on the floor, turning on his side as his body shuddered and heaved like he was trying to throw up.

And Toni? She stood up straight and started kicking the shit out of him.

"You think you can threaten us?" She kicked the back of his legs. "You think it's okay to beat up my sister-in-law?" She kicked his arms as he covered his head. "You think it's okay to terrify *children*?"

She was aiming for his head when Henry grabbed her around the waist and lifted her up and away from the man on the floor.

Megan reached for a pile of rope in the corner, and the end flew to her hand. She looked over at Nico as she held the rope with one hand and the semiautomatic pistol in the other. "Do you know how to tie stuff?"

Nico's eyes were saucers. "How did you—?"

"Can you tie shit up or not?" Megan wasn't playing. "Henry, do you hear Baxter and Katherine and my kids?"

"I don't. Sorry, I'm kind of trying to—"

"Let me fucking down I'm going to kill him!" Toni screamed and twisted in Henry's arms. "I'm gonna kill that piece of shit!"

Nico took the rope from Megan and started tying Ruben up. "What the hell is going on right now?"

A small part of Toni recognized that she'd absorbed all the anger of a homicidal maniac who thought dynamite was a viable solution to his problems, but she had a hard time feeling her way around it like she had with Henry.

Henry yelled, "Nico, I'm gonna take her out of here."

"Okay." Nico's gaze kept shooting to Megan while he tied Ruben up. "How did you do that?"

"Can we talk about it later?"

Henry carried Toni out of the cave and into the light where he finally set her down. Toni ran back toward the cave portal, but he just spun her around again.

"Do I need to throw you in the creek?" He was scratching his head, clearly trying to figure out how to get her out of the murderous rage. "Toni, you're gonna have to help me out on this one. I don't know what to do."

"I don't know either!"

"Maybe you should run back to your house."

"Run all the way back?"

"Try it." He waved her toward the road. "Last time, getting you really exhausted helped. I'll run with you. We'll find Baxter and Katherine on the way."

They ran toward the road and spotted the truck's dust in the distance. Baxter, Katherine, and Megan's kids were already halfway to Toni's house, which meant they'd be able to call the police soon.

When they were nearly halfway to the house, Toni started to feel sick to her stomach. "Henry?"

"Yeah?"

"I think I'm going to throw up, and I don't know if it's because of the baby or the crazy murderer I just sucked the emotions out of."

"Either way," he said, "you'll probably feel better if you puke. This might be the one case where it's better coming up than going down."

She was panting when she ran to the edge of the vineyard and puked her guts out. Breakfast, dinner, and lunch the day before. It was all gone.

And she felt... oddly better. Still revved with way more adrenaline than was probably healthy, but she didn't feel murderous anymore.

"Oh God." She heaved one more time, but there was nothing left. "I think I threw up all of Ruben's breakfast too. Not sure how that's possible, but there's no other explanation."

Henry stayed beside her, rubbing her back and holding out a bottle of water.

"How did I know" —he was panting from the run— "that I'd never be bored if I fell in love with you?"

"Probably the same way I instinctively knew it was a good idea to fall in love with someone large enough to physically remove me if I tried to kick an asshole to death." She took a giant mouthful of water and spit it out before she lifted her face to Henry's. "Kiss?"

He put his hand on her head and turned her face away.

He couldn't stop laughing even while he was panting. "You are so weird, and I don't know why I like you so much, but I do."

Toni smiled when she heard sirens in the distance. "Come on, Henry. This day just got interesting."

EPILOGUE

Two months later...

The party was at Toni's, and she and the kids were the only ones not drinking. The flagstone patio under the oak trees had been cleared, and lights were hung in the trees. Nico brought wine from the barrels they'd just started bottling at the winery, and Toni's mother and sisters brought mountains of pasta and salad while Henry and her father cooked an entire side of beef.

Katherine and Megan sat down at the old wooden table Toni had rescued from the barn.

"The place looks amazing," Megan said. "The garden is perfect."

"Goats." Katherine nodded in satisfaction. "I told you they'd do a thorough job."

The herd of goats belonging to the college had done extraordinary work eating the brush around the barn and along the creek, leaving clear the areas around the house that Toni had wanted to plant. The small vineyard between the house and the barn was neat and pruned; Henry had already taken cuttings from the old vines to propagate in Nico's greenhouse.

"The goats were a good suggestion," Toni said. "And the two of you... I cannot thank you enough."

After the craziness in the wine cave, Toni had been sick for over a week. She'd made it back to her house and been able to make a statement to the police, but when Henry led the officers to the cave where Megan and Nico were holding Ruben, Toni collapsed into bed and she could barely get out.

She was exhausted and overwhelmed. She hadn't known how Ruben's wild and violent emotional state would affect her, but it had been far worse than she'd imagined. Henry wanted to take Toni to the hospital, but she refused to go.

What was she supposed to tell them? *So I sucked the hatred and anger from a violent murderer, and it put me a little off the entire world for a bit.*

She made it to her obstetric appointment a few days later with Henry's help, but when she mentioned her exhaustion, the doctor cheerfully told her that was normal for an expectant mother "of her advanced age."

Bite me.

Toni was too tired to say it, but she was thinking it. Thankfully, everything with the baby looked completely normal, and all her blood tests came back showing the mini-human was perfectly healthy and right on target for a spring due date.

So Toni called her dad to cover for her at the garage, went home, and slept more.

Katherine and Megan had no explanation for her exhaustion, and Henry was getting desperate when she could barely keep her eyes open for more than an hour days after she'd drained Ruben.

Katherine had finally called their friends in Glimmer Lake. The only thing Robin, Val, or Monica could relate it to was the overwhelming state of exhaustion that sometimes plagued Robin after she'd spent a long time in communication with a troubled spirit.

Their advice? Sleep. Rest. And be in the healing outdoors as much as possible.

So Henry drove Toni to Moonstone Cove and sat next to her while she napped on the beach. She slept on a cot in the garden while he directed the goats and dug in the garden beds. And after days of sleep and more soup than she'd ever eaten in her life, she started to feel better.

And Henry? Well, he kind of never left. Toni needed him, so he stayed. And then one day about a month after the incident in the wine cave, Toni suggested he hang his clothes up in the closet she wasn't using, and Henry said that was a good idea.

And that was that.

"Note to self." Toni raised her glass of sparkling cider. "Do not suck out the emotions of a murderer ever again. It feels really gross and you won't want to eat for a week."

"Probably a good idea in general," Megan said. "Especially when I had it under control."

"I mean... the bricks were a good idea, but then you had to explain all our psychic stuff to Nico."

Megan craned her neck and caught sight of Nico standing next to Henry and Toni's dad at the barbecue. "I think he can handle it."

In truth, Nico seemed slightly scared of Toni and all her friends now. Not that he hadn't been busy himself.

As the party continued and meat was carved at the grill, Nico's son Ethan drove guests back and forth from the wine cave, which was in the process of renovation already.

Katherine said, "Baxter just went down to check on the progress. He was very impressed. He said your cousin already has power to the caves and it's even more impressive lit up."

"Henry and I walked down there a few days ago. It's going to be amazing. I'm not looking forward to the extra people, but it's going to launch Nico's business to the next level." She glanced at her cousin and her boyfriend. "Henry is over the moon."

"And how are things with your mom and dad?"

"Uh..." That one was more difficult. "About the baby? They've been surprisingly... chill. Very excited about a new grandchild. My mom told me, 'Toni, you could never do anything like the other girls your age, so what should I expect?' Which is..."

"Accurate?" Megan offered.

She shrugged. "Pretty much. And my mom has only brought up Henry and me getting married two or three times, so that's kind of nice."

"And you told her...?" Katherine reached for the steamed artichokes in the middle of the table. "Did you know that Romans preserved artichokes in honey and vinegar so they could enjoy them all year round? They were considered an aphrodisiac."

Toni frowned. "Are we talking about artichokes now? Because I'm fine with skipping over the marriage thing."

"Nope." Megan patted the table. "Focus. What did you tell your mom?"

"I told her that we're waiting until after the baby is born to decide anything."

"And she was fine with that?"

"I mean... no. But she knows if she lectures me, I'm just going to dig my heels in. I think she's probably going to switch focus and work on persuading Henry."

Megan laughed. "That sounds like a mom thing to do."

Katherine frowned. "And that doesn't feel manipulative to you?"

"If she were trying to be sneaky about it, it might feel manipulative, but she's just so obvious."

Toni relaxed in her newly painted garden chair, watching her nieces, nephews, and little cousins running around her house while the women gathered under the lit-up oak trees and the old men walked around the house, pointing out all the things that still needed fixing up.

Ah, her crazy, wonderful, nosy-as-hell family.

Mixed in with the gossip and shared news, Toni also heard her aunts talking about how thrilled they were about the baby and how well Toni was balancing her work and her personal life. She heard her uncles talking about what they could help fix before the baby came so she and Henry wouldn't have too much to do.

And of course her male cousins were already scoping out where they could fit in a horseshoe pit at her place.

Henry walked over, his long legs eating up the distance between the grill and the patio. He was holding a tray of steaming tri-tip and another bottle of red wine.

He set both in the middle of the table and pointed at

Toni. "Tell me when you're out of cider and I'll get you more."

Toni couldn't help smiling when she looked at him. "Hey, handsome. You're a sight for sore eyes."

His cheeks turned a little red. "Let me guess, because I feed you meat and keep you supplied in sugary, carbonated beverages?"

"Naturally." Toni crooked her finger at him, and he bent over and gave her a proper and full kiss on the lips, right in front of her friends and her entire family. "Best boyfriend ever," she whispered.

"Hmmm." He licked his lips and stood up. "I better get back to work."

"You're not gonna say I'm the best girlfriend ever?"

He pursed his lips and wiggled his hand in a so-so gesture as he backed away. "I mean... you're getting there. You're a little rough around the edges, but you're getting there."

Megan and Katherine started laughing.

"I'm making you pay for that later." He was so adorable, but she couldn't let him get away with too much or she'd turn into a hormonal pile of mush. "You're getting a little sassy, Durand. Don't make me sic the cat on you."

He winked at her. "I think I can handle it."

Megan snorted. "He's got your number, Toni."

"He thinks you're all talk," Katherine said. "Which you are. You are very much in love with that man, and I predict you're going to marry him."

"I might consider it." She sipped her glass of sparkling cider. "After all, he's useful to have around, and I am really busy. Plus he knows how to garden."

"I see." Megan nodded. "So it's a time-saving feature, living with Henry."

"Obviously." She rolled her eyes.

"It's efficient," Katherine said. "Sure. That makes sense."

They were both laughing at her, and Toni didn't care.

Her life was full.

So very full.

Too full?

Toni watched her friends talking and laughing under the oak trees, watched her man smiling as he served a mountain of food to her enormous family. She watched dogs and children running through the vines, and she caught her breath when she felt the tiny flutter of a kick in her newly rounded belly.

Too full? Impossible.

Sign up for my newsletter to find more information about upcoming releases like Fate Interrupted, coming Spring 2021!

AFTERWORD

Dearest Readers,

When I set out to write six books in one year, I did not realize that 2020 would shortly usher in a global pandemic, worldwide recession, and countless personal and national challenges.

In retrospect, maybe not the best idea!

On the other hand, being able to focus on this goal and this new genre has given me a lifeline. Not only has paranormal women's fiction been far more successful than I could have imagined, it's been creatively fulfilling, deeply meaningful to readers, and so much fun to write. For that, I will always be grateful.

I'm so pleased to end this year with Toni's story. She's a character I feel very connected to, a woman who has found success through hard work, juggled family and professional life, and handled big surprises with unimaginable grace—after the initial shock wore off, of course. I think a lot of working women can relate to Toni; I hope she's touched your heart in some way.

As I type this, my home state of California is deep in the worst wave of the Covid-19 pandemic. Our hospitals are crowded and stretched to capacity. Our healthcare workers have been challenged beyond their training. Our communities are reckoning with loss on many levels.

Yet in the middle of it all, we find happiness. Love finds space in people's hearts. Children are born. Pets are adopted. Home is found. Milestones are celebrated. Life, both beautiful and awful, happens all around us in the non-stop parade of time.

And so, we live.

We live and love and thrive and pass through this world, leaving our mark on the people around us. Our footprints leave tracks of hope, joy, or pain on the map of other peoples' lives.

I'm not telling you anything you don't already know. I write this only in the hope that in my own small way—through telling stories—I've left gentle footprints that have brought you joy. That you've found light when the world felt dark. That you've been warmed by happiness or laughter when circumstances stretched you to your limit.

If I have one wish for you at the end of this challenging year, it is this: I hope you do not feel alone. If my books have given you any kind of happiness, solace, or comfort this year, I consider that the best measure of success. If you have felt connected to my characters, then you have connected with me, and I am grateful to know you.

Thank you for reading. Thank you for loaning this book to a friend or a colleague. Thank you for giving it as a gift or reading that funny part to a friend over the phone. Thank you for the countless acts of good will I have witnessed in the reading community.

Some day soon, I will see you at a signing or a convention, and I will shake your hand or hug you, and we will know that we got through this time together. As readers. As writers. We found laughter and love in the pages of a book. We visited Moonstone Cove or Glimmer Lake or the Elemental universe or any of the countless fictional worlds out there that have given us joy.

We met there for a few hours or a few days, we found our friends, and we thrived.

Be well, stay safe, and have a magical holiday season.

And from the bottom of my heart, I wish you a happy new year.

Sincerely,

Elizabeth Hunter

December 6, 2020

ABOUT THE AUTHOR

ELIZABETH HUNTER is a *USA Today* and international best-selling author of romance, contemporary fantasy, and paranormal mystery. Based in Central California, she travels extensively to write fantasy fiction exploring world mythologies, history, and the universal bonds of love, friendship, and family. She has published over thirty works of fiction and sold over a million books worldwide. She is the author of the Glimmer Lake series, Love Stories on 7th and Main, the Elemental Legacy series, the Irin Chronicles, the Cambio Springs Mysteries, and other works of fiction.

ElizabethHunterWrites.com

The Force of Wind

A Fall of Water

The Stars Afire

The Elemental World

Building From Ashes

Waterlocked

Blood and Sand

The Bronze Blade

The Scarlet Deep

A Very Proper Monster

A Stone-Kissed Sea

Valley of the Shadow

The Elemental Legacy

Shadows and Gold

Imitation and Alchemy

Omens and Artifacts

Obsidian's Edge (anthology)

Midnight Labyrinth

Blood Apprentice

The Devil and the Dancer

Night's Reckoning

Dawn Caravan

The Bone Scroll

(Summer 2021)

Made in United States
North Haven, CT
30 December 2021

13884477R00195